After

Yesterday

After Yesterday

by

Bobbe Tatreau

iUniverse, Inc.
Bloomington

After Yesterday

iUniverse books may be ordered through booksellers or by contacting:

iUniverse
1663 Liberty Drive
Bloomington, IN 47403
www.iuniverse.com
1-800-Authors (1-800-288-4677)

ISBN: 978-1-4759-2640-8 (sc)
ISBN: 978-1-4759-2641-5 (ebk)

Printed in the United States of America

iUniverse rev. date: 05/31/2012

Chapter 1

Olivia Bennett was running late. First, it was the southbound traffic crawling across the Golden Gate Bridge, then having to wait twenty minutes for her manicurist, who had been stuck in traffic somewhere else. Once Olivia got to her office building, the elevator insisted on stopping at every floor even though she was the only occupant. As soon as the doors slid open on the ninth floor, she hurried down the hall to the imposing glass doors of Bennett Books, nodded to the new receptionist whose name she couldn't remember, and headed for Editorial's suite of offices, impatient to begin her day.

"Good morning, Ashley. Any fires that need to be put out?"

Accustomed to Olivia's cut-to-the-chase style, her twenty-something assistant held out a stack of messages and smiled calmly. "No fires. There's actually some good news on your desk."

"I could use some." Olivia closed the office door behind her, dropped her Italian leather purse into the desk's bottom right drawer as she sat down, and began searching for the extra pair of reading glasses she kept in the desk's center drawer. On top of the stack of letters waiting for her signature was a press release on expensive paper, announcing the 2010 finalists for the prestigious Milton Elgin Book Awards. On the fiction list was Kelley Jordan's third novel, *Spring Farm*. Launched in April, it was already in its second printing.

Since Olivia and her husband Kurt had founded Bennett Books ten years ago, they'd dreamed that one of their authors would someday get this kind of recognition. If *Spring Farm* won, the playing field for small publishing houses like theirs would be leveled, just a little. Winning would be huge. Ashley was right. Very good news.

And a potential nightmare.

Actually, it was the second potential *Spring Farm* nightmare. The first was movie producer Nate Pullman's interest in making the book into a major movie.

The Pullman offer was still in the negotiation phase, but Olivia was running out of time to present the project to Rebecca before the rumor mill got wind of it. The author should not be the last to know. And now that *Spring Farm* was an Elgin finalist, Rebecca would have to be brought up to speed on both issues as soon as possible. Emily too. Olivia shoved her reading glasses onto her head and pushed the intercom button. Almost immediately, Ashley opened the door, "Tea?"

"Gallons of it. And see if you can find Kurt."

"He's meeting with Henry Nash over in Burlingame. He won't be back until four."

No immediate help from that quarter. She'd either have to start sorting out this new development on her own or wait until tonight for Kurt's input.

She didn't feel like waiting. "Where's Kelley this week?"

Ashley moved over to Olivia's computer, clicked on the Kelley Jordan calendar and scrolled to the last week in October. "She's in town until next Tuesday. Then she'll be in Florida for five days—the Miami Book Fair, readings and signings at three libraries and four bookstores. Do you want me to call her?"

Though Ashley had only been working at Bennett for a year, she'd learned the office routine quickly, was adept at reading Olivia's mind and miraculously immune to her boss's brusque impatience. Initially, Olivia had thought Ashley was too young to handle the job. Kurt, however, had disagreed, and so Olivia finally gave in. She hoped his choice—admittedly a good one—hadn't been based on the fact that Ashley wore a size two, had shoulder length, natural blonde hair that bounced when she walked, and incredibly white teeth.

"See if she can come in this afternoon. Rearrange my schedule if necessary."

"I'm sure she'll be thrilled about the nomination."

Olivia wasn't in the mood for Ashley's optimistic half full glass because the half empty one was looming large. "Let me know what time she can be here and don't forget the tea." She picked up her pen and scrawled her signature at the bottom of the first letter.

The offices of *Twenty-First Century Magazine* were on the third floor of the Palmer Building, not far from Manhattan's ground zero construction site. Built in the 1920's, the red brick building had recently been remodeled but still had pipes that banged when the hot water faucets were turned on and an ancient elevator that was problematic. Every time Jake Hannigan took the stairs instead of the elevator, he told himself that he needed the exercise. Better than admitting his fear of being stuck between floors. Two months ago, three employees from the fifth floor had been trapped for over an hour.

It was already 9:25 when he picked up his mail from the receptionist and made the mistake of asking her how she was. After her five-minute monologue on how controlling her mother-in-law was, she added, "Max wants to see you ASAP."

Jake tossed the mail onto his desk, which was jammed into one of the dozen or so cubicles pretending to be offices, grabbed a notepad, and walked to Max's office, knocking but not waiting to be told to come in.

"Hey Jake. Bad commute?" Though Maxwell Adams had been Jake's boss for the last two years, fifteen years ago they'd been college roommates. Which meant Max knew Jake all too well.

"Slept through the alarm." No sense lying to Max, who was obsessively punctual. As far as Jake knew, Max had never been late to a college class or an editorial meeting. "What's up?"

"Sit." Max handed him a copy of the same press release that had been on Olivia Bennett's desk. "Something a little different for you."

Jake scanned the release, attempting to hide his dismay. Soft news. "The Milton Elgin Book Awards. Isn't Elgin something of a big deal in literary circles?"

"Not quite Pulitzer, but on a par with the National Book Awards. Sheldon wants an article on each of the finalists. Norman's taking the non-fiction list, Susan has the poetry, and Natasha's doing children's books; you have the fiction. We'll run one or two profiles every week until the winners are announced in early January. Then Natasha will do the follow up article on the ceremony here in New York. For your articles, we need interviews with the authors, the publishers, reviewers, as well as readers, maybe even the powers that be at Elgin though they might not be too forthcoming. Groups giving high profile awards like to play it close to the vest."

Jake would have preferred the non-fiction titles, but Norman had seniority. Actually, Jake would have preferred not to have this assignment. "Please tell me I don't have to read the books to write the articles."

"I think you should. Maybe not cover to cover, but at least get a feel for the style and subject matter. I know you hate features like this, but I don't have another reporter available right now, and Sheldon is currently hung up on expanding our coverage of what he calls the *cultural landscape*. Look at it this way, it's safer than the Gaza Strip."

"Hard to argue that." Until Jake joined the staff at *Century's* New York headquarters, he'd worked in the Middle East, initially as a stringer for any newspaper or news service that would pick up his material, later for *Twenty-First Century*. He'd thrived on being in the midst of the action—covering uprisings, interviewing the political leaders and the protesters—but after getting too close to a suicide bombing in Gaza and spending three months in rehab, he'd reluctantly settled for a safer venue. For the time being. Profiling authors was possibly carrying safe too far. On the other hand, he needed this job—there was the matter of Darlene's alimony payments and his own rent. "Can I keep the release?"

"Be my guest. I'd like a preliminary draft of your first article next week. Work these around the series you're doing on the NGO's."

"Any special order on the authors?"

"Your choice."

"Expense account?"

Max nodded. "This time, try to keep the paperwork in order. You're a terrific writer and you could research a rock and find a story, but you're a bit iffy on keeping track of your receipts."

"Yes, boss, whatever you say boss."

Max reached for the phone. "You're lucky I didn't assign you the poets."

The call from Olivia Bennett's assistant couldn't have come at a worse time. Emily Gerrard was sitting outside the principal's office at her daughter Claudia's elementary school.

It was the third time since September that Emily had waited on this wooden bench, wondering what Claudia had or hadn't done this time. Her younger daughter currently hated everything about school and about her life, so she found a thousand ways to be disruptive. Her attitude at home wasn't any better. No amount of cajoling or threatening had any effect.

She'd already been moved from one fourth-grade classroom to another. What was next? Suspension? Expulsion? If she were in high school, she'd probably be sent to a continuation school but, as far as Emily knew, there was no place to put a nine year old who was still traumatized by her father's death in Iraq over a year ago. The psychologist Emily had consulted hadn't been much help. *She's acting out, trying to take control of the one thing she has control over, her school work. Give her time.* Not the answer Emily was after. She still hadn't had the luxury of giving in to her own grief. She was too busy trying to assuage her daughters' distress. At the moment, putting food on the table and keeping Claudia in school were higher priorities than her own loneliness.

On top of everything else, Liv Bennett wanted her to be at the Bennett offices in downtown San Francisco this afternoon. So much for revising the new story she planned on debuting at this weekend's story swap. Since she'd been accepted for the Ojai Storytelling Festival next May, her first major festival, polishing new stories was crucial. In addition to the appearances she made for Liv, she was beginning to get regular Storytelling bookings at local libraries and school assemblies. After Ojai, she might have enough material and money to put together a CD of her material. Today however, she was cooling her heels outside the principal's office.

Emily arrived at Bennett Books just before three o'clock, dressed in what she thought of as her Kelley clothes, brown moleskin slacks, a cream-colored sweater, and high-heeled brown boots that made her 5'6" instead of 5'4". The successful author look. To avoid coping with downtown San Francisco's traffic, she'd taken the BART from Berkeley. It wasn't like Liv to call her to the office on such short notice. Hopefully, it didn't mean she was going to lose this job. It paid well, more than her Storytelling. Since *Spring Farm's* release, Liv had been sending her on the road approximately one week each month. The rest of the time, Emily took care of her daughters and picked up whatever Storytelling bookings she could, keeping Patrick's insurance money for major expenses like replacing the brakes on her Mazda and braces for Cristyl. If that reserve were used up before she could support herself with Storytelling, she'd be faced with finding a nine to five job or waiting tables. At least she didn't have to worry about paying for childcare. When she was out of town, her mother, who had moved in with them after Patrick's death, looked after the girls.

When Emily walked into the Editorial offices, Liv's assistant seemed genuinely glad to see her. A good sign. "Hi, Ms. Jordan, go right in; Mrs. Bennett's ready for you."

"Thanks."

Olivia came around the desk and kissed Emily on both cheeks—a European affectation that always made Emily slightly uncomfortable. It was so not California. As usual, Liv was smartly dressed in a designer suit and three inch heels—making Emily feel as though she should have taken another hour to pick out her clothing and work on her hair.

"Let's use the comfortable chairs. I've been sitting at that desk all day." Two Swedish style swivel chairs, upholstered in white leather, were arranged to take advantage of the view of San Francisco Bay where the afternoon fog was playing tag with the sun. "Ashley fixed us tea. It's Turkish; I hope you like it." Olivia handed Emily a delicate china cup and saucer from the table between the chairs and took the other for herself. "How was your day?"

Emily wasn't a big fan of tea but had gotten used to the fact that whatever Liv was drinking was the only beverage served. "Too much parenting. I spent the morning at Claudia's school."

"Again?"

"Again. Fortunately, this time it wasn't about her refusal to do something. For her composition assignment last week, she wrote about her father, about Patrick." Emily paused, "Her teacher showed it to the principal and he thought I should read it."

"What was in it?"

"Memories of Pat, how she misses him. It was touching. The principal hopes that putting her feelings on paper means Claudia's starting to deal with losing him in a healthier way, instead of glaring at the teacher and refusing to do her class work." Emily was quiet for a few seconds; she couldn't talk about Claudia's grief without her own pain closing her throat. Time to change the subject. "Anyhow, why am I here?"

"*Spring Farm* is up for a big award." Olivia handed her the press release.

Emily read it, "That's wonderful. Are you pleased? Does Kelley know yet?"

"I wanted to talk to you first, warn you."

"Because?"

"I'm uneasy." Olivia stirred more sugar into her tea. "If the book wins, it'll mean more sales and more readings." She was tempted to tell Emily about the possibility of a movie deal but caught herself in time. That was

Kurt's part of the business. Olivia's role was to keep the authors happy and the editors editing. Kurt liked to handle the negotiations.

Emily sensed a *but* was hiding in Liv's explanation.

"*But* it'll also attract more media attention."

Emily congratulated herself on being right.

"And too much attention could put our—this arrangement—at risk." The *arrangement* had been Olivia's idea. Book tours boosted sales, but Rebecca had adamantly refused to help promote the first two books. Passing Emily off as Kelley Jordan was a risky but rewarding compromise. Sales of *Spring Farm* had, in the first seven months, far surpassed the sales for the other two books.

"I've done several interviews. There's not much I can't answer about the books."

"I know. It's just that, if someone starts digging deeper, wants more personal information or—" It was unlike Olivia to be at a loss for words.

"What should I do?"

"Just be careful while you're in Miami. The announcement was made yesterday."

"Except for you and Kurt, and my mother, no one knows that I'm Kelley's public face. And since I don't know who she actually is, I can't very well give anything away. Even your employees think I'm Kelley."

"That doesn't keep me from being uneasy. Your hotel reservation is in Kelley's name as is the credit card you use on the road. But your airline tickets are in your real name. No sense upsetting TSA. If someone begins looking for Kelley Jordan's past, of course there isn't one."

Liv was making her nervous. "This isn't illegal."

"Absolutely not. Though Kelley's fans might not see it as playing fair. I'd hate to lose their trust. Word of mouth is crucial for sales these days. The Facebook/social networking generation sells more books for us than any ad campaign we could run. The news that Kelley isn't who they thought she was would spread like wildfire. I think the new term is going viral."

"And the real Kelley?"

"Might have her cover blown." And more important, as far as Olivia was concerned, Bennett Books would lose credibility.

Over dinner at one of her favorite restaurants in Union Square, Olivia filled her husband in on the possibility of *Spring Farm* winning the Elgin Award. Sandy-haired, still in good shape thanks to his gym membership,

Kurt Bennett was obsessed with trying to hold off the physical reminders that he was fifty-two. Most people assumed he was in his forties. He liked that. He'd bought a gym membership for Liv too, but she seldom went, didn't like getting sweaty. Not that she looked all that bad, but she wasn't as thin as when they married a dozen years ago, and lately she'd begun having the gray in her dark hair touched up.

"Now I not only have to present the Pullman offer to Rebecca, I have to tell her about Elgin. Hard to imagine that such good news—for most authors—will probably send her into a tailspin."

He sipped his wine, a rather acceptable Pinot Noir. He allowed himself just two drinks a day. Too many empty calories. "Be straight with her. I'm tired of the hand holding we've had to do with Rebecca. Granted this book has had phenomenal sales and reignited sales for the first two books, but all this cloak and dagger stuff seems rather silly. We need to be looking out for our own best interest, celebrating instead of worrying. The commission on the movie rights alone will give us a very good financial year."

"From Rebecca's point of view, it's not silly."

"Is she going to spend the rest of her life hiding from her past like a criminal? Supremely stupid if you ask me."

"I called to tell her I'll be at her place late tomorrow afternoon, ostensibly to talk about a timeline for her next book. I wish you'd go with me."

"She's your pet. I might just tell her what I think. Are you going to stay over?"

"Yes. Tomorrow morning, I have to keep a couple of appointments. I'll leave around noon. Ashley reserved me a room at one of the motels in town—there's not a lot to choose from."

Kurt signaled the waiter for the check. "Why don't you leave your car in the garage tonight? I have to come in early too. We can ride together for a change."

Chapter 2

Winter was hovering at the edge of the Sierras. The black oaks had already lost most of their golden leaves. No snow as yet, but it was cold enough that the resorts at Tahoe and Mammoth were making snow, anticipating help from the storm predicted for the weekend.

Raley's Supermarket was busier than usual for a Thursday morning, with residents stocking up in case the roads weren't cleared fast enough or the power went out. Fall had been dry and unusually warm in the Sierra foothills, so the abrupt shift into winter had everyone scurrying. Rebecca Sawyer's grocery cart was filled with candles, fresh flashlight batteries, and plenty of canned food she could heat up on the propane-fueled Coleman stove she kept for such emergencies. Since Olivia was arriving late this afternoon, Rebecca was also in need of fresh food for tonight's dinner—maybe fettuccini topped with shrimp, a garden salad and crusty rolls. She'd serve a good wine and a few appetizers. Liv rarely ate dessert, unless it was cheese and fruit. Her years living abroad had made her something of a food snob. Though Rebecca loved to cook, it wasn't often she cooked for her publisher because Olivia was always in a hurry to get back to San Francisco, making the eight-hour round trip to Oakhurst in one day, taking care of business while she and Rebecca ate lunch at one of the local restaurants.

Rebecca was looking forward to the storm. Winter was her favorite time to hunker down and write, especially when she was beginning a new book. This storm would keep her inside and force her to move beyond the opening chapters. Beginning was the hardest part, like getting a cold car to start on a winter morning. In long hand, on lined legal pads she bought at Costco, she coaxed words into the story she was currently carrying around in her head. On good writing days, the words raced onto the paper, almost dictating themselves. Then there were the days she threw away page after page of false starts and bad dialogue. She'd learned that, when a day's efforts ended up in the wastebasket, the next day would often produce better ideas, better words, as though failure had the power to breathe life into the project. The process was never tidy. Start—stop—start again and again. Add, subtract, move sentences, paragraphs and pages, then type a page or two into the computer.

Over many months, the book would be fleshed out. Far from finished but at least there was a structure ready to be endlessly rewritten—passages added or deleted, colorful phrases substituted for bland ones. There were always details she needed to check as she went along. She loved creating places and characters that she could team around. With the stroke of her pen or the cut/paste option on the computer, one character would succeed, another fail. She was never more content than when she was immersed in the process. She didn't let anyone, not even Liv, see her work until it was in the last stages of editing, not because she was a perfectionist but because she was leery about sharing her work too soon.

Rebecca—Becca to her friends—relished the privacy that writing demanded. She couldn't imagine how screenwriters collaborated without each losing the uniqueness of their own ideas and style. Solitude suited her, yet she wasn't a recluse. She liked people, had several good friends in town and plenty of casual acquaintances but, because people knew she was a writer, they respected her periods of creative hibernation. No one in town knew what she actually wrote, only that she wrote, swallowing the lie that she was a ghostwriter hired by those with a story to tell but without the skill to tell it. A perfect cover.

Only Liv and Kurt knew the truth.

At thirty-two, Rebecca's life was exactly the way she wanted it.

Well not exactly.

There was the problem of Alex.

Because the drive from San Francisco across California's Central Valley was unbelievably boring, Olivia always listened to an audio book when she went to Rebecca's; today it was *The Girl Who Played with Fire*. Enough action to keep her from fretting about the task before her. Just after four o'clock, she turned onto Highway 140, then took 49 into Oakhurst, drove to the north end of town, and checked into the Shilo Inn. Not really an inn, just an above average motel. Olivia would have preferred something classier, but this was all Ashley could find on short notice. Small mountain towns were almost as boring as the Central Valley. Impossibly provincial. Olivia preferred San Francisco's cosmopolitan atmosphere, shopping at Sak's, dining at Masa's.

Half an hour later, she drove back to the middle of town and turned east, following Crane Valley Road to the narrow road that led to Rebecca's house, a sprawling fifties style ranch house in a clearing ringed with pines. In Olivia's view, the middle of nowhere.

She sat in the car for a few moments, disengaging herself from the complexities of Larsson's storyline and, in truth, procrastinating. She dreaded telling Rebecca that the quality and popularity of her work might bring down the carefully constructed house of cards that tied Emily, Rebecca and Bennett Books together. As Olivia was locking the car, Rebecca walked around the side of the garage, carrying an empty wastebasket.

"Hi Liv. I didn't hear you drive up. Have you been to the motel already?"

"Yes. Not great, but not terrible either. I hope I'm not interrupting your work."

"Not at all. I'm waiting for the bad weather before tackling chapter four. Come in. Would you like some tea or wine?"

"Wine."

"The cats have been expecting you." There was a hint of amusement in Rebecca's voice.

Never quite sure when she was being teased, Olivia gambled that Rebecca was kidding. "Let me guess. They're afraid to come indoors."

Becca laughed. "Something like that."

The living room was designed for cozy comfort, at once rustic and modern, several deep leather chairs with footstools and a bright cobalt and lime green sectional stretched in front of a massive stone fireplace conveniently heated by natural gas. Rebecca had never mastered building a fire. The table lamps were already on. Olivia slipped off her high heels and curled into the sectional, letting the stress of the four-hour drive slip away.

Until dinner was ready, they sipped wine and talked about the weather, the Christmas specials that Bennett Books was promoting, and Rebecca's next book, which was set in Nova Scotia and Louisiana.

"I just got back from the Maritimes two weeks ago. I checked on additional locations, took pictures to record the geographical features, and spent more time in the libraries. A lot of the material is in French so that slowed me down. Winter sets in really early up there. It was freezing."

"Who takes care of the cats when you're gone?" Olivia didn't really care, but it was something to talk about instead of what she'd come to talk about.

"My neighbor Trudy; she lives a quarter mile farther along this road. Sometimes she brings her dinner over and stays with them for the evening so they don't get too lonesome."

The concept of lonely cats puzzled Olivia, but she kept her thoughts to herself.

After dinner, they drank more wine, spread imported cheeses on peppery water crackers, and laid out a publishing schedule for Rebecca's new book though Rebecca rarely met Olivia's deadlines. Ideas did not respect calendars.

When Olivia could no longer avoid the real reason for her trip, she pulled the Elgin flyer from her briefcase and handed it to Rebecca. "This was released to the press two days ago."

Rebecca skimmed it, immediately pleased when she saw *Spring Farm* listed. "Very nice. I'm up against some big names. Do you think I have a chance?"

Olivia shrugged. "Being nominated is no small thing. Camacho and Van de Veer are your major competitors. Stone's book is too intellectual. It requires a degree in the Classics and an unabridged dictionary. That said, anytime a panel of judges is involved, it's a crap shoot."

Rebecca refilled their wine glasses. "You've waited several hours to tell me about this—so there must be a downside in here someplace."

Caught.

"About the award itself, no major downside. Big for sales, probably more signings and readings for Emily." *The truth.* "If you win, however, you should collect the award in person." *The unwelcome truth.*

Rebecca's expression changed from pleased to panic-stricken, cold dread crawling along her spine. "If I do attend and my picture ends up in a newspaper or on the Internet, someone will say *I saw Kelley Jordan in Miami or L.A. and that's not the same person.* Even worse, *Isn't that Rebecca Kingston? Where has she been hiding all these years?* Game over. Have Emily accept it or you accept it. Tell them I'm ill."

"I haven't worried about Emily pretending to be you for the readings, but lying about who Kelley is in front of the Elgin people and most of the major publishing houses is a bad idea. I've got the company's integrity to protect."

Rebecca was fairly sure that, if it came down to a choice of saving Bennett Books or her, Liv would throw her to the wolves without a second thought. Studying her wine glass as though it contained an answer to this ugly dilemma, she felt fear close around her heart. She wasn't ready to face the media or the curious public—again. Her entire childhood, even her college and married years, had been picked over by the voracious media.

She was proud of her writing, proud of the responses from readers who visited her website, telling her how much they enjoyed her books. She loved waking in the morning to find a new line of dialogue or a twist of plot waiting to be added to the current manuscript, her subconscious having been at work while she was sleeping.

But attending the Awards was out of the question. Someone was sure to spot the star of *Mandy* and the paparazzi would be in hot pursuit, her carefully crafted disguise ripped away. Nowadays, her hair was shorter, her wardrobe was simpler, and she was no longer rail thin. She didn't need glasses but, whenever she traveled, she wore frames with clear lenses.

"Maybe I won't win. That would solve everything." She looked up from the wine glass and grinned. But beneath the grin, she was refusing to attend.

This was probably the best time for Olivia to explain the other potential nightmare. Might as well completely ruin what remained of the evening. "There's one more issue on the table. Do you know who Nate Pullman is?"

Rebecca did.

Her stomach tightened. Her *Yes* was barely audible. "A major movie producer. Won an Oscar several years ago for *Serious Doubts*." Her mouth was suddenly dry.

Olivia leaned forward, "He's interested in turning *Spring Farm* into a movie. Kurt has met with him several times in the last few weeks."

It took Rebecca several minutes to respond. In those minutes, she was remembering her fifth birthday, the birthday she spent at Disneyland. Her parents had been busy with a movie or play, so Nate Pullman had taken her on the rides and let her eat all the junk food she wanted—until she threw up. He'd had as much fun as she had. Nate had been one of the best parts of her childhood. The substitute parent who paid attention to her.

Her voice was firm. "I won't give my permission."

"Even if we write into the contract every kind of confidentiality protection our lawyers can think of?"

Rebecca summoned up enough energy to shake her head. "There's no such thing as complete confidentiality in that world. I should know. Besides," she took in extra air, "he's my godfather."

"Oh Lord."

"So you see, it's impossible, a Pandora's box. Nate would want to work with the author—he always does. I don't want to—correction—I can't go there."

As Olivia digested the word *godfather*, she realized there was little hope of getting Rebecca to sell Pullman the movie rights. Since she and Kurt had been publishing Rebecca's books, Olivia had learned that there was an impenetrable wall Rebecca had built between her past and present. It did no good to try to breach it. Getting her to allow Emily to promote *Spring Farm* had taken three trips to Oakhurst. The first two books had had to rely on traditional advertising.

They talked until after eleven, not arguing but not compromising. Rebecca adamantly refused to consider attending the award ceremony, and she would not enter into negotiations about the movie. End of discussion.

Kurt was right; there'd been too much handholding. Rebecca wasn't a criminal. She'd simply been famous and had famous parents. But that life, that childhood had permanently scarred her.

When Olivia ran out of rational arguments, she retreated to the Inn and called Kurt, unloading her failure and frustration on him. He reminded her that Rebecca's contract allowed Bennett Books to act as her agent. They could legally sell the movie rights without Rebecca's permission. Kurt wanted this movie deal badly enough that he just might close the deal with Pullman in spite of Rebecca's refusal. But if he did that, they could lose her as an author.

That possibility kept Olivia awake until almost three.

After Liv left, Rebecca sat huddled on the sectional, wrapped in a fleece throw, contemplating the news that the anonymity she so cherished was about to be destroyed by her own success.

Her first instinct was to flee.

But she couldn't think of anywhere to go. Oakhurst was her safe harbor.

To anyone not living it, Rebecca's childhood seemed the stuff of fairy tales. Talented, famous parents who had stayed married, an obscene number of toys, a beautiful bedroom in the ocean front house at Malibu and another in the Manhattan penthouse overlooking Central Park. Tutors, piano and dancing lessons, expensive summer camps, skiing in the winter.

When she was eleven, her father cast her in a movie he was directing in Spain—a bit part with one scene and just four lines. She did it to please him. The media quickly picked up on the story: *Only child of Peter Kingston and Hillary Wallingford begins her own career.* Though other small parts in movies and on TV followed, she didn't much care whether she acted or not. She would have preferred hanging out with friends, but then she didn't have all that many. She'd attended private elementary schools, one in New York, another in Santa Monica, but was seldom in either of them for a full school year. When her parents were working on location, she accompanied them, so she never played on a soccer team or belonged to the Girl Scouts. It was hard to find friends if you were something of a gypsy. At fourteen, she was offered the lead in a new TV series entitled *Mandy* about a teenager with famous parents. Not much of an acting stretch. The show was an instant success. The public and the media had a new darling, and her parents were thrilled that she was following in their footsteps. Rebecca, however, was not thrilled.

"You promised that I could go to high school full time in L.A. or New York. No more tutors or racing around the universe."

Her father couldn't see what the problem was. "Any child can go to high school. Not everyone can be a TV star." When the promise about high school was broken, Hillary was appearing on Broadway, too busy to take her daughter's frantic phone call. And so Rebecca became Mandy. There were fan clubs, magazine articles, and a female bodyguard when she went out without one of her parents. Instead of attending high school, she was tutored on the set. She vowed never to forgive what she saw as her parents' treachery.

Mandy lasted four seasons.

When she turned eighteen, Rebecca had had enough and confronted her father. "Screw my career, actually screw your careers too. I want to go to college and be normal for once in my life. It's almost impossible to be normal in this family."

She had already instructed her agent to break her contract. Being eighteen gave her that power. *Mandy* went into reruns and, having been accepted into Wellesley's undergraduate writing program, Rebecca moved to the East Coast. She cut her hair, left her glamorous wardrobe behind, and settled into a dorm instead of joining one of the sororities that were falling all over themselves to have *the* Rebecca Kingston as a member. It took a couple of semesters to convince her new friends to forget—most of the time—who she had been. The first step in the reinvention of Rebecca Kingston.

When she graduated from Wellesley, her parents' arrival on campus had, of course, turned the day into a celebrity circus, students and parents alike trying to get a look at Peter and Hillary, sneaking photographs and asking for autographs. Thus Rebecca's day, like so many other days in her life, was all about her famous family. The Wellesley students, who had almost forgotten that Rebecca was a *Kingston*, were reminded that she wasn't really one of them.

The second step in reinventing herself came soon after her college graduation when she eloped with her college roommate's older brother. David Sawyer was Ivy League handsome, came from old New England money, and was already working for his family's brokerage house. After a two week Hawaiian honeymoon, Rebecca found herself playing a new role: the Junior League/Country Club wife, who entertained her husband's clients and was seen at gallery openings and the opera. Though she'd tried to stay out of the spotlight while she was a student, she still had enough star power to be an asset to the Sawyer family. She'd foolishly jumped from the non-stop scrutiny of the entertainment world into the snobbish scrutiny of the East Coast social register. And of course the paparazzi were back.

It took three years to admit that marrying David had been a mistake. For once, she couldn't blame her parents for what was happening in her life. Misunderstanding her unhappiness, David accused her of missing the bright lights of Hollywood. "Aren't we good enough for you?"

"I just want to be myself." A response that didn't come close to explaining the complexity of her feelings, but it was the best she could do at that moment. All her life it had been impossible to know whether people really liked her for herself or were simply in awe of who she was, who her parents were. She craved invisibility. The freedom to walk down a street without someone recognizing her. To buy groceries or go to a post office without attracting attention.

David's family made sure she received a handsome settlement in lieu of alimony, and she disappeared from their lives, though she kept Sawyer as her last name. *Kingston* had always attracted too much attention. The settlement money, along with the royalties from the *Mandy* reruns and the investments her father's broker had made with her TV earnings, gave her enough income to experiment with being invisible. She wanted time to write and carve out her own life.

Chapter 3

On Saturday, wind-whipped rain kept Rebecca indoors, but by Sunday afternoon the wind had died down, leaving two inches of wet snow on the pines surrounding Rebecca's house. A temporary Christmas card that would vanish with the first touch of sun.

Perfect writing weather, yet Becca sat in her studio, staring at the yellow pad, unable to say anything to the paper. Since Olivia's visit, her brain had gone dead. Why bother to write? It was writing that was about to destroy her sanctuary. In one evening, the past she thought she'd successfully escaped had arrived on the doorstep, masquerading as praise.

She'd probably over-reacted to Liv's news, been unnecessarily stubborn. After all, she reasoned, she wasn't about to die or go to prison. She was not going to be destitute. In fact, nothing had actually changed—so far. The wood stove with its pale blue soapstone sides still warmed the studio and the cats were, as usual, fussing about going outside in the wet weather. They were always neurotic during a storm.

Halfway through Sunday afternoon, when the yellow pad was still in pristine condition, Tinker, a seven-year old tom who was fairly certain he was in charge of the house, gave up trying to get Rebecca's attention and decamped to the living room in a sulk. The two younger cats, Matilda and Kitkat, shared the upholstered window seat in the studio's bay window, Matilda making low, threatening gurgles at the birds she suspected were hiding just beyond her vision. Kitkat was bathing; Kitkat was always bathing, never entirely sure she was clean enough.

Rebecca hadn't set out to have pets. The cats had, nevertheless, found their way to her house and heart in very different ways. Tinker had belonged to the mother of the contractor she'd hired to knock out the wall between two small bedrooms to create her studio and install the French doors opening onto the front patio. The woman was going into an assisted living facility that didn't take pets. Would Becca adopt the cat? She'd never had a pet before. Might be nice.

Matilda had wandered into the patio on her own, much too thin, her eyes running. She'd probably been abandoned, surviving only because she was an annoyingly good hunter, proudly bringing her kill into the house, expecting something other than Rebecca telling her in no uncertain terms to *Get that damned mouse out of here!*

Then, a month after she'd slept with Alex for the first time, he conned her into taking Kitkat. As a member of the Foothills Search and Rescue team, Alex had gone on a call to rescue two horses from a barn in the path of a wildfire. A mother cat and four kittens needed rescuing too. If Becca would take one of the kittens, Alex would install a cat door. She agreed, lured by the opportunity to get rid of the litter box.

And so there were three cats in residence.

Her studio, as well as the guest room, occupied the south L of her ranch house; the master suite was in the north L. The living room, dining room, and kitchen connected them. From every room but the kitchen, she could walk onto the front patio through French doors. The shortest way between the studio and her bedroom was directly across the patio. The house was her greatest treasure. She couldn't imagine how she had ever lived anywhere else. There was no housekeeper, no cook or gardener. All those people her parents couldn't live without. She didn't mind scrubbing the sink, loved putting bulbs out in the winter and experimenting with new recipes. Ideal invisibility.

The house she and David bought during their second year of marriage was a Cape Cod bungalow. What her mother-in-law had called a starter house. It didn't take long for the house to become a battlefield. Her mother-in-law lived by a rigid, unwritten code of East Coast correctness. *There is only one right way to furnish a Cape Cod style house.* Never mind that Becca truly hated Geraldine Sawyer's *right way*: brocade upholstery, occasional tables with spindly, carved legs that curved out at the bottom. Mahogany everywhere. It had taken Becca eighteen years to stand up to her parents' view of how she should live her life. In the three years she was married, she'd never successfully stood up to her mother-in-law because David thought his mother's opinion about almost everything mattered more than his wife's. Despite Geraldine Sawyer's belief that only druggies and surfers lived in California, she often used Rebecca's Hollywood connections to her advantage: *This is our daughter-in-law, Rebecca Kingston, yes that Rebecca Kingston.*

Leaving the Cape Cod house—and her marriage—had been embarrassingly easy.

Once the snow stopped falling, Rebecca put on her hiking boots and followed the road into the forest beyond Trudy's house, hoping the hush of the snow would ease the tension in her neck and shoulders. She needed to move, be outside, away from the memory of Liv's voice telling her that Nate was on the horizon and that an award for her work might force her to come out of hiding and face a world she'd abandoned nearly seven years ago in favor of cats, writing, and new friends.

Like Alex.

Oakhurst had provided a fresh page on which to write her life. As a child and teenager, she hadn't made many friends. As a college student and wife, she had a few but, once she went off the grid, she lost contact with them. People living in the Sierra foothills didn't pry. Who you were today was all that mattered. That attitude allowed her to grow into herself.

As she left footprints in the wet snow, Rebecca conjured worst-case scenarios. She could show up to accept the award—egotistical to assume she'd win—and, as Kelley Jordan, say thanks and run for home. After all, there was no paper trail from Kelley Jordan or Bennett Books to Oakhurst. How important could a book award be to the media? It wouldn't make the nightly news or the pages of *Time*. The award was probably not as dangerous as Nate Pullman's interest in *Spring Farm*. His films always made a splash as well as huge sums of money. They weren't, however, the kinds of films her father made. Peter Kingston's films made statements—edgy, iconic stories that were discussed in university film classes. The dangerous part of the movie offer was that Nate's staff always did their homework. They would eventually discover who Kelley Jordan really was. There were no secrets in Hollywood.

Then, she'd have to explain herself to her parents, who thought she was living in England. One of Rebecca's favorite tutors, Megan, had married a Brit and was living south of London. Rebecca sent birthday and Christmas gifts destined for her parents to Megan, whose husband Hugh traveled regularly and mailed them from different locations within the UK. It was too risky to give her parents her real address. They might just show up on her doorstep. She kept track of them on the Internet, occasionally calling them from a phone that couldn't be traced to her. She didn't hate her parents. She simply couldn't be anywhere near them. They were larger than life and sucked up all the air in the vicinity. Rebecca shivered at the thought of giving them access to who she was now. They would think she'd lost her mind, living alone in an obscure town, feeding kindling into the soapstone stove, poring over cookbooks for recipes, and sleeping with an ex-ski racer.

It was getting dark. Not wise to keep walking without a flashlight, and the cats would be wanting their dinner. She hadn't eaten all day and still wasn't hungry, thanks to the knot in her stomach.

After leaving David, Rebecca spent a few months in Milwaukee—surely no one would track her to Milwaukee—seeing a therapist three times a week, gradually coming to terms with some of the issues from her past. In trying to escape being Rebecca Kingston, she'd married David, naively assuming that, when she entered his world, she'd be safe—a married woman, no longer answerable to Peter and Hillary or Mandy's adoring fans. As Mrs. David Sawyer, she wouldn't have to figure out what to do with her life. Marriage would figure it out for her. An assumption born of too many years having others make her decisions. At twenty-two, she had few life skills and no idea who she really was or what she was capable of.

The weeks of therapy helped a little, letting her talk honestly about herself and how she felt. The next step was to find a place to practice being herself.

She remembered having been with her parents on location in the Sierras when she was twelve, remembered how comforting the mountains felt—majestic, solid, resisting the pressures surrounding them. Perhaps living near them would give her strength. Eager to find a new home, she headed for Yosemite, rented a room in a small hotel in Groveland just outside the park, and began scouting the area for the right house, eventually buying the house in Oakhurst—her first real home—with a substantial mortgage and furniture she'd chosen. No mahogany in sight. For the first time in her life, she was content.

She was not willing to lose any of this.

Jake Hannigan's desk was strewn with folders, books, and to do lists. When he was developing a story, he was thorough and organized, bordering on obsessive. The rest of his life never received the kind of structure he established when he was writing—which probably explained why his marriage fell apart. Chasing stories was more interesting than remembering to pick up milk on the way home or that he and Darlene were having company for dinner on Friday. Too late, he'd discovered he wasn't ready for domesticity. He escaped by quitting a perfectly good job at *The Record*, a small newspaper on Long Island, to become a stringer in the Middle East. Hurt and angry, Darlene continued teaching second graders and waited for Jake to come home. After he'd been gone a year, sending an occasional e-mail message to let her know he was alive, Darlene sued him for divorce which, ironically, became final three days before the Palestinian bomber interrupted his war correspondent career and sent him home. When she visited him in the rehab facility on Long Island, she was already seeing someone else.

In the ten days since Max had given him the Elgin assignment, Jake had finished the first article on Norene Camacho, a well-respected author of three other novels. Her book *Wrong Side of the Border* had been on the bestseller list for months. It was the story of a brother and sister whose parents had been deported to Mexico, leaving the children, who had been born in Texas, on their own. Jake had only intended to skim the book. He seldom read fiction of any kind—maybe a Michael Connelly mystery on a long flight—but he found himself drawn into Camacho's story and quickly finished the book. Getting an interview with her had been simple. Her agent and publisher were delighted she would be featured in *Twenty-First Century*. Jake flew down to Dallas one afternoon, interviewed her the next day, and caught the red eye out of Dallas that night. Piece of cake. He was satisfied with the article, ready to give it to Max and start Kelley Jordan's book. Because it was longer than Camacho's, he doubted he'd have the time to read all of it.

Now he was impatiently waiting for Olivia Bennett to return his phone calls. He'd left several messages with her assistant. In the meantime, he searched in vain for information on Kelley Jordan, finding little more than the brief paragraph on the back cover of her books.

Kelley Jordan's books are an intriguing blend of human strengths and weaknesses set against the panorama of history. She has written two other best sellers: Impossible Secrets and The Lost Years.

The people at *Publishers Weekly* and *Booklist* couldn't add any information. Google and Wikipedia weren't much help either, and there was no photo on the book jacket. Frustrated, he contacted the two historians who were quoted on the book's back cover. They were quick to confirm that her research on the Oregon Trail was impeccable. Bennett Books had asked them to write their reviews, but they'd had no direct contact with Jordan. In this day of proliferating information, he'd come up dry.

Nowhere was there anything that told him where she had been born, what her education was—nothing personal. Her website only listed her upcoming appearances to promote the books and provided space for comments from her readers, most of whom seemed to love her work. He printed out the website's promotional material and her personal appearance schedule. She was currently in Miami and would be there for three more days.

Going to Miami was a gamble. He'd rather confer with the publisher before talking to the author, but he was wasting time. The expense account could handle a flight to Miami and a hotel room for a couple of nights. He left a message for Max, booked a flight for the next afternoon and went home to pack.

Olivia had left firm instructions that, if any calls came in about Kelley Jordan, Ashley should take the messages but make no promises about Olivia returning the calls. She hadn't yet worked out just how she should field the inquiries about Kelley and the Elgin nomination—what the spin should be.

Since the announcement of the finalists, there had been ten or eleven requests for interviews—four from someone named Jacob Hannigan of *Twenty-First Century*. After his fourth message, Olivia called the magazine, only to be told that he was on assignment in Miami for the next couple of days.

Miami!

Not good news. Public appearance information for Bennett's authors was easily available on each author's website and on Bennett's. She pushed the intercom. "Ashley, find Kelley."

Chapter 4

Emily rather enjoyed being Kelley Jordan for a few days each month. She could relax into the role, do a few readings, sign hundreds of books, smile, and ask what the fans liked about *Spring Farm*. Being Kelley was much simpler than being Emily. Bennett Books put her up in good hotels, made sure the rental car had a GPS, and never complained about how much she spent on food, though her tastes were rather simple. The Gerrard household thought it was a big deal if they could afford dinner at Applebee's. Being on her own gave her time to work on new Storytelling material. Except for the nightly calls to the girls—who usually saved up a day's worth of problems to share—the trips were peaceful interludes.

A few minutes before Kelley Jordan's 11 a.m. reading at the Borders Bookstore on Biscayne Boulevard, Jake slipped into an empty seat at the back. There was no hope of being inconspicuous since he was the only man in the audience. Though he'd brought his laptop for notes, he left it in the zippered case. No sense attracting additional attention. Kelley was scheduled for two readings today, this one and another at four in the library in Miami Beach. He had no intention of trying to interview her this morning but, after her second reading, he planned to introduce himself and suggest they have dinner. Before he left the hotel, he'd asked the concierge to recommend a restaurant in Miami Beach—*Clarke's is very popular*—and made a reservation for two at six o'clock.

Promptly at eleven, a balding block of a man wearing a pink shirt and tie introduced himself as the store manager, apologized that there were no more chairs, and encouraged the audience to stay after the reading to have their copies of *Spring Farm* signed. "And now, here's our lovely author, Kelley Jordan."

As the audience applauded, the attractive blonde who had been standing off to the side came forward, thanked the manager, laid the hardback book she was carrying on the lectern, and adjusted the microphone's height. Her smile swept across the audience. "Good morning. I'm so glad to see all of you."

Jake found himself smiling back, only half-listening to her introductory comments while he searched for the right words to describe her. *Hot* was the first word that came to mind but probably was not a good choice for this kind of article. She was perhaps in her mid-thirties, about 5' 3" or 4", shoulder length hair that fell softly around her face. Pretty in a wholesome way. Though pretty and blonde often translated into empty-headed, he was fairly sure her head wasn't empty. Suffice it to say, Kelley Jordan was definitely not what he'd expected. With a twinge of disappointment, he took note of her wedding ring.

"I'm going to read from the fourth chapter of *Spring Farm,*" she paused as she opened the book. "This is the morning Harriet and her physician father are leaving Independence, Missouri, adding their wagon and two cows to a wagon train heading toward Oregon. Harriet is twenty-three, an accomplished portrait artist. Since her mother's death last year, Harriet has had to abandon her dreams of having her own studio to help her physician father in his clinic. And now her father wants to start over out West. He has not listened to Harriet's pleas that she be allowed to stay in Chicago on her own.

> *Harriet hadn't slept. It was her final night in civilization—if you could call this crude jumble of unpainted frame buildings and dusty streets civilized. It had taken all of her control not to climb out of the wagon while her father slept and find someone who was traveling east and beg a ride. She had a little money of her own, earned from her painting commissions. Let her father go on this adventure by himself. She had friends in Chicago, and her art teacher was there. She desperately wanted to be back in the two-story brick house that didn't belong to them anymore, in her bed with its down comforter and fat feather pillow."*

In Jake's experience, most authors read their own work badly. The few readings Darlene had dragged him to had been deadly dull; poets seemed especially awkward when confronted with their own words.

Kelley, however, had a rather husky voice that embellished the story. She was poised, comfortable in front of the crowd. He was already looking forward to having dinner with her.

For half an hour, her voice owned the room; then she moved over to the table the store had provided and spent the next hour autographing books. Jake stood near the magazine shelves, positioned so he could watch her without watching. She seemed to be enjoying her fans, asking them questions, paying attention to their answers. Just before she finished, Jake chanced taking her picture with his cell phone, quickly checked that the picture was in focus, then left the bookstore. He'd make notes in the computer while he ate lunch.

As Emily was leaving her hotel room to drive to the afternoon reading, Olivia called.

"A problem?" Emily gathered up her purse and the book, taking a last look in the mirror.

"Maybe. I've had several messages from a reporter named Jacob Hannigan, who writes for *Twenty-First Century*. When I finally returned his calls, the magazine told me he's in Miami for a couple of days—on assignment. I doubt it's a coincidence."

Emily let the hotel door click shut behind her and headed for the elevator. "You think he's looking for Kelley?"

"I just wanted you to know. I won't keep you."

"Don't worry; I'll be cool."

Emily saw him the moment she sat down at the table in the library's fiction section and clipped on the body microphone the young librarian handed her. Light brown hair, khaki Dockers, a brown sport jacket—too heavy for Miami weather—no tie. She was fairly sure he'd been in the back row at this morning's reading. So Olivia wasn't paranoid. Emily gave the audience her usual smile and hoped she would be able to keep her cool if he wanted to interview her.

Two hours later, she was seated across from him at one of the polished pine tables in the pub-like restaurant called Clarke's. She hadn't had dinner with a man—alone—since Patrick's death, yet accepting Jake Hannigan's dinner invitation had been strangely easy. "I'd like to interview you if you're free for dinner." *Smooth.* Of course this wasn't a date. This was part of her job description. She was simply having dinner with a man chasing a story about someone who didn't exist. For the briefest of moments, she wished it were more than an interview. He was rather charming, at once boyish and assertive, blue eyes that seemed to be smiling even when he wasn't. As they ordered drinks and dinner, and admired the restaurant's old world ambiance, he was gently probing for information without probing. What was her favorite wine, was this her first time in Miami, where had she grown up? Siblings?

Chardonnay, yes, San Francisco, an older brother.

Not answering his questions would have been rude, especially since he was paying for dinner, so she offered him unimportant and untraceable information: Where had she attended college. *Berkeley—Communication major, Library Science minor.*

But when he asked what her husband did, whether she had children, she suddenly heard Olivia's warning, and Emily's guard went up. She'd given interviews as Kelley before, mostly for local papers, but Jake Hannigan was in a different league. Good looking and clever. It would be easy to fall under his spell and answer his questions too truthfully.

Time to be cool. "I don't answer those kinds of personal questions. They have no bearing on my work. I'm happy to answer anything about the books."

He didn't back off. "Who a writer is, what his or her past life has been, shows up in what they write—it can't be avoided. Your book is about a difficult father/daughter relationship. Do you get along with your father?" The blue eyes challenged her.

"I did. He died when I was in college." Two could play at this game. "Do you show up in what you write?"

His eyes registered surprise. *Good.* She felt less pressured.

"Journalism is reporting what you see and what people tell you. We're trained to keep ourselves out of what we write. If I didn't, I wouldn't have a job for long or I'd get moved to the op/ed page."

"Fiction writers can't be objective?"

"Of course not. Fiction is based on emotion."

"Where did you get that idea?"

He liked her spirit. It had been ages since he'd enjoyed talking with a woman. Jake was accustomed to enjoying women in a number of other ways. Conversation wasn't usually one of them.

Two hours flew by. They discussed a couple of recent movies they'd both seen, debated the possible reasons for the way the East Coat hated the West Coast and vice versa, and ended up talking about art. They both loved the Old Masters. As they were leaving the restaurant, Jake suggested taking a stroll toward South Pointe. He wasn't ready to end the evening. The air was warm, a slight breeze playing with her hair. "When do you leave Miami?"

"Tomorrow, three o'clock. You?"

"Noon. How do you ever find time to write if you're flying all over the place signing books?"

"I only travel during the six months after a book has been released—a few days a month." Time to redirect, "Do you travel much?"

"Depends on the assignment."

"Overseas?"

"Sometimes. Most of what I write has to do with politics in the Middle East."

"How did you end up with this assignment?"

"My boss was desperate."

"Have you been to Iraq?"

"A few times, not recently though."

"Because?"

"Because when I was working in Palestine two years ago, I nearly got blown to smithereens. Spent a few months in rehab. The doctors almost got rid of my limp."

She stopped walking and turned to face him. Though the darkness made it hard to see her expression clearly, she looked as though she was going to cry. "It's okay. Really. The doctors put my leg back together with pins and plates. Of course, my football career is probably over."

In the faint light cast by the streetlight, he saw that there actually were tears on her cheeks.

"What did I say?"

She rubbed at the tears, embarrassed. "Sorry. It's not about you. You just said it so casually—*smithereens*. Patrick was killed by a land mine. They told me there wasn't much left of him—someone used the same word—and so they sealed the casket."

Jake remembered the wedding ring.

"Patrick was your husband?"

She nodded.

"How long ago?"

"Sixteen months."

"Iraq?"

Another nod. "Not military. He was a surgeon helping reopen one of Baghdad's hospitals." She stopped. "I should get back to my car, find my way over the causeway. Thanks for dinner. I apologize for—the tears. Sometimes they just show up."

"No apology necessary." They retraced their steps to the restaurant parking lot in silence. The evening had taken a solemn turn. As she unlocked the car door, he risked "Will you have breakfast with me tomorrow?"

She hesitated. "I have to be at the book fair by 9:30. My publisher has a booth."

"Eight o'clock?"

"Doubletree Grand. There's a coffee shop."

Jake smiled. "I'll be there."

As she drove off, the GPS told her to turn right in one hundred yards, guiding her onto the causeway that connected Miami Beach to the city.

Not until she turned the lock on the inside of her hotel room did she admit to herself how badly she'd compromised the whole Kelley Jordan secret. Because she'd given Kelley part of her own life, Liv might fire her. Jake would undoubtedly use everything they'd talked about, give Kelley a husband who'd been killed in Iraq. Jake Hannigan was good at extracting information and she'd been ridiculously gullible. If she had any sense, she'd check out of the hotel before he arrived in the morning.

But she was looking forward to having breakfast with him.

Standing in front of the Departures board in Miami International Airport, checking that his 12:06 flight to New York was on time, Jake skimmed ahead to three o'clock. The only California bound flights were to Los Angeles at 1:45 and 4:30, and a 3:02 flight to San Francisco. Flight 1447.

Chapter 5

Emily usually slept during plane flights but not this time. She spent the five plus hours between Miami and San Francisco replaying her conversations with Jake Hannigan, remembering his concern about her sudden tears, remembering the way his eyes crinkled at the corners when he smiled. A young Harrison Ford. Sort of. In the midst of remembering their conversations, she struggled with how best to tell Olivia that Kelley Jordan had acquired a San Francisco childhood, a brother, a university and a dead husband. Emily hadn't actually given anything important away, but the blank sheet that had been Kelley Jordan wasn't so blank anymore. There was, however, no need to confess that she'd been attracted to Jake, had enjoyed his company in spite of the fact he was probably only interested in interviewing her—the Kelley Jordan part of her—for his article.

During their breakfast at the hotel, she'd let down her guard and became more like the Emily she'd been before Patrick died. That Emily had been full of laughter, comfortable in her own skin. Today's Emily was too often weighed down by the complexities of single parenting and the need to make a living. But while she was talking to Jake Hannigan, she hadn't once thought about the girls or whether she would have enough cash to get through the month.

As soon as Jake's plane landed at JFK, he caught a cab to *Twenty-First Century's* office. He needed a favor from Carson, the computer geek who kept the magazine's software up and running. Time and opportunity permitting, Carson could hack his way into almost anything. In this case, Jake needed Carson to take a look at the manifest for United's 3:02 flight from Miami to San Francisco. He also asked him to check the July 2009 casualty lists from Baghdad for a civilian doctor, Patrick Jordan. Jake told himself he was only chasing a story, but he knew there was now much more at stake. He wanted to see Kelley again and, unless he was misreading her, she felt the same way. There was no mistaking the subtle stirrings of attraction between them.

It would take him a few days to rough out the information he'd already accumulated, then fly out to San Francisco to talk to Olivia Bennett. Since she hadn't returned his calls, he'd simply plant himself on her doorstep. Max would probably go ballistic about the expense of two plane trips, but there was something about Kelley Jordan that didn't quite add up. It wasn't that she was lying. It was more a matter of being very careful about what she told him and didn't tell him. One of the skills Jake possessed was an instinctive ability to separate the truth from lies. Unfortunately, lies of omission were harder to detect.

Just in case this story was bigger than it was supposed to be, he started work on the Van de Veer article. It might have to be second in line.

Olivia listened to Emily's explanation about the interview with Jake Hannigan, not responding until Emily finally asked, "Have I ruined everything?"

Instead of screaming *This is what I warned you about!* Olivia reined in her anger. "I don't know. We'll just have to wait and see how he presents the material. He'll probably contact me again. I sidestepped his calls last week."

"If he does uncover the truth, will you lose Kelley as an author?"

"I don't know that either. I'm certainly not going to tell her about any of this until I have to. Perhaps he'll simply assume Emily Gerrard and Kelley Jordan are the same person and that you're using a pen name. I can live with that. *Not that I want to.* But if he looks into the chronology of the books and your marriage, he'll see a disconnect. Five or six years ago, you were busy being a wife and mother, not writing historical novels."

"Hiding who the real Kelley is seems like a lot of trouble."

"No argument there, but her books have sold millions of copies in several languages, and this subterfuge keeps your kids in shoes."

As soon as she hung up, Olivia pushed the intercom. "Ashley, more tea please—strong."

Business at Sierra Sports always picked up after the first snow, even if it melted right away. The promise of ski season brought the Oakhurst locals in to get new bindings or replace broken ski poles. Day trippers on their way to Yosemite stopped in to look around, check on this year's ski rental prices, maybe buy new gloves or a fleece ski hat.

The week after the storm, Alex kept the store open until nine o'clock every night. Sierra Sports needed all the sales it could get. For several years, business had been shrinking as the large sporting goods chains and the Internet siphoned off customers. Alex kept pushing for TV ads, but his father, who insisted on running the store the same way he'd run it in the '70's, refused to spend the additional money. He'd only agree to buy an occasional full-page ad in the *Sierra Star* or maybe a quarter page in the *Fresno Bee*, the way he always had. Even more important, the store needed a webpage but, whenever Alex brought it up, his father acted as though his son were speaking in tongues. Alex and his parents had been arguing about how to bring in more business ever since he came home to help out.

He had not come willingly.

Eleven years ago, Alex had dropped out of college after one semester to become a ski racer, gradually working his way up through regionals, finally earning enough points to qualify for the U.S. ski team two years in a row. His best year—the year he won two World Cup Slalom events—was the same year his father had his heart attack.

Alex was needed in the store.

When he got the call from his mother, he was in Innsbruck, preparing to race the next day. "Why can't Randy help? He lives over in Mariposa."

"Your brother has a law practice, a wife and two kids. He hasn't got time to help in the store."

And I do? But then ski bum and member of the U.S. ski team were synonymous in the Zimmermann household.

It took two more phone calls from his mother to guilt him into returning. "Someday the store will belong to you and Randy."

"I don't know about Randy, but I'm not ready to spend my whole life waiting on customers who can't make up their minds. And I doubt Randy's interested either."

He promised himself he'd stay a few months, then resume training for the next season. However, Eldin Zimmermann's recovery had taken longer than expected and now, almost two years later, Alex's chances of rejoining the ski team were slim to none. He was out of shape and not getting any younger. The World Cup circuit was tough. He didn't think he'd be able to compete at that level any more.

From the time Alex was eight and Randy was twelve, they'd worked in the store, unpacking sports equipment and running errands. The upside was that they always had their own skis; whenever the slopes at Badger Pass were open and they could find a ride, they skied. At sixteen, Alex was good enough to teach one of Badger's children's classes during Christmas vacation. Randy's skiing was strictly recreational; he'd set his sights on finishing his undergraduate degree at Cal Berkeley and eventually getting into a good law school.

While Alex was stuck in Oakhurst, the Search and Rescue team provided an escape from the tedium of working in the store and gave him time outdoors. His father was getting better but was not quite as energetic as he'd once been, coming in at ten and leaving by four. Eldin still did most of the ordering while Mae Zimmermann kept the books and fretted about her husband's health.

And so at thirty, Alex found himself doing what he'd promised himself he would never do: working for his parents and living in the tiny apartment above the store.

There were only two positive aspects to being stuck in Oakhurst. His work with Search and Rescue and his affair with Becca Sawyer.

Alex had been home three or four months when she brought her skis in to have them sharpened and the bindings replaced. They were top of the line European skis. Not the kind that ordinarily came into the shop. She'd asked about his father's health.

"Not quite ready to come to work, but he's better."

Her smile caught his attention. "Bet getting him to stay away from the store isn't easy."

Alex wrote up the work order and handed her the claim check. "He assumes that leaving me on my own will bankrupt the store."

"And will you?"

"Possibly. Retail isn't my thing."

"You're the son who skis?"

"The family ski bum at your service."

She had a nice laugh, gorgeous red-gold hair and coppery eyes. How had such a beauty ended up in Oakhurst?

"Nice to meet you. I'm Becca Sawyer, the oddball East Coast writer who lives out in the woods."

"Great skis. Are you any good?"

"Fair. More guts than skill. Not nearly good enough to make a ski team."

Over the next few months, they met for coffee, occasionally went to a movie in Fresno. Sometimes Becca cooked dinner at her place. They skied at Badger, not because the runs were all that challenging but because it was only an hour's drive from Oakhurst. Once or twice, he took time off so they could go to Tahoe.

They laughed at the same things, didn't especially care what others thought about them, and were not interested in a relationship that had a future. In the current jargon, they became friends with benefits.

"As soon as my father's able to manage on his own, I'm out of here. Places like Tahoe or Aspen are always looking for ski instructors. Off-season, I can probably tend bar; I've done it plenty of times. My dad's right actually. I'm addicted to the slopes."

"No more ski team?"

"Doubtful. It's grueling and I'm not in shape."

"Don't leave without saying goodbye." At that moment, she was teasing but she was acutely aware that he was only on loan and that she shouldn't let their relationship be too important.

Carson Tyler's computer skills gave Jake two important pieces of the Kelley Jordan puzzle. Dr. Patrick Gerrard—not Jordan—a Berkeley surgeon who had been donating his time in a Baghdad hospital was killed on July 10, 2009, leaving a wife, Emily, and two daughters. And the manifest for the San Francisco flight listed an Emily Gerrard. The on-line White Pages for San Francisco and environs gave a Berkeley address for P. Gerrard.

Kelley Jordan must be her pen name.

Jake lost no time reserving a seat on a Thursday flight to San Francisco; then he presented the new information to Max, outlining what he planned to do in San Francisco. Well not everything he planned.

"Do you honestly think there's a bigger story here?"

"Could be. The fact that Olivia Bennett seemed to be avoiding my calls makes me a bit suspicious."

"Or it's just the pen name thing. Writers have been using pen names for centuries. That's not front page news."

Ignoring Max's skepticism, "So I have your blessing?"

"Not because I think you've uncovered a big mystery but because the Camacho article is terrific, so I'm cutting you some slack. It runs next week. When do you think you'll have the Jordan piece ready?"

"Could take a while. That's why I've been working on the Van der Veer profile. It's almost done. All the people were local and happy to get the publicity. A slam dunk."

"As long as all four are done by Christmas. The award ceremony is the second weekend of January."

"You'll thank me if I end up with something more than a soft feature story."

Jake arrived at Bennett Books Friday morning just before eleven without an appointment. He'd called earlier to ask if Olivia Bennett was in her office, thanked the girl on the other end of the phone, and hung up before she asked his name.

He preferred surprise.

Before he left New York, he'd researched Bennett Books. *A small publishing house with a growing reputation, despite being a continent away from the New York publishing scene.* Kelley Jordan was one of six big name authors on Bennett's list, along with thirty or so secondary authors. The company had a solid financial rating.

The young man at Bennett's reception desk asked Jake to wait until he checked with Olivia Bennett's assistant. Ten minutes later, a stunning blonde in a form-fitting skirt entered the reception area, her hand outstretched. "Mr. Hannigan, I'm Ashley, Olivia Bennett's personal assistant. Please follow me."

Showing up unannounced had worked.

As Jake Hannigan entered her office, Olivia cautioned herself to sit back and let him tell her what he thought he knew. No sense doing damage control until she knew just what the damages were. If he thought Emily was Kelley, so be it.

Jake shook Olivia's hand. "Thanks for seeing me without an appointment."

He was younger than she expected, roughly handsome. No wonder Emily had succumbed to his questioning so willingly. "Have a seat." She ignored the comfortable chairs by the window—better to let the formality of her executive desk set the tone. "What can I do for you, Mr. Hannigan?"

"I'm interested in Kelley Jordan. *Twenty-First Century* is doing a series of articles on the authors vying for the Elgin Award. I'm handling the fiction list."

"I understood you had already interviewed Kelley in Miami."

"A preliminary interview. I still have some questions for her—as well as questions for you." He pulled a slender digital recorder out of his jacket pocket. "Do you mind if I record our conversation?"

"Not at all." Refusing would invite suspicion. "What can I tell you?"

"When did you first read Kelley's work? Did it come through an agent or over the transom?"

"She actually brought it to us herself. My husband and I had a smaller office then—in East Bay." She went on to describe that first meeting; there was nothing dangerous in recreating that afternoon. Rebecca hadn't explained who she was until a week later when the Bennetts agreed to publish *Impossible Secrets*. She'd been adamant that there be no picture or biography on the book jacket. Before Olivia could protest, Rebecca pulled out a picture of herself at sixteen. Olivia instantly recognized Mandy, and so Kelley Jordan became part of Rebecca's contract.

"She doesn't have an agent?"

"No. We act as her agent and publisher. Simpler."

"How many years ago?"

"About five."

"I've located many of the early reviews of her work, but I'm sure your file is more complete. Would you be willing to let me have copies of them?"

"Of course," Olivia pushed the intercom and explained what Jake needed, grateful he only wanted printed background information.

"But more important, I'd like your perspective on why her books are so popular. The writing itself? The stories? Did you know that her first book would be a bestseller?"

Olivia took a few minutes to choose her words carefully since he would probably quote her.

"She does her homework. Her research is thorough. Before and during the writing process, she visits the settings, sometimes spends weeks doing on-site research, and she has a gift for integrating that research with a powerful sense of storytelling." She paused, "Though her characters live in the past, they connect with today's readers. The bottom line is that she loves what she's doing. That love communicates itself to her readers. I believe *Spring Farm* is her best work. Have you read it?"

"Most of it." No need to admit that historical fiction wasn't really his thing. "Is Kelley easy to work with?"

"Generally yes. Of course, all authors have their special idiosyncrasies." *Major understatement in this instance.*

"She certainly charms the audiences she reads for. Do you know the subject of her next book? I'd like to include it in the article."

"She's currently researching the Acadians' expulsion from eastern Canada in the eighteenth century. I don't know the specifics. She doesn't share what she's doing until she's well into the project. I've learned to trust her instincts."

"One thing I forgot to ask her was whether she writes straight into the computer or does she work in long hand first?"

"Long hand. Then a great deal of revision."

"How long does it take her to finish a manuscript?"

"It varies. Around two years. This last one is quite long, so it took two and a half. I'm surprised you didn't get this information from her in Miami."

I kept getting distracted. "Will you be with her for the ceremony in January?"

"I plan to be there" *with or without her. Someone needs to represent Bennett Books.* For the next ten minutes, they discussed the other three authors, contrasting their work with Kelley's. Olivia was careful to tell him that her evaluation of the other three writers was off the record. "I don't want to see these opinions in print. We try to play nice when it comes to the competition."

"Understood." He switched the recorder off.

During their conversation, Jake had been tempted to ask about Emily Gerrard's relationship to Kelley Jordan. Get Olivia Bennett to admit they were the same person. He was good at extracting answers people didn't want to give him but, he reminded himself, Emily was more than an assignment. No sense making too many waves until he had a chance to talk to her face-to-face again. Instead, "Is there a way I can contact her? I have a few more questions I'd like to ask." *And I'd like to spend time getting to know her in ways that have absolutely nothing to do with this article.* Pretending he didn't know, "Does she live in the Bay Area? I'll be in town through the weekend."

He saw Olivia's mouth tighten ever-so-slightly and knew he'd presented her with a dilemma. She really didn't want him to have access to Emily, but he hadn't left her much of an out.

Reluctantly, she picked up her pen. "Give me your cell number. I'll have her call you."

Emily was in the midst of doing laundry when Olivia phoned. By the sound of her voice, it was apparent that Jake's visit had blind-sided her. "Play along. I get the feeling he's already decided Kelley is your pen name." She sighed, "Be as honest as you wish without letting on that someone else wrote the books. It's okay with me if he thinks you're the author. We can keep our fingers in the dike only so long."

Excited at the prospect of seeing him again, Emily copied Jake's cell number. There definitely had been a connection between them in Miami. When she called, he suggested a Berkeley restaurant for lunch. Evidently, he knew where she lived. And if he knew that, he also knew what her real name was.

Chapter 6

Sitting at a table that gave him a clear view of the street, Jake watched Kelley/Emily walk toward the restaurant. She was dressed in black slacks and a pale blue sweater, her hair scooped back into a silver clip. Though it had only been a week since he'd seen her, she seemed prettier than he remembered. As the hostess led Emily to the table, Jake stood, put out his hand and, when she took it, he felt a rush of warmth.

His eyes wrapped themselves around her, and the first words out of his mouth were "I like your hair that way." He hadn't intended to be so personal so quickly, but his mouth and his brain weren't quite in sync. His heartbeat was interfering. *Hannigan, stay on task. You didn't come three thousand miles just to hit on this woman.*

Or had he?

Giving no hint that she'd felt the same warmth when their hands touched, she slid into the chair across from him, carefully placing her purse on the floor next to her. "Liv said you wanted to continue the interview. I thought you'd finished it in Miami."

"I have some more questions about your work—about you." *Not all of which involve the article.*

The waiter brought a basket of warm sourdough bread slices and took their order.

As soon as he was out of earshot, Emily asked, "What questions?"

He'd planned on working up to the question of her identity, but she left him no alternative except the truth. "I did some checking. Kelley Jordan is actually your pen name."

"That's not a question."

"True. Your real name is Emily Gerrard, you live here in Berkeley, and you have two daughters." Jake watched her eyes, measuring the effect of his words. Though he wanted her to admit the truth, he didn't want to drive her away.

Not ready to concede, Emily tried to redirect the conversation. "My writing should be the focus of your article, not me personally." A line that had served her well in other interviews, but Jake wasn't like other interviewers. Jake was clever—definitely intriguing.

"Readers like to know about the people who've created their favorite books." *Like he'd know that.*

Grateful that Liv had given her permission to admit to being Kelley, Emily took a long breath and let him be right. "I adopted the alias for privacy. There's nothing wrong with using a pen name."

He hadn't meant to put her on the defensive. "Please, don't apologize. I can understand you not wanting to put your daughters in the spotlight." Of course, if he truly understood, he'd keep the secret, but reporters spent most of their time uncovering secrets. It was what he did. What he was good at.

Hoping he didn't know she wasn't the real author, Emily asked, "How did you get this information?"

"You said your husband Patrick died sixteen months ago. Checking the military's casualty lists was fairly simple. Not many doctors named Patrick died during that month."

Until their meals came, he explained about Carson Tyler's computer skills. When she seemed more comfortable with his having invaded her privacy, less defensive, he softened his approach. "How long were you and Patrick married?"

"Almost thirteen years."

"You must have gotten married at twelve."

That made her smile, a good sign. "Not quite."

He asked her some of the same questions he'd asked Olivia Bennett—checking that the answers matched; though Emily said she'd gone to Bennett Books four years ago, not five, the answers were close enough.

As they talked, she felt herself relaxing. He'd had that effect on her in Miami too. When they finished eating and had ordered coffee, she decided to go on offense to keep him from asking more questions. "Okay Jake, my turn. Where did you grow up?"

"A small town in Southern Illinois."

"Please be specific." Her eyes challenged him.

"Tough interviewer! Alton—on the Mississippi River. Hideously hot and humid in the summer but historically interesting."

"College?"

"University of Missouri at Columbia. The Harvard of journalism schools."

"My, my, such lofty credentials. Siblings?"

"Two older brothers. One is career army, the other teaches elementary school."

"Parents?"

"Yes."

"Very funny. Are you married?" Something she should probably have asked in Miami.

"No, divorced. I was married three years. The last two I was bouncing around the Middle East. We were hardly ever together. We shouldn't have gotten married in the first place. Darlene wanted the picket fence and backyard barbecues. I wasn't ready to settle down. Still looking for adventure."

"So how many years abroad?" Emily was rather enjoying putting him on the spot, teasing him just a little, finding out about this man who had been crowding her thoughts for the last week. Besides, as long as he was answering questions, she didn't have to.

"Off and on for four or five years." *The best years of his life, so far.*

"What happened to your leg?"

"A crushed fibula. Lots of hardware to reconstruct it. Getting through airport security is complicated. In the cold and damp, I limp like an old man, but I can at least walk." He folded his arms on the edge of the table and leaned forward, "Enough history." He went out on a limb, "Do you have something planned for this afternoon?"

"Why?"

"I'm contemplating a drive over to Marin and beyond. Maybe take a walk through Muir Woods. I've read about the Coast Redwoods but haven't seen them."

She hadn't expected an afternoon in the redwoods with Jake Hannigan. Very tempting. As she was considering his invitation, she was studying his face. Strong jaw, faded blue eyes. Was this a date or an excuse to extract more information from her? She surprised herself by not caring which it was. "I'd enjoy that, but I need to do something about my car. It's parked a couple blocks away, and it may already have a ticket on it."

"Why don't I pick you up at your place in half an hour?"

She didn't give him her address. He undoubtedly knew it.

Jake liked the way she'd turned the tables on him. She could stand up for herself. The rental car's GPS talked him to the narrow, two-story frame house on an equally narrow lot—almost a row house. White clapboard with green trim, rose bushes in the front yard instead of grass. When he parked at the curb, Emily was talking to an older woman who had pruning shears in one hand and a basket in the other. Emily kissed the woman's cheek, walked to Jake's car, and got in.

"I'm ready."

"Your mother, aunt, housekeeper?"

"My mother, Mildred. She'll be here when the girls get home from school. Even though Cristyl is almost fourteen, I don't want them home alone."

"Understandable."

"Do you know how to get to Marin?"

"No. But Herman—that's my name for this pushy GPS voice—will sort me out."

The interview was over. They were on a new page—still empty but exciting. As Jake negotiated the traffic, Emily was careful not to look at him because the car suddenly seemed too small for what she was feeling and thinking.

Jake Hannigan rarely tolerated indecision. His own or anyone else's. Yet, by the time he drove Emily Gerrard home Friday evening, he was tied up in mental knots over what to do about the whole Kelley/Emily issue. He had enough material to begin the article, but writing the truth might cost him this fragile connection with Emily. Jake now knew the ages of her daughters, knew that the younger one had been something of problem since her father's death, knew Emily's mother had rented out her own small house in Oakland so she could move in to help her daughter. The reporter in him was puzzled by Emily's house and car. Her books surely brought in a solid income, yet the house was unremarkable and needed painting, she drove a 2003 Mazda, and her wardrobe wasn't particularly expensive. Though these were personal parts of her life, not meant for an article, they were things that didn't add up. An even bigger question was how she'd managed to write three long novels and raise a family—for the last year and a half—on her own.

Once the article was published, her day-to-day life would change; her daughters' privacy would be compromised. Granted, authors' families could live below the radar of public attention more easily than families of movie stars or musicians, but there would be increased attention. And Jake would be the whistle blower. That fact could end what hadn't quite begun between them.

Everything that he wanted to begin. Picket fences and roses were looking better.

They walked among the giant redwood trees until the drizzle turned into rain and sent them in search of an early dinner at a snug seafood restaurant in Sausalito. For the next two hours, they talked about nothing and everything—he liked Rhythm and Blues, she liked classical, he loved Sushi, she hated it. They didn't talk about Kelley Jordan. They had more important things on their minds. He didn't touch her, even casually—didn't kiss her goodnight, though everything in him wanted to. Wanted much more than just a kiss.

Friday melted into Saturday. Emily invited Jake to the girls' soccer games. Cristyl's was at eleven, Claudia's at one. Cute girls—with their mother's fair coloring. Claudia pretty much ignored him, but he could see Cristyl covertly watching him. She was old enough to suspect he was interested in her mother—which of course he was. He tried to be friendly but not too friendly. He wasn't used to being around young girls. His brothers each had two boys—much easier to relate to. Saturday night, they took the girls and Emily's mother out for pizza. Still no touching and no kiss.

Sunday morning, Emily met him for breakfast before his one o'clock flight.

"When and where are your next readings?" He'd already checked the Kelley Jordan website for the dates but didn't want her to know that.

"Chicago. December 6th through the 11th."

"I have some vacation time coming. May I meet you there for a day or two?" He felt like a nervous teenager asking a girl out for the first time, afraid she'd say no. He desperately wanted Emily to say yes—but perhaps he was moving too fast, reading too much into these last two days. "Separate rooms of course."

She was stirring cream into her coffee. Stirring and stirring. Her eyes held onto his as she evaluated the implications of his request. The two of them in the city.

By themselves.

Whatever was happening to her—and him—them—might require that she stop being the grieving widow and remember what it was like to be a woman. Was she ready to let another man into her life?

She realized she hadn't answered his question and was still stirring her coffee. He deserved an answer.

"I don't know. Perhaps. I'll have to think about it. Well, there's my schedule, of course. I don't have the details from Liv yet. But maybe." She couldn't get her thoughts or words in order.

He smiled. "I'll take that *maybe* as a yes. I'll keep in touch." She knew what he was suggesting and she was flustered.

Another thing he liked about her. The list was getting longer.

Mildred McGee knew her daughter very well. Since Pat's death, she'd watched Emily's grief, watched her crawl slowly out of the pain so that the girls could move on with their lives. Emily had always had strength, had set her own dreams aside until Patrick finished his residency. Raising two children while working the night shift at a high-end restaurant hadn't been easy.

The appearance of this reporter was more than business, more than an interview. Mildred saw the way they watched each other while they thought no one was looking. Rather sweet actually. This weekend, Emily had more color in her cheeks than usual; she laughed more easily when Jake was around. And he clearly was smitten, his eyes following her—nice eyes, kind. Emily deserved to have love in her life again. Mildred had been afraid her daughter wouldn't be able to let the past go. Perhaps Emily was ready.

When the girls were in bed Sunday night, Mildred joined her daughter in the kitchen where Emily was laying out the dishes for tomorrow's breakfast. School mornings were always frantic.

"Cereal or scrambled eggs?" Mildred was in charge of the girls' breakfast.

When Emily didn't answer, Mildred asked again.

"Oh—whatever."

"When are you coming back to earth?"

"Sorry." Hiding anything from her mother was hopeless. "Do you like him? Jake?"

"One day isn't much time for me to make a valid judgment. However, I think he likes you."

Emily blushed. "Fix eggs."

Not ready to let Emily off the hook. "The question is do you like Jake?"

"I do."

"And?"

"He wants to meet me when I'm in Chicago next month."

"What did you say?"

"Well, I wasn't prepared for that question exactly. I stumbled around." She looked embarrassed, "I said maybe."

"You left the door open, good."

"I couldn't just say no."

"Because?"

"Because I like him. A lot."

"Then let him meet you."

"He said separate rooms."

"How chivalrous." Mildred grinned at Emily's discomfort. "Do you want to have sex with him?"

Leave it to her mother to call a spade a spade. Even though Jake had kept his distance, Emily's insides had been sending clear signals all weekend.

"Yes."

"Then erase that maybe."

Chapter 7

Rebecca and Alex had been lovers for over a year. He was the icing on the cake—the cake of course was living and writing in Oakhurst. No one handing out shoulds and shouldn'ts. No expectations but her own. She was grateful Alex didn't expect her to be anyone but who she said she was—a thirty-two year old divorced ghostwriter. She'd been semi-honest about her life with David and the divorce—leaving out the way the Kingston glitter had followed her into the marriage.

Fortunately, Alex wasn't given to asking questions about her past or, for that matter, revealing the details of his lifestyle on the ski circuit. Every week a different country, a new competition, and new groupies drawn to the glamour surrounding skiing.

Becca didn't ask questions either. Her own version of *don't ask, don't tell*. If she didn't ask, no one would force her to tell. But sometimes she wished she could tell him the truth.

Explain her double self.

Triple self if she factored in the fictitious Kelley.

In the beginning of their affair, she hadn't worried about honesty. But lately, she'd begun to wonder what it would to be like to peel away the layers of herself, let him see all of her. No one had ever known her completely. Certainly not her parents, who saw her only as a reflection of themselves and had no idea where she was or what she was doing at this moment. Certainly not David, who had been more in love with the glamour of the Kingston name than with Rebecca. Ironically, the Bennetts possessed more information about her—and she hardly knew them.

Though Alex had made it abundantly clear that he was just passing through her life, some of his clothes had migrated to her closet and into one dresser drawer. A Pisa-tower of ski magazines cluttered the floor on his side of the bed; his toothbrush and shaver were in the second bathroom.

She'd been wondering whether she wanted their relationship to be more than sex, cooking dinner, and long walks. Wanted permanence. If she were honest about herself, would Alex wonder why she hadn't trusted him enough to tell him months ago? Perhaps he wouldn't think it was a big deal. They had different lifestyle priorities. He couldn't wait to get out of Oakhurst, out of the store and back to skiing, even though he'd be relegated to teaching. She only wanted to stay in Oakhurst.

Writing and Oakhurst had, until now, satisfied her, yet she was beginning to want more in her life than sitting in front of a computer, creating worlds for people who only existed in her head. She'd left her marriage and her past to create her own world, but she was alone in it—except for Alex—and he wouldn't be around for long. Though she'd been certain another marriage wasn't for her, lately she found herself watching couples and families—wondering whether she was wrong about what her life should be. But expanding the boundaries of this life might mean facing that other life.

A catch-22 if ever there was one.

Alex had no doubts about what life he wanted. The day after Thanksgiving, he finally hired his replacement. Raised in Mariposa, Jorge Reynolds had one year of community college classes, a young wife and a baby daughter. He needed the job, and Alex was hoping Jorge could take over the majority of what Alex was responsible for in the store. Though the apartment over the store would be a tight fit for three, the young couple was looking forward to having their own space, instead of living with Jorge's parents.

Alex had his escape plan.

There was a job waiting for him in Squaw Valley. An old friend, Jay Williams, who owned the ski school, needed another instructor. Alex could sleep on Jay's couch until he found his own place. By the middle of December, he'd be back on skis. There was light at the end of the tunnel he'd been living in. He hauled out his ski gear, fixing bindings, cleaning goggles, making sure all his equipment was in working order. He even treated himself to new ski pants.

Miraculously, his father hadn't objected to hiring Jorge or Alex leaving, "You've put your life on hold long enough," but his mother was still sulking.

He was, however, running out of time to tell Becca about his plans. He told himself he just hadn't found the right time or the right words. When it came to relationships, the right words never came easily. He and Becca were—comfortable. He stopped short of the word happy. A couple without actually being a couple. No strings. He'd told her often enough that he planned on leaving Oakhurst as soon as he could—she knew that.

Don't leave without saying goodbye.

But he had to tell her about the job—he couldn't simply walk away as he so often had walked away from other women. While he hadn't been paying attention, Becca Sawyer had become more important than the others.

Just not more important than skiing.

Over their usual Monday morning coffee and croissants, Becca's friend Karen, who owned The Oak Tree Gallery, asked, "When's Alex leaving?"

For a fraction of a second, Becca wasn't sure she'd heard correctly. "Leaving for where?"

"Sorry." Karen added more sugar to her coffee, "I thought you knew. Rumor has it that Alex hired his replacement at the store. A handsome young man from Mariposa. He started last Friday. Too bad he's married." As Oakhurst's resident cougar, Karen always knew which men were available. Becca suspected Karen had had her eye on Alex before Rebecca took him off the market.

Rebecca struggled to hide her surprise about the news behind the professional smile her parents had taught her to use when caught off guard. *Never let anyone see that you're hurt or afraid.* And then she lied. "I don't know exactly. What with the Thanksgiving holiday and all, I haven't seen much of him." Except that she'd had dinner at his parents' house on Thursday, and he'd spent Saturday night at her place without saying anything about leaving. Karen's news did, however, explain his sorting through the old ski magazines—throwing away all but the most recent ones. She hadn't given it a thought. The magazine stack had been a sweetly private joke between them.

When she and Karen finished their coffee, Rebecca headed for Sierra Sports. Besides learning to smile when she didn't feel like smiling, she'd also learned to stay ahead of emotional curves that might catch her unaware. No sense waiting for him to show up on her doorstep to collect his clothes and wave goodbye.

As she entered the store, Alex and a young man with jet black hair pulled into a ponytail at his neckline were intently studying the computer screen at the check out counter. The store was empty except for a man trying on down jackets.

Her smile firmly in place, "Good morning, gentlemen."

The deer-in-headlights expression on Alex's face told her she'd successfully stolen a march on him and that Karen had been right. With the innocence of the fictional Mandy, "I came by to meet your new employee."

Alex stumbled over the introduction.

Rebecca extended her hand. "Nice to meet you, Jorge. Are you from Oakhurst?"

"No, Mariposa, but we'll be moving here soon."

"Do you have a family?" From the corner of her eye, Rebecca could see Alex fidgeting with a stack of papers on the counter, probably wishing he were somewhere else. Served him right for letting her hear the news from Karen.

"My wife Julie and I, we have a baby girl, Celia. She's six months old."

"How nice. Where will you live?" *As if she couldn't guess.*

"When Mr. Zimmermann, Alex leaves, we'll move into the apartment upstairs."

"I look forward to meeting your family." She smiled at Jorge, nodded in Alex's direction and left the store. She was fairly sure Alex wouldn't follow her. He hated scenes of any kind, especially in public. She'd forced his hand. No doubt he'd show up at the house after the store closed.

Except for his subdued "Hi" and a light kiss when he arrived just after nine, Alex and Becca had barely spoken to each other. He'd brought his battered duffle bag with the US Ski Team logo on the side. She was sitting in the maple rocking chair by her bedroom window, Matilda curled on her lap, watching him fold his clothes before putting them in the bag, then add the ski magazines he hadn't thrown away and retrieve his toothbrush and shaver.

She'd spent the afternoon trying to figure out what to say when he showed up but had failed to write appropriate dialogue for being dumped. Too strong a word perhaps. While he was packing, she struggled to swallow the tears collecting in her throat. She rarely cried personal tears, only those required by a script and a director.

When Alex finished, he zipped the bag and forced himself to meet her eyes. Then, as though it were an ordinary evening, he asked, "Is there any wine left?"

She set Matilda on the floor and headed for the kitchen. The cat beat her there, hoping for a late snack. "Not on your life," Rebecca grumbled. "Trudy says you're too fat."

Her hands were suddenly unsteady. She poured two glasses of white wine and carefully carried them into the living room. She hadn't bothered to turn on the fire; fires were for happy, comfortable evenings. This was not that kind of evening.

Alex dropped his bag near the front door and picked up the wine glass she'd placed on the coffee table. Rebecca chose one of the leather chairs—eloquently isolating herself. He pulled the footstool away from her chair, sitting with his elbows on his knees, leaning toward her but not touching her. Waiting for him to try to explain what was already *fait accompli*, she let her eyes roam his face, memorizing the gray eyes, straight nose, his thick, dark hair tumbling over his forehead.

"Becca, I'm sorry you had to hear it from someone else."

"From Karen Sutter, actually. She thought I knew." *Do not cry.*

"My bad. I couldn't seem to find the right time, but that's no excuse."

Thick silence. She wasn't about to help him.

"I'll miss you."

Probably not. "When?" Without permission, her voice wavered.

"Day after tomorrow. I've got a job at Squaw Valley. All the runs are operating. They need another instructor."

"Jay's school?" She'd met Jay on one of their ski trips last winter.

"Yeah."

"That's nice." *She didn't mean it. None of this was nice. She wasn't ready to lose him.*

"Becca, I'm not going to be that far away. Six or seven hours, depending on the driving conditions. I'll be getting time off. This isn't the end." She was watching him, listening to him, but not moving a muscle. He repeated, "I don't want it to be the end of us." Yet he had to admit it must look like the end to her. He'd handled everything badly. In the past, he'd casually broken up with a long list of women. Those leavings had been easy. This time was different; he wasn't prepared for the strained look in Becca's eyes, the tight line of her mouth. He'd never left a woman he'd known this long—and cared about this much. His thoughts stopped short of using the word love. With Becca, sex was only part of the attraction. She was smart, funny, strong without trying to prove her strength.

And he was hurting her.

Eventually she looked away. "I don't want it to be the end either; but distance will change things."

No argument there. He finished his wine and stood up. "Should I go—or?"

She didn't move from the chair, couldn't look at him. "You might as well go. No sense prolonging this." Much too melodramatic. She'd have deleted a line like that from a manuscript.

She wanted him to argue with her, to protest that they needed tonight together, that he'd come back as soon as he could. She needed loving words to smooth the jagged edges of this parting because she knew in her deepest self that, once he was caught up in the siren song of the slopes, he was lost to her.

He'd just been on loan.

From an impossible distance, she heard the door shut quietly.

Even though she needed groceries, she didn't go into town until Thursday. Someone might ask about Alex, and she was not capable of talking about his leaving, not ready to wear her *I'm just fine* smile. She hadn't realized how deeply entangled her life was with his. At some hidden level—and she was an expert at hiding things—she'd hoped he would call to tell her goodbye or stop on his way out of town. But he hadn't. He'd probably left before dawn Wednesday morning. She wondered whether he'd followed Highway 49 or gone over to the Interstate, wondered what the weather was like—whether he was thinking about her. Wondered how she was going to get along without him.

When he didn't call Wednesday night to tell her he'd arrived safely, she knew she needed to stop dragging herself around the house like a zombie and get back to writing. But writing demanded a clear head, and she couldn't get his eagerness to leave out of her mind. Over and over, she reminded herself she'd known what Alex wanted for himself. Known the rules of their affair.

He was undoubtedly rejoicing that he'd found his way back to the ski slopes he missed so much and perhaps the personal freedom that lifestyle offered him. As soon as she stopped feeling sorry for herself, she'd be angry. But right now she couldn't move past the shock of realizing she loved him.

She hadn't known that.

The world she'd carefully constructed was beginning to fray at the edges.

First, the Elgin Award
Then Nate Pullman
Now Alex.
The rule of threes.

Chapter 8

As she did every weekday, Olivia scrolled through the e-mail messages on her laptop while eating her breakfast—two slices of wheat toast, orange juice and Chai tea. She always liked to get a jump on the day's business. Ashley had flagged the message from Jake Hannigan. The subject line read *Preliminary Draft of the Kelley Jordan Article.* Under her breath she muttered, "Damn," and opened the file.

Across the table, engrossed in *The Chronicle's* business section, Kurt didn't look up, "Damn what?"

"Damn Jake Hannigan."

"Umm." He turned the page and kept on reading.

Olivia skimmed through the article's teaser reminding readers that this was the third of the four profiles on Elgin's fiction nominees.

Spring Farm, the third novel published under the name Kelley Jordan, is a deftly layered journey of a young woman enduring the impossible hardships of the Oregon Trail while trying to break free of her father's control over her life. The language is simultaneously powerful and beautiful. A modern tale of family expectations and limitations. Set in the nineteenth century, Jordan's 623 page novel immediately grabs the reader, refusing to let go until the final page. No wonder this book is a finalist for the 2010 Elgin Fiction Award.

This reporter set out to interview Kelley Jordan, only to discover that Kelley Jordan is actually the pen name used by Emily Gerrard, a young widow who lives with her mother and two daughters in Berkeley, California.

"Thank God."

Kurt looked at his wife. "What?"

"Hannigan didn't dig any further than Emily. He believes she's Kelley. Maybe he was distracted. I had a feeling he was interested in more than an interview."

"Interested romantically?"

"I think so. He seemed very eager to get in touch with her while he was here."

Kurt folded the newspaper and stuffed it into his briefcase. "The whole Kelley masquerade has been stupid from the beginning. Fifty years ago, it would have been easy to keep a secret like that. But in this century, hiding personal information is virtually impossible. I'm surprised he missed the truth. The real answer—the Rebecca Sawyer answer—isn't that hard to find. Granted getting to the Kingston part is a bit trickier." He stopped at the kitchen door. "Are we riding together this morning?"

She nodded. "Give me ten minutes. I need to send this to Becca."

Clicking *Forward*, Olivia quickly typed in Becca's e-mail address and sent Jake's e-mail without comment. Silence was simpler. There wasn't anything in the article that led to the real Kelley Jordan. Essentially, Rebecca had nothing to be upset about, yet she would be. Frankly, Olivia was tired of being the gatekeeper for *The Kingston Secret*. Kurt's *It's time for her to get over it* stance was looking better all the time. She rather wished Jake had looked further.

Assuming Hannigan hadn't shared the article with Emily, Olivia forwarded it to her too, adding *So far, he hasn't found the whole story. Please be more careful.*

Since Alex's departure, Rebecca hadn't written anything—hadn't even bothered to turn the computer on—so it was two days before she found the Jake Hannigan article Liv had forwarded. Lately, Rebecca sensed that Liv was tired of playing watchdog, tired of passing Emily off as Kelley Jordan, though Emily's salary and expenses came out of Rebecca's royalties, not out of Bennett's profits. Hiring Emily to be Kelley had been Liv's brainchild, and the readings had certainly helped sell books. The *Spring Farm* sales were triple those of the first two books. Ever since Rebecca had said *No* to the movie deal, Olivia had kept her distance. That *No* would cost Bennett Books a lot of money and, because Kurt was always focused on the bottom line, he might take matters into his own hands and ignore Rebecca's wishes.

She opened the e-mail's attachment—a PDF file with the *Twenty-First Century* logo across the top. She had no idea who Jacob Hannigan was but *Preliminary Draft of the Kelley Jordan Article* certainly caught her attention. On the first page, there was a picture of an attractive blonde woman signing books in a large bookstore, smiling up at the women standing in line for her autograph. That must be Emily. The caption read *Kelley Jordan/Emily Gerrard at a signing in Miami.* So Hannigan had figured out that Kelley Jordan was a pseudonym—but assumed Emily was the author.

That should be good news.

Why didn't it feel that way? When Emily was hired to give readings as Kelley, Rebecca hadn't minded. She was grateful that she didn't need to go public, to risk someone saying "Has anyone ever told you that you look like Rebecca Kingston? You know, the girl who played Mandy on TV."

Now, in one of the most widely read news magazines, Emily would officially become Kelley Jordan and was getting credit for what she—Rebecca Sawyer—had written. According to the article, Kelley Jordan had two daughters, Claudia and Cristyl, a deceased husband, a mother, and a house in Berkeley. In the space of the article, Rebecca had been replaced.

Whoever this Hannigan was, he at least wrote well—for a reporter—and had obviously read the book, researched the reviews of her previous books and knew what the literary world was saying about *Spring Farm*. From an objective point of view, it was an excellent article, fair and complimentary.

Yet, at this moment, Rebecca did not feel objective.

If she won the Elgin Award, and Emily—as Kelley—accepted it, Rebecca would feel cheated. Admittedly an irrational response. Because she'd hidden behind the pseudonym, she'd never experienced the pleasure of people telling her in person how much they liked her work. She'd read compliments on her website, but that wasn't the same. Her writing mattered to her more than acting ever had, and her ego suddenly wanted to stand on a stage and hear applause for the book. So much for believing she was okay with being invisible.

If, however, she came forward and accepted the award, then Rebecca Kingston might once again inhabit her life. Privacy and winning couldn't exist simultaneously.

The week after Jake returned to New York, Emily was scheduled for Storytelling appearances at six different kindergarten classes. Thanksgiving programs. When Claudia was in kindergarten, her teacher had asked Emily if she could prepare a telling for a holiday program, so she'd developed a version of the first Thanksgiving, as told by a Native American girl.

A child's eye view of the Pilgrims—minus the romanticized view some teachers promoted. Every year since, the school district invited her to give the program in the district's kindergarten classes and paid her. She was in the process of preparing a similar program for Presidents Day and Martin Luther King Day. Last year, her Storytelling had brought in twice what it had the year before, but she still couldn't survive without Bennett Books. Someday, maybe she could concentrate on her own career instead of Kelley Jordan's, but not anytime soon.

Packing for her Kelley trips—she'd made nine this year—was usually simple. Slacks, a couple of casual jackets, a sweater or two. The upcoming trip to Chicago was way more complicated. She packed and repacked. Perhaps she'd need a dressy outfit for dinner—that is, if Jake showed up—and comfortable shoes for walking; he liked to walk. She definitely needed a new nightgown—a pretty, sexy one. At home, she slept in Patrick's old t-shirts.

Emily had spent the last sixteen months convincing herself that she would never need or want another man in her life. Yet the sheer black nightgown she bought on sale at Macy's was the first item she put in the suitcase. She and Patrick had had a good marriage—the only downside was his trips to Third World countries to use his surgical skills. The painful irony was that, before he went to Iraq, he'd promised it would be his last trip.

The San Francisco weekend Emily had just spent with Jake had been tantalizing, reminding her what it was like to have a man around—a very attractive man. He'd tried, with little success, to make friends with her daughters—that failure was not his fault—but had successfully charmed her mother. For those three days, Emily felt—actually *felt*—desirable. And now he wanted to meet her in Chicago. No children or mother in the mix. However, spending more time with him came with risk. He might just be pursuing her to get at the truth about Kelley Jordan. Playing her for a fool.

Risk or no risk, she hoped he'd be in Chicago.

The draft of Jake's article and Olivia's e-mail warning her to be careful didn't help Emily's nerves. This lucrative job with Bennett Books might be in jeopardy. The Kelley Jordan lie and Emily's attraction to Jake were a dangerous combination. She read and reread the draft of his article—flattering in every way—but it was creating a new lie: that she was

Kelley, not just pretending to be Kelley. How would this lie impact the original lie she'd been contributing to for nearly a year?

As soon as Olivia e-mailed the schedule for Kelley's Chicago trip—eight signings—Emily forwarded it to Jake with a simple FYI on the subject line in case he hadn't changed his mind.

He answered the next day: *I'll meet you at the airport.*

His promise made her catch her breath. She visualized him waiting as she left the secure area, smiling at her—he had a quiet, thoughtful smile. Since their San Francisco weekend, she'd thought about him a lot. In those three days, he hadn't made a pass, only held her hand and kissed her goodbye. Despite his restraint, she knew he was attracted to her, and she certainly was attracted to him, wanted to touch him and be touched. It had been so long since she'd been touched by a man.

In the midst of imagining their next meeting, imagining more than just the meeting, she bought a package of condoms.

Emily's flight was scheduled to leave San Francisco a little after nine Monday morning. Her mother and the girls drove her to the airport at seven, Cristyl complaining that the family's traditional Christmas tree shopping would be delayed. "All the good ones will be gone by the time you come home." Everything was a drama lately. Cris had Emily's coloring and Patrick's dark eyes, but her temperament was definitely her own.

"This trip will pay for Christmas shopping. It's not like I'm enjoying myself. It's work." *Not quite true this time.*

Mildred stopped in the loading zone. Emily pulled her suitcase from the trunk. "Mind your grandmother. I'll see you in a week." She kissed her fingers to them and extended the handle on her suitcase, grateful the children hadn't noticed she was taking a bigger suitcase than usual.

No sooner had Jake sent Olivia Bennett the rough draft of the Kelley Jordan article, than he decided not to give it to Max just yet. Instead, he went to work on the Samuel Stone piece. Changing the publication order meant Kelley Jordan's article would appear just before Christmas. He told himself the adjustment was better timing for *Spring Farm*—closer to the awards banquet. But that wasn't the real reason. Something was still buzzing around in his head, something that hinted he'd missed a crucial aspect of the story.

He spent the time between San Francisco and the trip to Chicago getting the majority of the Stone article fitted together. In some ways, it was harder to write than the others because Stone's prose style was impossibly sluggish. He told a good story, but wading through his language was exhausting, and Jake did not even try to finish the four hundred pages. He read the beginning, middle and end, gambling that the intervening details wouldn't affect the way he wrote the article. On the plus side, Stone lived in Connecticut and proved to be an excellent interview, very open about his work and his life. By concentrating on Samuel Stone the writer, Jake could soft-pedal his own tepid response to the writing style and soft-pedal some of the negative reviews the book had received. More than once, Jake wondered why *The Enigma* had been nominated at all. He resisted the temptation to open the article with *It's an enigma why The Enigma is on this list.*

Max would have apoplexy.

As soon as Emily entered O'Hare's baggage claim area, she saw Jake leaning against a wall, smiling at her. He was wearing his usual Dockers topped by a heavy yellow sweater and carrying a rust-colored parka. She smiled back. He'd really come. How lovely to be met. On most of her trips, she was on her own, wrestling her luggage off the carousel, searching for the taxi stand or car rental counter.

"Hi." He kissed her cheek. "Good flight?"

Emily's "Yes" was soft, unsteady. His lips on her cheek and the fresh scent of aftershave sent tiny shock waves through her, interfering with her breathing.

"Which carousel for your bag?"

"Supposedly number four."

As though they had done this numerous times, they stood side-by-side, not touching yet, watching the luggage from the San Francisco flight bump onto the belt. Finally her plain black Samsonite, its handles wrapped in green fluorescent tape, dropped.

"That one." Emily pointed, and Jake retrieved it, setting it upright.

"Always good to have your luggage arrive when you do. Let's go. My rental car is in the lot." He took her hand and, with his other hand, pulled the suitcase.

By the time they found his car, Emily had relaxed a little. Her voice was surer now. "When did you get in?"

"Around noon. I checked into the hotel, had lunch, and then drove back out here. I also scouted out a fairly decent Italian restaurant a couple blocks from the hotel—if you're not too tired."

"Not at all." In fact, massive doses of adrenaline were being pumped through her body.

"How're the girls?"

"Upset because Christmas tree shopping has to wait until I get back. Excessive whining about my being gone so often. But I don't think it's my absence that's really the issue. More a knee-jerk memory that their father didn't come back from Iraq." As soon as she'd said it, she was sorry she'd resurrected Patrick. She didn't want him to be part of this week.

It was just after five when Jake left her outside her sixth floor hotel room.

"Dinner at 6:30?"

"That's fine. I need to get sorted out." *And have a leisurely bath.*

He smiled, "I'll be back," and strolled to the elevator. His room was on the third floor.

Her heart was racing as she unpacked, shaking out the dress she planned to wear for dinner—a simple black wool that she could dress up or down. She'd never had this kind of a rendevous with a man, each of them staying in separate rooms in the same hotel but not intending to *stay* in separate rooms. This was unchartered territory. She was no one's mother this week.

As good as the restaurant was, neither Jake nor Emily paid much attention to their food. The atmosphere between them was charged with what they hoped would come afterward. They discussed all the things that weren't actually important: her schedule, the locations of the readings/signings—one day in Winnetka and Evanston—the rest of them in the city. While she was working, he planned to visit museums, look up a couple of college friends. He'd bought tickets for *Wicked* on Thursday night, but hadn't made any other specific plans. Better to improvise as the week went along.

They lingered over their coffee, then walked hand-in-hand back to the hotel. It was so comforting to have her hand curled into his. As they entered the elevator, Jake punched the sixth floor button.

At her door, "May I come in?"

Without answering, she slid the key card into the slot—it took two tries before she caught the green light in time—and turned the handle. She'd left only one of the lamps on. A more romantic look.

In the middle of the entryway, she stopped, suddenly uncertain. What had before seemed so enticing was now unsettling. In a few moments, he would be looking at her body, touching it. No one but Pat had seen her body since she'd given birth twice, her figure softer than it had been. There was Pat again.

Jake was standing behind her, barely three or four inches between them. She could feel him waiting for a signal from her, could feel his breath brushing against the back of her neck. A shiver of anticipation cascaded along her spine.

If she turned around, he would kiss her and expect her kiss to match his. She remembered the condom she'd slipped under her pillow before they went to dinner. At that moment, she'd been completely sure about tonight, eager to feel his weight on her, feel him in her.

But now she couldn't bring herself to turn around. She was frozen. How had she gotten to this unfamiliar place?

"Emily?" His voice was low, "What's wrong?"

You're not Patrick.

When she didn't answer, Jake gently turned her around so she had to look at him. "It doesn't have to be now—or even tomorrow. There's no hurry."

"I thought I could. I want to, I do, but—well, maybe not tonight. This—us—it's bigger than I thought."

"Patrick?"

Grateful she didn't have to explain, she nodded.

"The first woman I slept with after Darlene and I were divorced, all I thought about was Darlene, even though we hadn't been especially happy, hadn't actually built much of a life together. Physical memory's hard to erase. You had a longer, better life with your husband." He paused, "Don't stress about it."

His kiss didn't ask anything of her. "I'll call in the morning."

It was impossibly hard to meet his eyes, "Breakfast?"

"Absolutely."

Though she'd gone to bed as soon as Jake left, Emily didn't drift off to sleep until after midnight. She replayed every word—every touch. Heard the echo of the door closing behind him, leaving a vast, embarrassing emptiness.

She hadn't meant to panic, had planned on more—craved more. But unexpectedly Patrick had shown up, bringing with him the memory of their wedding night and honeymoon—delicious moments and days. They'd stayed in a bed and breakfast outside Mendicino on California's northern coast. It had rained for the first two days, gray sheets of rain driven by the wind, enclosing them in the Victorian room that overlooked the Pacific, the surf crashing on the rocks below.

When the sun eventually reappeared, they strolled the New England style town or drove through the surrounding countryside, always returning early to their room to close themselves away. She'd been hypnotized by her wedding band—the one she still wore. She was Emily Gerrard, no longer McGee. Gerrard sounded more exotic. Morphing her into another person. It was both terrifying and perfect to be a wife. They told each other that this was forever, that as soon as he finished his surgical residency, they would start a family. She was, however, already pregnant with Cristyl when they left Mendicino.

There had, of course, been no forever.

And tonight, another man—not Patrick—had wanted to make love to her. Jake was—himself. His touch wouldn't be Patrick's, the scent of Jake's skin would be different. Would she always be comparing and contrasting men to Patrick, depriving herself of the physical and emotional pleasure of being with someone else? She told herself over and over she didn't need to love Jake in order to sleep with him. She could simply enjoy him. Enjoy having sex with him.

Hanging onto the past did very little for the present.

It was a little after 4 a.m. when she knocked on Jake's door. She'd slipped on a pair of slacks and a sweater, not bothering with a bra or underwear. Her room key and the condom were in her pocket.

Jake pulled the door open a crack, blinking against the bright light of the hall, then swung the door wide and wrapped her in his arms. "This is what I call room service."

The door shut.

They kissed as though they were starving, took a few steps toward the bed, then paused as Jake pulled her sweater over her head, chuckling as he realized she wasn't wearing a bra. He kissed her breasts, his mouth traveling down to her belly as her insides began to explode. Fumbling, she unzipped her slacks, letting them drop down to her ankles.

Short of breath, he managed "You dressed in a hurry."

She pulled away from his hands for a moment to retrieve the condom from her pocket. "I remembered this."

He laughed. "No worry. I have a supply."

Chapter 9

Rebecca had been dreaming that Alex was snoring; she could feel him against her back, snug and comforting. Then, little by little, the sound of rain lashing against the windows woke her and replaced the dream with reality.

Alex was gone.

Had been gone for one miserable, lonely week.

They'd been apart when she was in Canada doing research, but this time the separation was different. She was still in Oakhurst and he was in the Sierras, restarting his life.

Without her.

She rolled onto her back, displacing the snoring Tinker, whose indignant howl woke Kitkat, curled on what had been Alex's pillow. Matilda, spread out at the foot of the bed, yawned and began cleaning a paw. Rebecca stretched and watched the three cats take their morning baths. Once they finished, they'd be pestering her for their milk and fresh handfuls of dried food in their bowls, and she'd have no choice but to get up.

The storm clouds outside the window matched the massive psychological ones that had been piling up in her head. Persistent, menacing clouds that had begun building when Liv told her about Nate and the Elgin nomination. Now, there would be an article indentifying Emily Gerrard as Kelley Jordan.

Rebecca was being stalked by the truth or—depending on how you looked at it—by the lie about Kelley Jordan. About who she really was.

Actually, if Hannigan had searched the Library of Congress copyright record of her first novel, he'd have found the link because Rebecca had copyrighted *Impossible Secrets* herself before she took the manuscript to the Bennetts. The author line read Rebecca K. Sawyer. Kelley Jordan didn't become part of the equation until the Bennetts purchased the rights to the book. Though there must be countless women named Rebecca Sawyer, she'd been afraid her parents or someone in David's family might get curious. And so Kelley Jordan was born. Neither she nor Liv had bothered to file a name change for the first novel. In hindsight, a mistake.

On top of everything else, Christmas was on the horizon.

Rebecca hated Christmas. It was invariably filled with frantic people trying to squeeze too many tasks into too little time, spilling good cheer all over her. The first Christmas after her divorce taught her that being alone during the holidays sucked, so in the years before she met Alex, she'd spent her holidays at various resorts in the Caribbean. Plenty of warm weather and anonymous strangers also escaping the holiday madness that infected the western world each year.

Last Christmas, she and Alex had driven up to Squaw Valley, skiing in two feet of new snow. It had been her best Christmas except for the Christmas her parents had rented a house in Stowe, Vermont, when she was nine.

Instead of feeling sorry for herself, she should use the upcoming holidays to settle down and work on the new book but, since Liv's visit, she hadn't been especially productive. Still only three chapters.

Alex had finally e-mailed her, explaining that his phone wasn't working. He was looking for a place of his own and, as soon as he bought a new phone, he'd call. At least he'd surfaced. But an e-mail wasn't the same as hearing his laughter. She longed to talk to him.

Emily had forgotten what happiness felt like. This morning, she was definitely happy and definitely behind schedule, with barely enough time to buy coffee and a bear claw at the coffee bar in the hotel lobby. While she ate the pastry, licking the sweet frosting off her fingers, Jake drove to the bookstore on Jackson Boulevard, kissed her goodbye, and promised to pick her up for lunch at two o'clock.

In the minutes before she was introduced to Kelley's fans, Emily sat quietly in the small alcove near the podium, trying to focus on the reading instead of on Jake, rehearsing what she needed to say to the crowd that was rapidly filling up the chairs. She was still floating in a soft haze; every part of her body charged with whatever endorphins had been turned loose in her. Memories of the hours since she'd gone to Jake's room raced across her vision.

His gentle passion had taken her mind and body to places she'd almost forgotten about.

Sometime after eight this morning, she'd fallen into a soft, dreamless sleep. At 10:30, Jake was kissing her awake; her body, remembering the last few hours, was instantly warm and willing.

"Yes, please."

"I'd love to oblige but, if I do, you'll miss your noon reading."

"Oh hell."

He pushed pillows behind his head, watching her slide her sweater over her naked breasts.

"Any idea where my slacks are?"

"Try the entry hall."

Once she had them zipped, she checked the pocket for her room key. "Did I have shoes?"

"Nope. Just the sweater and slacks—very practical."

His grin made her blush. "I probably should be embarrassed about my—well, all that—but right now I don't have time."

"I'll come by your room in half an hour. Will that work?"

"Yes." She slipped out the door, looking a bit like a waif, barefooted, her hair in a tangle, hoping the elevator was empty.

"Ms. Jordan," Emily saw the bookstore manager walking toward her, "we're ready for you."

The next two days were a blur of sex, bookstores, romantic dinners and more sex. After dinner Wednesday night, they strolled State Street, enjoying the lavish Christmas displays in Macy's windows.

"Claudia would love these. I should have brought my camera." Emily had called home every night, struggling to sound normal, to find something to talk about that didn't include Jake, who was usually nearby.

Her mother, however, picked up on something: "You sound different, Em. Are things going well?"

You have no idea just how well. Emily quickly launched into a description of the Christmas windows, hoping to deflect any more difficult questions.

Thursday, the two readings were at independent bookstores in Winnetka and Evanston, a pleasant change from the likes of Borders and Barnes and Noble.

Jake attended both readings, allowing himself the luxury of simply looking at her, remembering what having her in his arms felt like. These few days had made him possessive. Proud of her. Grateful he'd found her. What he felt for Emily was infinitely deeper than what he'd felt for Darlene. The complexity and suddenness of his emotions surprised him. He caught himself imagining the picket fence he'd run away from before.

The late afternoon commute into The Loop made them late getting back to the hotel. They barely had time to change, arrive in time for their reservation at the Italian restaurant they'd gone to the first night, then grab a cab to the Cadillac Palace.

It had been years since she'd attended a live theater performance; the last time was when she'd taken Cris to see *How the Grinch Stole Christmas*. Claudia had been too young to sit still that long, so Patrick had stayed home with her.

Now Emily was watching the magic of *Wicked*, holding Jake's hand, her arm brushing against the roughness of his tweed jacket, trying to keep her mind on the performance. It was the first time she'd seen him dressed up. He was even wearing a tie. She was glad she'd brought a pearl trimmed sweater to wear with the plain black dress. A real date with the man she'd been sleeping with for the last three nights. A man she hardly knew. They weren't yet sharing their pasts; they were content with exploring the present. She knew he preferred beef to chicken, hated hummus, was a Yankees fan and preferred making love to her with the lights on.

As they were leaving the theater, a tall, gray-haired woman called, "Emily? Emily Gerrard."

Surprised that someone in Chicago recognized her, Emily turned around. The elegantly dressed woman in three-inch heels and a full-length evening coat was one of the movers and shakers in the National Storytelling Network, but Emily couldn't remember her name.

The woman quickly came to her rescue. "Marjorie Astin."

"Oh yes, sorry, last year at Ojai." Marjorie had been giving a workshop that Emily spent extra money to attend.

"I thought you lived in San Francisco."

"Berkeley. I'm here on business." A partial truth. Since Jake was quite obviously attached to her hand, Emily added, "This is Jake Hannigan."

Marjorie and Jake shook hands.

"Emily is one of our rising stars on the Pacific Coast Storytelling circuit. Are you involved in Storytelling too?" Jake shook his head and was about to ask what Storytelling was, but Marjorie was again talking to Emily. "I see you're scheduled at the Ojai Festival in the spring. I do hope you'll be doing that charming Thanksgiving piece you performed at the story swap."

"I'm not sure what I'll use. I'm working on several new pieces. Where have you performed this fall?"

"I was at Jonesboro, of course, then Kansas City in early November. We're here visiting our son and his family." She looked away for a moment, "I must go; my husband has snagged a taxi. So good to see you." And Marjorie was swallowed by the crowd.

What were the odds of meeting someone from the NSN on a sidewalk in Chicago? Now Emily was going to have to explain her involvement in Storytelling, and Jake being Jake would ask questions like *how do you find the time to write novels, raise children, and tell stories?* Unfortunately, she didn't have a believable answer prepared. Besides, she didn't want to lie to him any more. Not after the last few days.

"What's Storytelling? And where's Ojai?" Jake was understandably puzzled.

Emily sighed. There was no way to dig herself out of this situation. "Can we go someplace for a drink?"

"Sure. Or we can go back to the hotel." His eyes were smiling, teasing her.

Tempting as the hotel was, she needed to keep her wits about her. "To explain everything, I need to be sitting across a table from you, otherwise—"

"Duly noted. There's a bar across the street."

Though the bar was crowded, they found a booth at the back. Jake ordered a gin and tonic; Emily chose white wine.

"Okay. What's Storytelling?"

Emily took a sip of the wine—too dry for her taste—and began, knowing she sounded as though she were delivering a classroom lecture. "Storytelling's a performance art that's been around for about forty years. At a festival, several Tellers perform their own material. Sometimes, the material is distilled from old fables or legends, but mostly it's original. A story can last anywhere from ten minutes to half an hour, rather like having a one-on-one conversation with the audience. Stories can be very personal. Often humorous. Some Tellers include music or props."

"And you go to festivals and tell your stories?"

"This will be my first major festival. Ojai is just east of Ventura, California."

"How long have you been telling stories?"

"I started telling in college. I was a Communication major; one semester I took a Storytelling class as an elective and got hooked. I was beginning to get bookings when I met Patrick. Because he did his residency in Boston, it was a while before we came back to the Bay Area. By then, I was raising two children and didn't have much free time. When Claudia started kindergarten, I began performing again."

"Do you get paid or is this a voluntary sort of thing?"

"It pays—some gigs pay more than others. Not enough yet to support me and the girls. Maybe someday. Being accepted by Ojai is a big deal for me." And with that admission, she'd opened the way for Jake's next question.

"But your books must earn—"

He stopped.

The missing piece of the Kelley Jordan puzzle slipped neatly into place. He suddenly understood Olivia Bennett's cat and mouse game with the telephone calls and her reluctance about giving him Emily's number.

The truth about the books arrived before they were ready, "You don't write the books."

Very softly, "No."

With that truth, so many things were different.

At least she hadn't volunteered the truth, hadn't said, *I'm not the author.* She could honestly tell Liv that Jake had guessed on his own. However, in the long run, that fact wouldn't matter. It was going to be much harder to explain having an affair with the man who could—probably would—reveal the Kelley Jordan charade.

On the other hand, Emily didn't want the world to believe she was a bestselling author when she wasn't. A few readings and signings hadn't seemed particularly dishonest—a tiny white lie that had stayed below the radar. But *being* Kelley in a major magazine article was another matter entirely. That lie would only complicate an already complicated situation. "Bennett Books pays me to promote the books. I started doing readings for the second book a few months before *Spring Farm* was released. Olivia has good instincts. She was sure the new book was going to take off and used my readings of *The Lost Years* to jump start *Spring Farm.*"

Jake signaled the waiter for another drink. He was fairly sure one wasn't going to be enough. Emily hadn't touched hers.

"Why doesn't the real author do the signings?"

"I don't know. And I have no idea who the author actually is, so don't bother to ask." Suddenly, she was exhausted.

"Who does?"

"The Bennetts."

Jake took a sip of his second drink, briefly savoring the sweet satisfaction of having been right about the story behind the article. He hadn't lost his touch. Following up on this new information—perhaps discovering who the author was—would, however, cost Emily her job. But if he didn't publish what he knew, then he'd lose credibility within his profession. If it should come out that he'd buried the truth, Max would skin him alive—just before he fired him.

The weight of what Jake now knew effectively silenced them. On the way back to the hotel, they didn't speak, didn't touch.

Emily was irrationally angry with Marjorie Astin. *How dare she show up and destroy this idyllic week.* In less than one hour, their joyous interlude had crash landed, scattering emotional debris everywhere.

She was struggling to assess the potential fallout. Olivia would explode and this trip would surely be Emily's last. But then she'd known from the beginning that the job had a short shelf life. The hardcover edition had already been on the market for seven months. Even though it was still on the bestseller list and the trade paperback was due out in February, the value of the signings had probably peaked.

She told herself she had no right to punish Jake for being clever enough to unravel the story. He was, in truth, simply doing his job.

The one question she did need an answer to—before anything else—was whether he'd been pursuing her just to get information for the article. If he had, then she needed to cut her losses, chalk this week up to stupidity and lust, and move on. Except she didn't want to move on. She liked Jake—a lot. If it was possible to fall in love in the space of a few days, then perhaps she loved him.

Jake's thoughts were even more chaotic than Emily's because the decision about revealing or not revealing the truth lay with him. Should he protect Emily and this new relationship or protect his job and professional reputation? He was fairly sure that jeopardizing his job was not really an option. He'd spent a dozen years working his way up the journalistic ladder, was proud of his abilities and not ready to go job hunting. But Emily was very important too.

The real author would, of course, be the one to take the heaviest hit. Why she—he assumed *Kelley* was a she—chose deep cover he had no idea.

The Bennetts might take some criticism for having devised the plan—but if he was any judge of what publicity could accomplish, book sales would probably increase once the story came out. The public's reaction was the wild card.

Once inside her hotel room, Emily confronted Jake. "Has this week simply been part of your research for the article?"

As soon as she'd asked, she was sorry. The stricken look on Jake's face answered her question.

He folded his arms around her, not saying anything for a few seconds. Then his lips were against her hair, whispering, "I wouldn't do that." He paused, "I think I'm falling in love with you. This week has nothing to do with the article. I swear."

It felt like the truth. She prayed it was the truth.

"I had to ask."

She moved out of his arms because she couldn't think clearly when she was so close to him—and sat in the only chair in the room. Jake sat on the foot of the bed. For the next few hours, they dissected the problem from every possible angle, finally agreeing Jake should finish what he'd started, regardless of the fallout.

She was pretty sure, however, that he'd have gone ahead with or without her support.

The next morning, while Emily was at her first reading, Jake called *Twenty-First Century* and asked for Carson. "Can you find the copyright information for all three of the Jordan books?" Jake was mad at himself for not having thought of the copyrights before.

"That's a no-brainer. The Library of Congress is on-line. Anything else?"

"Is there a way you can hack into the publisher's financial records, check to see where the royalty checks go for *Spring Farm*?" He already knew what Carson's answer would be.

"Not unless we want to go to jail."

Chapter 10

On Sunday, before the Gerrard family went Christmas tree shopping, Emily faxed Bennett's Accounting Department copies of the receipts from the trip. Though Jake had tried to pay for her meals, she'd insisted on charging all her expenses as usual. Accounting would expect a paper trail.

Before leaving Chicago, she and Jake agreed not to tell Olivia anything—yet. She'd find out whenever the article was finished. Jake didn't want the Bennetts to threaten a lawsuit of some kind to stop publication. If the company filed one later, at least the article would have made it into print. It occurred to Jake that reporters had a warped moral code: *regardless of the repercussions, run the story.*

Saying goodbye at O'Hare was bittersweet, both wishing the truth hadn't intruded on what had begun so beautifully. "Call me when you get home." Jake's flight would land two hours before Emily's.

"I will; take care." Their kiss was full of promises.

Jake picked up his laptop. "I have to get through security."

One more kiss and he was lost in the confusion of people taking off coats and removing shoes.

By the time Jake walked into his office on Monday, Carson had already forwarded him the copyright form for *Impossible Secrets*: Author: Rebecca K. Sawyer. The forms for the other two novels listed Kelley Jordan. Since the publisher had filed for those copyrights, the address on the Jordan forms was Bennett Books. The address for Rebecca K. Sawyer was a San Francisco post office box. That was five years ago. Odds were it was no longer valid, but he had at least eliminated forty-nine states and half of California.

He sat quietly for a few moments, digesting the information, then called Emily.

Her voice was sleepy, a bit confused. "Jake? What's wrong?"

"I have the name."

"You do realize it's only 6:20 here."

"I wanted you to know." *And I wanted to hear your voice.*

"Sorry. I'm just not awake yet. What is it?"

"A Rebecca K. Sawyer is listed on the copyright for the first book. The other two show Kelley Jordan."

"Interesting shift." Her voice was waking up.

"Ring any bells?"

"No, should it?"

"Just wondered. I found fifteen different listings for the name Rebecca Sawyer on Facebook and Google. Not sure any of those are the right one. The Sawyer copyright shows a San Francisco post office box. I'm going get Carson to run the property rolls for the Northern California counties to see whether she owns property. It's a long shot."

"When's the article going to run?"

"This Friday. I may have to be satisfied with just the name and San Francisco."

"Are you going to alert Olivia?" Emily did not relish being the messenger.

"I'll e-mail the article to her—and you—on Friday morning. New subject. I miss you."

"I miss you too." She kept thinking of things she wanted to tell him.

"Everything okay at your place?"

"The moment we bought the tree, the whining stopped. You?"

"I'm good—glad I have the right name, but that's not good for you."

He heard her sigh, "I suppose not," and he wished he could put his arms around her, smell the lemon shampoo on her hair, feel her relax against him. It surprised him how important she'd become in such a short space of time.

"Try not to worry."

"Easy for you to say."

"I'm sorry."

"Me too."

Jake laid the copyright forms he'd printed out on Max's desk. "I was right. There's more story here."

In the midst of slathering a bagel with cream cheese, Max was not especially happy about being interrupted.

"And?"

"Carson is looking at the property records for Northern California. The publisher certainly isn't going to give her up. They're the ones who hired Emily and created the charade."

"Whether you have any more information or not, I need the final copy of your article in my e-mail Thursday morning. By the way, this Emily—who's admitted she didn't write the books—did you get the information from her fair and square?"

"What constitutes fair and square?"

"Not sleeping with her."

Jake was instantly on the defense. "I didn't sleep with her to get the material. I like her and I think she likes me. We were in Chicago so we could be together without her kids. I wasn't expecting to find out anything new." *He hoped that was the truth.*

Emily had a busy week ahead of her: two Christmas Storytelling dates, one on Wednesday for the Berkeley Rotary Club, another on Friday night at the Methodist Church. However, she was having trouble concentrating on preparing for the performances because Jake's face kept getting in her way, and she felt guilty about not telling Olivia what was about to happen. Jake probably wouldn't appreciate her calling to warn Liv. He was a journalist with a job to do. Guilt wasn't an issue for him. At the same time, she didn't like being caught up in this ridiculous tangle. Funny how pretending to be Kelley had never bothered her before, even though she'd been as involved in the lie as Liv and the mysterious Rebecca Sawyer. The emotional roller coaster she'd been riding since Chicago was wearing her out.

Alerting Liv could jeopardize Emily's relationship with Jake since she'd agreed not to say anything until he sent the article. But she'd known Liv longer, worked for her. When Emily couldn't stand it any longer, she called Bennett Books.

Once again, Olivia listened without commenting until Emily finished her confession. "The article will be in this Friday's issue. He only has her name and the San Francisco post office box."

"So far." Then, "What in the hell were you thinking? You know damned well he seduced you to get the information. Oldest trick in the book. So stupid!" Silence. "You do understand that I won't need your services any longer. I'll have payroll mail your final check." Olivia was spacing out her words in lieu of shouting them.

"Yes."

"And mail me the company credit card." Because Olivia was using a cordless phone, nothing actually slammed when she hung up, but she'd desperately wanted to slam something. The Kelley Jordan arrangement had just gone south.

Since he'd been in Squaw Valley, Alex had only called Rebecca twice. The first time was when he finally bought a new phone, the second time to tell her he was renting a studio apartment. He sounded happy, full of anecdotes about the ski classes, the snow, the difficulty of getting back into shape. "Thank God for hot tubs."

Rebecca didn't want to imagine the other reasons he might thank God for hot tubs. She pretended she didn't care what he did in the hot tubs.

"Can you drive up after Christmas? I'll be moved in by then."

They agreed she'd come the Tuesday after Christmas. She didn't know whether she should be pleased at the prospect of spending time with him or put off by the fact that he didn't want her to come for Christmas. *Don't go looking for trouble.* Since he'd been gone, her emotions had been all over the place like a hormonal teenager's. She alternately missed him and wanted him back or didn't care if she never saw him again.

The next day, Olivia called to tell Rebecca about Hannigan's revised article.

"When?" was all Rebecca could manage.

"Tomorrow's edition."

Rebecca didn't bother to ask how Hannigan had uncovered the truth. Didn't want to know. She hung up without saying goodbye.

Until long after dark, Rebecca sat in her studio, not bothering to turn the lights on. Tinker finally came looking for her, his meows complaining that she was late with his dinner.

"Sorry baby." She picked him up and buried her face in his fur. "I wish my world were as simple as yours": *Eating, sleeping and more eating. And of course bathing.* Tinker's response was to lick her ear. "Hey, that tickles." She carried him into the kitchen where Matilda and Kitkat were waiting beside their empty bowls. A feline sit-in.

At least the cats didn't care what her real name was.

In the middle of the night, she decided to get out of town—temporarily—and called Megan. It was noon in Surrey.

"Yesterday I mailed the Christmas gifts you sent for your parents."

"I'm also sending myself."

Megan paused, not quite sure she'd heard correctly. She was always encouraging Rebecca to visit. "You mean you're actually coming?"

"I need to be somewhere else. You're the safest place I can think of. Do you mind?"

"Of course not. Please come. It seems forever since I've seen you. Hugh will be delighted, the kids too. When?"

"Don't know yet. Thank goodness, I renewed my passport last year. As soon as I have a ticket, I'll e-mail you my arrival time. Do trains still run from Gatwick to Dorking?"

"Yes. I'll check the schedules and e-mail you."

It took three days for Rebecca to get herself organized and packed. She had to stock up on cat food, alert Trudy, and close up the house.

Though she didn't plan on writing while she was gone, she copied the chapters she'd finished onto her laptop, packed the charger and hoped she could buy a converter once she was at Megan's. It occurred to her that she should call Alex but, in the end, chose not to. She didn't feel like telling anyone where she was going. Certainly not Liv. She only told Trudy that she would be out of town for a week or two, and left extra cash for cat food. Trudy would e-mail her if there was a problem.

Plane trips from Oakhurst were never easy. She drove to Fresno, parked in the long stay lot, flew to San Francisco and finally into Gatwick. By the time she landed, she'd been traveling twenty-one hours. She'd bought the Friday edition of *Twenty-First Century* at the San Francisco airport but hadn't looked inside. She was afraid of what it said and what it was going to do to her life.

It had taken Jake only two hours to revise the Jordan article because he didn't need to rewrite the material about the book itself and its reviews; he simply wrote a new introduction. He included Emily's picture and the essentials of her personal life, some of which had been in the original article, adding the fact that she was a Storyteller.

> *At first, I thought Emily Gerrard was simply using Kelley Jordan as her pen name. But a chance encounter with a woman who knows Emily's Storytelling work made me realize she wasn't the author. When I asked her straight out whether she wrote the books, she said no. She was quite honest about being hired by Bennett*

Books a year ago to promote the Kelley Jordan books. Once I had that information, I began my hunt for the real author. So far, I know that the author's name is Rebecca K. Sawyer and, though I don't have proof yet, she probably lives in Northern California. If anyone reading this article thinks they know where Rebecca K. Sawyer lives, let me know."

He included his e-mail address at the magazine.

Jake sat across the desk as Max read the article on his computer screen, carefully watching his friend's expression. Max closed the file and looked up, "I'm thinking we could run this in the news section instead of on the book page."

"Good idea. It'll get more attention. Someone out there knows a Rebecca Sawyer who writes but doesn't use her own name."

"Your e-mail is going to be stuffed with false leads."

"That's okay. I'd love to have the answer before the awards banquet. Carson's still running property rolls."

"Revealing the author's real identity will wreck havoc in her life. Clearly she does not want to be identified with her writing."

"If we worried about fallout, we'd never write anything that exposes secrets."

"Just thought I'd mention it. Good work. And now that you're finished with your soft news assignment, I'm sending you to Tunisia the day after Christmas. Your reward for a great series on the authors."

Jake smiled his thanks, not bothering to mention that he'd already been rewarded in ways that had nothing to do with journalism.

Chapter 11

Megan Sutherland was the older sister Rebecca had always wanted. Taller than Rebecca, almost 5'10", Megan's dusky skin and jet black hair contrasted with Rebecca's fair coloring. When the young Rebecca had asked Megan why her hair was so black, Megan had explained, "One side of my family is Welsh, the other is Jewish and Cherokee. No other color choice with that mix."

She was in her sophomore year at UCLA, a 4.0 General Studies major preparing for a teaching career. Typically, an on-set tutor would have to have a valid teaching credential, but the show's producer felt Rebecca would do better working with someone closer to her own age. All Megan had to do was follow the school district's curriculum and lesson plans and keep up with her own college classes.

From the beginning, they were a perfect fit, and Rebecca trusted her. That trust was the reason Rebecca was sitting in Megan's kitchen in Dorking, drinking Lady Grey tea and watching eight-year old Sara frost Christmas cookies. Nigel, three years older and too grown up for frosting cookies, was in the lounge watching a football match with his father. Rebecca was struggling to stay awake until nine or ten o'clock, a necessary step in adjusting to the eight-hour time difference as soon as possible. Realistically, however, she wasn't going to last that long.

Noticing Rebecca's battle with jet lag, Megan reached for the table knife her daughter was using. "Sara, my love, why don't you take a few of those to your father and brother. I'll put the frosting in the refrigerator and you can finish tomorrow."

"But—" a scowl appeared.

"Scoot."

"You just don't want me to hear what you and Aunt Becca are going to talk about."

"Grown-up talk. Very boring."

Sara took her time arranging six cookies on a plate and slowly left the kitchen.

As soon as the kitchen door closed, Megan shook her head. "She already knows how to make a point without saying a word. I can hardly wait until she hits puberty. Nigel is much easier. Feed him, give him as much football as he can handle, and he's happy."

"They've grown so much. I might not have recognized them if you hadn't been standing with them at the station."

"You haven't been over for two years."

Rebecca ignored the complaint. "Was I easy or hard when I was a teenager?"

Megan reached for a handful of cookies and laid them on the table between herself and Becca.

"As far as I was concerned, you weren't any trouble, but then I was hardly out of my teens so I was more teenager than adult. Sometimes I still am. But for your parents, you were trouble because they didn't have a clue who you were and didn't take the time to find out. They assumed you were just like them, wanted the same things. My mother suffers from the same delusion. On the set, you were always ready with your lines and worked hard. Sulky sometimes. But what teenage girl isn't?"

"I didn't want to be there." Rebecca hadn't known how to fight against her parents' wishes. She wasn't given to throwing tantrums or running away from home—which, in retrospect, she should perhaps have tried. In a family that was overly dramatic about everything—even deciding what wine to serve with dinner could escalate into Oscar winning performances—Rebecca learned early to stay on the sidelines.

"Don't take this the wrong way; I'm delighted you're here, but why are you here?"

Because I don't know where to be.

"I'm about to be ratted out." Rebecca reached into her purse and found the copy of *Twenty-First Century* she'd purchased at the San Francisco airport. She skimmed the table of contents, turned to the article, and handed Megan the magazine. "I'm up for a big writing award."

"Congratulations."

"Unfortunately, it comes with a curse. The journalist assigned to profile the four nominees has figured out that Kelley Jordan is a pen name. Initially, he thought Emily, the woman who has been doing the readings for me, was actually the author. Now he's discovered that Rebecca K. Sawyer is the author."

"Has he gotten to the Kingston connection?"

"No. But it's only a matter of time."

"Have you read the article?"

"Not this version. I saw the preliminary draft, written before he discovered the Rebecca Sawyer connection. At some point, the rest of the story will come out, and the media will be all over it—and me. On top of that, Nate Pullman is trying to buy the movie rights for *Spring Farm*."

"Does he know it's yours?"

"Not yet." She sighed, "I feel like The Furies are closing in on me. All of a sudden I'm fourteen again and have no control over my life." She bit the head off a Santa cookie, briefly wondering if there was symbolism in the beheading. Jake Hannigan's head perhaps.

Unsure whether she should play Devil's Advocate or offer comfort, Megan did neither. "And so you're spending Christmas in England with us."

Rebecca almost smiled. "I have a cowardly streak. At the first hint of confrontation, I run."

"Not always. I remember when you stood your ground about college and refused to do another year of *Mandy*."

"I was desperate to stop doing that show so I could go to college. I never wanted any part of acting or all the crap that goes with it."

"You're not fourteen now. You've lived your own life for a long time."

"True. And had the pleasure of making my own mistakes, David for instance." She took another cookie. Sara had used bright orange frosting on a Christmas tree. How lovely not to care about what something should look like. "I'm afraid." She finished the cookie. "I'm not sure what I'm afraid of. Discovery or myself. Sorry. It's too late in the day to be philosophical. Time for bed. I'm fading fast."

Megan walked her up to the small attic room that doubled as a sewing room and guest room, and hugged Rebecca. "Sleep as late as you want. The kids and I have some shopping to do in the morning. Every shop in town is out of brussels sprouts so I need to try the shops in Reigate. Can't have an English Christmas dinner without sprouts."

"The good English wife."

Megan laughed—Becca loved her friend's deep laugh, nothing held back. "Hardly. Personally I hate brussels sprouts. I bury them in my mashed potatoes."

Two days before Christmas, Carson Tyler found a trust deed for a Rebecca K. Sawyer in Oakhurst, California. Unfortunately, Jake didn't have time to enjoy the discovery. He was in the midst of preparing for his trip to Tunisia—getting the necessary papers and press credentials, looking forward to being back in the Middle East. He'd been saddled with safe stories far too long. The day after Christmas, he would fly out of Kennedy to Cairo, then to Tunis. As much as he wanted to finish what he'd begun with the article on *Spring Farm,* he couldn't go to California now. When he made his nightly call to Emily—seven o'clock Pacific time—he asked a favor. "How long is the drive to Oakhurst from where you are?"

"I don't know. Several hours at least. I'll have to look at a map. Is that where she lives?"

"There's a Rebecca K. Sawyer on the title of a house on half an acre outside Oakhurst." He gave her the address. "That's the only Rebecca Sawyer listing in Northern California. I'd do this myself, but I'm leaving Monday night."

"When will you be back?"

"No idea. Uprisings don't keep schedules."

"What should I say if I find her?"

"Just ask if she's the author. By now, she's seen the article, so she knows who you are. Maybe she's known your name all along. See what develops. She can only throw you out." He was only half kidding.

"Something to look forward to. I've never interviewed anybody, though I admit I'm curious about her. I've been her alter ego for a year."

"I apologize for dumping this on you."

Emily didn't think he sounded especially apologetic. Ever since he'd told her about Tunisia, she'd sensed a difference in him—he was energized by the opportunity to be in the midst of the upheaval. This was a Jake she hadn't met before. Rather like Patrick whenever he'd been tapped by the World Health Organization to go on a mission. "As soon as I get back, I'll take a few days off and fly out to do a real interview with her."

"Why don't we just wait."

"Somehow I have a feeling we need to keep looking for the answer in case I'm gone longer than a couple of weeks. I trust your instincts."

Longer than a couple of weeks was not what she needed to hear. Of all the men she might have met, she'd found another one who went racing off to the ends of the earth.

"I'm not sure going to Oakhurst is a good idea, but since it's you—"

"I'll make it worth your while."

"I'm counting on it."

But not too much.

The weather in Southern England was unseasonably dry but cold, hovering around freezing. Perfect for walking. Her first day at Megan's, Rebecca woke to an empty house, fixed herself toast and juice, then followed the road into Dorking, strolled the streets and stopped for a coffee. She wasn't ready to focus on finding Christmas gifts for Megan's family. Jet-lag fog was interfering with her thought processes.

After a second night's sleep, she walked the High Street with more purpose. She bought Sara a bright red purse, little girl size, and Nigel a football, having first made the mistake of asking for a soccer ball. The clerk at Seymour Sports was, at first, confused and then said *You must be American.* For Megan and Hugh, she settled on a basket of imported cheeses. Not an especially personal gift, but it was the best she could do at the last minute in a small market town.

Rebecca had always loved the feel of Dorking. Brick buildings, some whitewashed, clustered in the Mole Valley, the Surrey Hills framing the scene. Picture postcard England. Since Medieval times, it had been a place people could count on. Solid. Slow to change. She was only one of the thousands and thousands of people who had walked these same streets. In the grand scheme, Rebecca Sawyer was a bit player on the town's stage. In the tick of time, what was worrying her didn't count for much.

The next day, Megan drove Rebecca and the children to the Druid's Grove; they hiked among the ancient Yew trees then stopped in Norbury for lunch. Christmas Eve day they took the children to Dorking Halls to see *The Chronicles of Narnia.* Rebecca finished wrapping her gifts just before the family left for the Midnight Communion Service at St. Martins. Snow was in the forecast and the temperature was already below freezing. The glow of the Christmas candles reached beyond the church windows, a warm and welcoming English Christmas. For a little while, Rebecca let herself feel safe.

Jake called Emily on Christmas night. "Merry Christmas. Did you have a good day?"

"I did, and I love my present."

He'd sent a delicate silver bracelet with tiny pearls.

He would have loved to see her face when she opened it. "It reminded me of you."

She was tempted to ask how, but that might sound as though she were fishing for a compliment. Instead, she tucked his words away to be cherished later.

"I thought about sending something for your mother and the girls, but I didn't want to get ahead of myself." *And he had no idea what to buy for young girls.* "Thanks for the DVD's." She'd sent two recently released movie DVD's she was pretty sure he hadn't seen. "North African TV isn't all that great and watching CNN loops in the hotel gets old. I'll think of you when I watch them and wish you were with me."

"Were you at your parents' house today?"

"Yes. I left about seven. My brother Ned, the one who's the teacher, and his brood were there too. I left early so I could finish packing."

"Will Tunisia be dangerous?"

"Yes and no."

"I hate that part of the world. You've already been injured once." If she could have talked him out of going, she would have.

He could hear worry in her voice. "I promise I will keep safe and come back in one piece."

"Good. I don't want to lose you." She stopped short of including *too.*

Maybe she wasn't just worrying about him. She was undoubtedly remembering all the times she'd worried about her husband. Hard to compete with someone who had died doing heroic work. "If you don't have time to go to Oakhurst, I'll understand. I wish I could follow up on Rebecca myself."

"I'll try to go. Will your phone work over there?"

"Yes, but the timing will be tricky. There's a nine hour difference."

"Even if it's the middle of the night, please call." *I need to know you're okay.*

"I will. Em—well—we'll talk as soon as I get back. About us—about this whole thing." *Thing. And he called himself a writer.* When it came to his own feelings, he was hopeless at expressing them.

"Yes we should."

Neither knew whether it was time to use the word *love*, but there it was dangling in the air. Implicit in what they weren't saying.

"I'll call when I get to the hotel in Tunis. Sleep well." His voice was gentle.

Chapter 12

Thank goodness for Google. Emily printed out the Oakhurst map and located the street name Jake had given her. With an old Auto Club map, she planned a route across the Central Valley to Oakhurst. She wanted to make the trip not only because Jake had asked her but because she was personally involved in the secret. He'd warned her that the media might come asking questions once the article was in print but, so far, nothing had happened.

Perhaps it wasn't as big a deal as Jake or Olivia thought.

Perhaps Rebecca Sawyer was just paranoid.

Her mother invited herself along. "It's a long trip. Why don't I come with you to share the driving? I'm curious about her too."

Cristyl already had a Thursday sleepover with a school friend, so she had no interest in going. And being cooped up in a car all day didn't sound good to Claudia either. "Why do you have to do this for *him*?" There was no good answer for the tone of that question, but Emily answered anyway. "Because he asked me and because I was pretending to be this woman when I went on all those trips." She'd given the girls the article, though she doubted they'd read it.

A phone call to the mother of one of Claudia's friends provided a sleepover for her too. A full day with an unhappy nine year old in the car would not be fun.

They dropped the girls off at their friends' homes and were on the road by seven, stopping for breakfast around nine. During the drive, Emily was mentally rehearsing what she should say when she found Rebecca Sawyer. "Hi, I'm Emily Gerrard. I wanted to meet you." An eight hour drive just to meet her? Not plausible. "Jake Hannigan wanted me to find out if you're the Rebecca Sawyer who wrote *Spring Farm*. He's in Tunisia right now and couldn't—" Not much better. Halfway across the Central Valley, she was already sorry she'd agreed to track down this mysterious woman who didn't want to be found.

As soon as they left the Valley and began climbing into the foothills, there were patches of snow along the edges of the road and beneath the trees. She hadn't considered the possibility of snow. A good thing the roads were clear because she didn't have chains.

It was almost noon when they drove into Oakhurst. Her mother was studying the Google map. "This is when a GPS would come in handy. We could let it talk us to the right house without having to read the addresses on the mailboxes."

"Not in my budget."

"There it is." Mildred pointed to a wide gravel driveway on their right; the rural mailbox had R. Sawyer lettered on the side.

Emily pulled into the driveway and parked alongside a black, mud-splattered Explorer with a ski rack on the top. "Looks like she's here." Something in Emily's tone must have given away her hesitancy about this errand.

"Were you hoping she wouldn't be?"

"Sort of." Emily could feel her stomach tighten.

"Come on," her mother opened the passenger door, "let's get this over with. You're making me nervous."

Emily grabbed the copy of Jake's magazine and followed her mother into the patio. A gray tabby was sleeping on the doormat. As they approached, it got up slowly, stretched, and sauntered away, more annoyed at having its nap interrupted than frightened.

A tall, dark-haired man dressed in ski pants and a heavy jacket with a Squaw Valley logo answered the door, looking as surprised to see them as they were to see him.

"Hello," Emily hesitated, "is Rebecca Sawyer home?"

"No, no she isn't. I'm looking for her too. Do you know her?"

"Not exactly. I'm Emily Gerrard. This is my mother. We've driven from Berkeley."

Mildred extended her hand. "Mildred McGee. And you are?"

"Alex Zimmermann."

No one seemed to know what the next step should be. Finally, Alex stepped aside. "Come in for a minute. I was about to call the woman who takes care of the cats when Becca's gone. See what she knows." He flipped his cell phone open.

Emily and Mildred followed him into the spacious living room with a picture window framing the pine trees just beyond what was, in summer, a lawn. The green of the pines and the blues and greens in the room made it seem like outside and inside were one.

Alex punched a number and waited, "Trudy? Alex Zimmermann."

He listened, then "I'm still teaching, but I drove down this morning. I've been trying to reach Becca since late Monday. At first, I thought she was avoiding me, and then I got worried. Do you know when she left?"

More listening. "Any idea where?"

Listening.

Finally he closed his phone, "Trudy says Becca left on the eighteenth but didn't mention where she was going. Trudy thinks she's planning to be gone at least two weeks because she stocked up on cat food and left additional cash for emergencies. Becca's car is gone. If she flew, she probably left it at the Fresno airport."

In spite of her nervousness about this meeting, Emily was disappointed. "It was a gamble, trying to catch her, I mean."

"If you don't know her, do you mind telling me why you came all this way?"

"It's rather complicated." Emily wasn't certain she should confide in this stranger, though he did have a key to Rebecca's house and Jake's article had already made much of the story public. Since she'd already lost her job with Liv, she saw no reason she should keep the secret the Bennetts had so carefully guarded.

"Please, sit down. Can I get you anything, water?"

"No thanks."

He sat in one of the deep leather chairs. "I know it must seem strange that I'm in her house. My family owns the local sporting goods store. Becca and I have been seeing one another for a while, but right now I'm at Squaw Valley teaching skiing. She was supposed to come up this week, but she didn't. I haven't been able to get her to answer her phone or her e-mail. I was worried so I took the day off. I have to be back at work tomorrow."

Emily rather liked his face, sunburned except for his raccoon eyes, compliments of ski goggles. Nice eyes that seemed to be telling the truth.

An orange marmalade cat had jumped into his lap, rubbing its head against his chest until he scratched behind its ears. "Hey there, Kitkat. Lonesome?"

Emily leaned over to hand him the magazine. "There's an article on page thirty-two about a Rebecca Sawyer—and, well, about me—and about the award her novel has been nominated for. I'm trying to find out if the Rebecca Sawyer in this article is the one who lives here."

"A novel?" He shook his head. "It must be a different Rebecca Sawyer. Becca's a ghostwriter. She only writes other people's memoirs."

"I don't know anything about her ghostwriting, but the Rebecca Sawyer in the article has written three historical novels. The one that's up for the Elgin Award is called *Spring Farm*. It's a terrific story about the Oregon Trail." Emily could tell by Alex's expression that he was genuinely confused by what she was telling him. If the Rebecca Sawyer who lived in this house was the author of *Spring Farm*, she was keeping secrets even from the man she was undoubtedly sleeping with. "She's been using a pen name. Kelley Jordan." *In for a penny, in for a pound.* If Rebecca Sawyer didn't want her boyfriend to know, it was too late now. It took only twenty minutes for Emily to tell the whole story—or as much of it as she knew.

When she finished, Alex asked, "Are you sure about all of this?"

"I can't prove she's the right Rebecca Sawyer, but if you don't mind, could I see her office or wherever she does her writing? I know that she's begun a new novel about the Acadians. Perhaps there's something in the office that will show what she's currently writing. Or would that be intruding too much?"

He stood up. "At this point, I want to know what the truth is too. The studio's this way."

The wood-paneled room had a bay window where another cat slept on the window seat cushions. Obviously Rebecca Sawyer loved cats. Her desk was piled with books and stacks of paper, a desktop computer in the midst of the clutter. Rather messy for Emily's taste. She could only work on her own stories if her desk was tidy. She picked up one of the books beside the computer, *The Acadian Journey to Louisiana*. She handed it to Alex. He took note of the title and set the book back on the stack. "Looks like you have the right Rebecca Sawyer. She's taken a couple of trips to Canada this year and was planning to go again this summer."

Since Emily had begun explaining her relationship to Becca, Alex had been trying, unsuccessfully, to absorb all these things that he didn't know about Becca. In truth, she never talked about her past or her work in any detail, dodging even the simplest of questions. Not knowing all the bits and pieces of her life had never concerned him. After all, he wasn't planning on spending the rest of his life with her. Whenever she did mention something about herself, it was in general terms. *I grew up in Southern California. I'm an only child. My parents are in the entertainment business so they travel at lot. I don't see them often.* About her life since her divorce, she'd always seemed more forthcoming; however, she'd never mentioned being a novelist. Evidently a good one. As a general rule, he didn't read novels, didn't read many books at all. He'd have to find a bookstore before he got back to Squaw Valley. Once he'd teased Becca about her ghostwriting. "Don't you even get an acknowledgement on the last page of the book?"

"Nope. A ghost remains a ghost. I prefer being invisible."

Obviously.

When he stayed overnight, she usually kept the door to her studio closed and never worked. "It's a mess in there." Alex simply assumed ghostwriting required secrecy.

There was a lot about his years in international skiing he didn't care to share either.

He'd seldom dated a woman longer than three or four months. Casual relationships had always suited him. No questions asked or answered.

Being with Becca was his first long-term, monogamous relationship, and he surprised himself by being content—even happy. Cooking with her, watching TV, having dinner with friends in town. Skiing. Yet he never let himself think about their relationship as anything but temporary. Neither of them had ever used the L word.

Since he'd been in Squaw Valley, he missed the simple rhythms they'd established together, but he hadn't called her as often as he should have—telling himself he was busy. A lot of that busyness included enjoying the daily happy hour at one of the ski lodges after a day on the slopes. Unlike his ski team days however, he always went back to his apartment alone. He hadn't hooked up with any of the single women who would have been more than willing to sleep with a handsome ski instructor. This behavior was different for him. If he'd been given to introspection, he would have realized he was being faithful to Becca.

He'd spent the week before her scheduled arrival getting the small studio he was renting ready for her visit. Shopping for groceries in Tahoe City, hunting for the special foods she liked. Buying the Pinot Grigio she favored. But she hadn't come. He'd called both her cell and landline numbers, e-mailed her several times. Assuming she was still pissed off about his leaving, he didn't call Trudy right away. Finally, he checked with the CHP to find out if there'd been any accidents on the roads she might have driven.

And now he was listening to Emily Gerrard tell him that Becca wasn't who he thought she was. Unsure whether he should be worried about her disappearance or angry about the deception, he asked, "Would this publisher—Olivia—would she know where Becca is?"

"I don't know. Liv definitely wouldn't approve of my being here. She's always careful to keep Rebecca's secret and was not happy about my seeing Jake Hannigan—the author of the article—because inadvertently I played a role in his discovering that Kelley Jordan was a pen name and that I wasn't Kelley Jordan. I called Olivia to tell her when the article would be published and that Jake had found out who Kelley Jordan really was. Liv probably warned Rebecca."

"Do you have this Olivia's phone number?"

Emily scrolled through her contact list and read the number.

When Bennett Books answered, Alex asked for Olivia Bennett. "I see. Will she be back today? Please ask her to call Alex Zimmermann," he recited his cell phone number. "It's about Rebecca Sawyer."

Chapter 13

In the ten days Rebecca had been in Dorking, Megan had been trying in vain to get her to talk about the crisis that brought her to England, but Rebecca didn't want to have that conversation—yet.

"You're avoiding the issue." Megan accused.

"You're right. I haven't decided what to do. When I know, I'll run it by you."

Maybe.

"Let me help."

"I'm not ready for help. Before all hell breaks loose, I need to get my head on straight."

"Have I ever mentioned that you're stubborn?"

"Frequently, but I don't take it personally." Rebecca pulled her coat from the peg in the front hall. "I'm going for a walk. Fresh air helps me think." She wound a blue wool scarf around her neck and pulled on matching gloves. Christmas gifts from the Sutherlands. "Don't wait lunch. I'll grab something in town."

She wasn't, however, planning to go into town, preferring to walk into the countryside. She craved the tranquility of snow-covered fields while she forced herself to revisit that first hell—the one she'd taught herself to stay away from—and then figure out how to survive the new hell on the horizon. For seven years, she'd successfully avoided everything and everyone from her past, except Megan. A past that had made her feel like a pawn pushed around by those who supposedly had her best interests at heart. Though she sometimes missed her parents, she was deathly afraid of spending even one day with them or doing anything that might put her in the spotlight again.

As it had been everyday since her arrival, the English sky was various shades of gray, not ready to snow again but thinking about it. She tugged the scarf up so it covered her nose and mouth, jammed her hands into her coat pockets, and began replaying the scene that had followed telling her parents she was not renewing her *Mandy* contract.

Always on stage, even when there was no stage, her mother began with high drama. *You're throwing away your career. No one will hire an actor who cavalierly walks away from a hit show. Mandy has made you a star!* Hillary Wallingford was still a beautiful woman; at forty-eight, she looked forty. Rebecca had inherited her mother's coloring but not her delicate features and certainly not her flair for dramatizing everything. Rebecca resembled Peter's mother, a wider mouth, doe-shaped eyes, more exotic than fragile.

Once her mother ran out of steam, Rebecca tried presenting her own case, angry about her parents' power over her but with no faith in her own power. Probably because she'd never before tried to exercise it. This time would be different. Things had to be said. "I don't want this damned career. I intend to go to college." She'd been practicing this speech for days. "I deserve a life I choose. Not the one you assume I should want. You've never paid attention to what I want." Expecting her mother to launch into another monologue, Rebecca was surprised it didn't come.

"Which is?"

"To live a normal, ordinary life instead of being gawked at and talked about 24/7."

"Your fans love you."

"I don't care. I'd rather have friends."

"You have Megan."

"Megan's my tutor. You pay her."

"I don't understand you, Rebecca." *Of course you don't.* "You have a life most young women would kill for." *They're welcome to it.*

When it was clear Rebecca wasn't giving in, her father—theoretically more rational than his wife—took over. Peter Kingston tried arguing that she could go to college later; *Mandy* probably had another year or two in it. "And you know that Nate is negotiating a remake of *Rebel Without a Cause* with you in the role Natalie Wood played in the original. A once in a lifetime opportunity. It's almost impossible to move from TV to the big screen, and you're going to walk away from a major movie? I thought you were smarter than that."

If she compromised—waited a year or two—there'd be something else getting in her way. Nate's movie, more TV, a contract that couldn't be broken. She had to get out completely. Now.

That she knew.

At the beginning of the battle, Peter had fixed himself a scotch on the rocks. He believed he argued better with a drink in his hand. Six years older than Hillary, he was already turning gray. He'd started out as an actor but, early in his career, had switched to directing and producing, preferring to create films and plays that had *meat on their bones*. Two Oscar nominations and one win gave him the ability to pick and choose his projects.

"Darling child, you know we love you and want the best for you."

Their best was not her best. She'd heard that line all her life and was not falling for it this time. "Then let me go to college. Now."

Peter fixed himself another drink.

Two days of turmoil—icy silences and another dramatic monologue by Hillary. Rebecca remembered being so angry at one point that she began shaking and then threw up all over the expensive Turkish carpet in her father's study, effectively putting an end to the Kingston war of wills. Her parents capitulated—not gracefully or quietly—but *Mandy* was not renewed.

She was free.

Rebecca's agent released a brief statement on her behalf. *I've enjoyed playing Mandy, but I now want to concentrate on my education, find out what the rest of the world is like. I'll be attending Wellesley in the fall. I hope all of you will give me the space and privacy I need to complete my degree.*

Fat chance of that. The supermarket tabloids had a field day.

Rebecca Kingston Going into Rehab.

Rebecca Kingston Pregnant.

Kingston Family at War. That one was true.

Rebecca Kingston to Marry Her Mandy Co-Star. Justin Blake's current girlfriend was not thrilled with that one.

In the days after the announcement, reporters camped outside the Kingston house in Malibu. It was impossible to appreciate her newfound freedom when, just to leave the house, she had to run a gauntlet of shouted questions and cameras clicking like mechanical piranhas. Her father conveniently left for Toronto where he was shooting exterior scenes for a new film; Hillary simply put on her outsized sunglasses and waved as she drove out of the driveway. Because she'd had years of dealing with the media, they didn't faze her.

Even now, fourteen years later, Rebecca's blood ran cold remembering the lies that were published and the in-your-face harassment whenever she was spotted on the street, effectively cutting off her ability to breathe or think.

To its credit, Wellesley refused to comment on Rebecca's enrollment and barred the media from campus, though policing the ban was virtually impossible. In the four years she was there, reporters fabricated stories whenever they had a slow news day—*Rebecca Kingston flunking out, binge drinking, sleeping with her professors.* Never anything positive, but at least she was doing what she wanted to do.

While she'd been walking, the clouds had gradually settled themselves into the valley, obscuring the hills beyond town, threatening more snow. Time to turn around.

Revisiting her youthful declaration of independence hadn't gotten Rebecca any closer to deciding whether or not to attend the Elgin Award ceremony. If she did, she'd surely have to confront the media head on. *Here I am. Do your worst.* Which they certainly would. Yet getting recognition for her writing would be a validation of what she'd chosen to do with her life. She was proud of *Spring Farm*, had buried herself in it for over two years, and wanted the book to win. Of that she was sure. Winning would be tantamount to saying to her parents and the world: *Look at what I've accomplished without the Kingston name.*

Not attending would be admitting she couldn't take the heat. And perhaps she couldn't. Her skin still didn't feel thick enough to withstand an onslaught of paparazzi and cameras.

Emily and Mildred left Oakhurst just before three o'clock. They'd stopped in town for lunch, spending more time than they meant to reviewing the conversation with Alex Zimmermann. He'd thanked them for filling him in. "At least, when she turns up, I'll be ready to ask the right questions." He and Emily exchanged cell numbers. "If Olivia Bennett calls me back with information, I'll let you know." He locked up the house. "I have to be at work early tomorrow morning."

Mildred drove the first part of their return journey, both women lost in their own thoughts. While they were at Merced buying gas and getting coffee to go, Jake called Emily's cell.

She walked a few steps from the car so she could talk in private. "It must be after midnight where you are."

"One-thirty to be exact. My sleep cycle is messed up. Where are you? I hear traffic."

"Mom and I are at Merced, buying gas. Jake, I found her. I'm pretty sure it's the right Rebecca." She gave him an abridged version of her meeting with Alex, told him about asking to see Rebecca's studio and finding the research material for the Acadian book.

"Very clever." Suddenly he didn't sound as tired. "You're a better detective than you think you are."

"I really feel sorry for Alex. He was already worried about her disappearance, and then I presented him with a totally different view of her. He had no idea about the novels."

"She must have left town as soon as the article came out."

Emily hesitated, "She had a heads up before it came out."

Several seconds passed, then "You called Olivia Bennett."

"I felt like I owed her that." Would he be angry? She'd done the very thing he'd asked her not to do.

"Rebecca would probably have disappeared anyway." He sounded resigned.

"Jake, I'm sorry."

"It's okay. Do you think this Alex will really call if he finds her?"

"I do. He seems like a good guy. Really nice eyes. Handsome, athletic."

"Now I'm jealous."

"No need. I miss you."

"I miss you too."

Mildred was getting into the passenger side of the car. "I need to go. It's my turn to drive. We still have about three hours before we're home. Get some sleep."

"I wish."

Though being free of her first eighteen years was what Rebecca had fought for, she had no idea how to take charge of her life.

She had few coping skills to help navigate her newfound freedom. All her life she'd been waited on by servants and told what to do by directors, publicists, nannies and, of course, her parents. Suddenly, she had to learn to take care of herself. Do her laundry, pay bills, though her credit card statements still went to her father, and keep her car running.

At the end of her college years, despite graduating with honors, she wasn't qualified for much of anything. English majors, especially those with an emphasis in creative writing, weren't easily employable unless they wanted to teach or work for a publishing house, so graduating felt like stepping off a cliff into empty air. A reality check that Rebecca wasn't entirely prepared for.

When her parents attended her graduation, the media predictably invaded the campus. Rebecca had initially been pleased that both parents were coming, momentarily forgetting that nothing they did went unnoticed. *Peter Kingston and Hillary Wallingford Attend Daughter's Graduation. Kingston Family Reunited. Will Mandy Return to Hollywood?*

Her day was ruined.

Enter David Sawyer, who was conveniently waiting in the wings, dancing attendance. Two years older than Rebecca, already working for the brokerage where his father was a partner, David had been courting Rebecca ever since his sister Peg brought Rebecca home for Thanksgiving their junior year. Before taking a close look at this new script, Rebecca convinced herself that her next role should be David's wife. She naively believed that, if she were married, she'd be spared the media's harassment. Instead, her marriage unleashed a new media invasion that lasted several months. She hadn't expected David would enjoy the attention, but he did. "I don't see why you're upset. They're not hurting anything, and my clients are impressed with my famous wife."

That was the moment—barely two months into her marriage—when Rebecca began to wonder if her celebrity status was part or all of the reason he'd married her. David loved visiting her parents and often invited them to the house in Connecticut. After each visit with them, there'd be a new round of tabloid stories speculating about Rebecca's comeback, about their marriage, whether or not she was pregnant.

As soon as she and David had settled in Hartford, they joined a country club and Rebecca enrolled in cooking classes. They bought the Cape Cod house with Rebecca's money, and his mother began dictating how the house should be furnished. Rebecca was struggling to learn everything all at once, to do everything at once, and failed much too often. Determined to learn how to take care of her own home, she refused to hire a housekeeper, took up gardening, even tried her hand at quilting.

She'd never been especially good at handling money. Her credit cards were typically maxed out. David had no patience with her spending habits. "I'm not as rich as your father."

In the end, she had to admit marrying David had been a huge mistake.

The Monday after New Year's, Nigel and Sara returned to school, Hugh flew from Gatwick to Belfast on business, and Megan went on the attack. "Are you going to the Awards or are you planning to live here permanently?"

"Your attic is rather cozy."

Unlike Liv, Megan knew when Becca was putting her on. "Be serious; what are you going to do?"

She sighed. There was nowhere left to run. "I suppose I need to make a plane reservation."

"California or New York?"

"I'm damned if I go to the Awards and damned if I don't, so I might as well go to New York. I'm just not ready to turn back into a Kingston."

"Would that be so terrible?"

"You of all people should know the answer to that."

"I know *your* answer, but I've never had to deal with that kind of scrutiny. What I do see is that you've shut yourself so completely away from the person you were that you've become a fugitive, and you're stuck in that mode. You don't want to look back but you can't move forward either. That's not healthy."

"I love Oakhurst and I love writing."

"I get that. Is that all you'll ever do? Never marry again, not have kids, not see your parents? You might as well join a convent."

"I'm not Catholic."

"Hey, you came to see me—remember? If you didn't want my input—"

Rebecca should have known that Megan would be totally honest. No punches pulled. That's what she loved about her. But handling that honesty wasn't always easy. Megan measured detergent into the dishwasher, closed the door, and turned the dial to heavy wash. Its low hum was the only sound in the kitchen.

"Becca, what are you so afraid of? Your parents aren't ogres. Overly dramatic perhaps, seriously self-absorbed, but not evil. You've been out of the acting business for a long time, so you can't be that valuable a target anymore. Maybe you're fighting a war that doesn't exist."

Rebecca considered the question. "I'm afraid everything will be different. Two of the best parts of my life are doing my own grocery shopping and having coffee and a croissant every Monday morning with

Karen, the biggest gossip in town. No one notices *me*. It's miraculous. But if Rebecca Kingston becomes visible, people—my friends—they'll treat me differently. I'll be a curiosity. And Alex, well Alex. I've never told him who I am, and I'm pretty sure it would make a difference. It always made a difference with David."

"Who's Alex?"

"Alex Zimmermann. I met him nearly two years ago. His family owns a sporting goods store in Oakhurst. He moved back to help out in the store after his father's heart attack. He was a ski racer on the U.S. team for a year or two. Loves skiing more than anything else, including me. He left town just after Thanksgiving to teach at Squaw Valley."

"Are you two serious?"

"On one level, yes. Realistically no. Alex isn't a forever-after guy. I've always known he wanted to go back to skiing. Because he was up front about that, I didn't have to commit too much of myself." *A perfect fit.*

"But?"

"When he left, it hurt more than I thought it would, and I haven't seen him since. I was supposed to visit him the week after Christmas."

"Does he know where you are?"

"No."

"Jeez, Becca, maybe you are still fourteen."

"He's busy swooshing down the slopes. My guess is there are plenty of females at a ski resort willing to occupy his time."

"And his bed?"

Rebecca blanched, then "Possibly. I don't know if our relationship was anything more than convenient sex and, if it is more than that, he's going to be in for a whole new view of me whenever *Rebecca Kingston's Years in Hiding,* hits the tabloids. He might not like the new Rebecca. Actually the old Rebecca."

"But you haven't called him." Megan reached into her purse on the kitchen counter and pulled out her cell phone, "No excuses that your phone doesn't work from here. Call him. At least let him know you're alive," and left the kitchen. Rebecca could hear her footsteps on the stairs.

It was 4 a.m. in California. Alex had his phone turned off so she left a message, "I'm in England," and hung up. She probably should have said she was sorry she'd bailed, but she didn't.

When Alex heard Rebecca's brief message, he was both relieved and annoyed. *England for God's sake!. What was she doing all the way over there?*

Only one of the dozens of questions he wanted to ask her. He left a message on Emily Gerrard's cell but, since Olivia Bennett had never returned his call, he didn't bother to call her.

The day before Rebecca flew from Gatwick to JFK, she and Megan drove into London to shop for a dress to wear to the Awards. It had been years since Rebecca had needed a dressy outfit—not as glamorous as her mother would choose, but something more than denim pants and a leather jacket, which was high fashion in Oakhurst. Four hours and three boutiques later, Rebecca had a simple black dress with a gored skirt that swung seductively round her calves and a v-neck accented with a mosaic of turquoise stones and pearls. Classy but not too showy. Black was always good with her hair, which had grown since her arrival in England. Rather than gamble a haircut that might not work, she would push it behind her ears and wear silver hoop earrings—the only jewelry she'd brought with her.

On the morning of the Awards, Megan drove her to Gatwick for the one o'clock flight to JFK. Outside of security, they hugged for a long time. "Thanks for putting up with me."

"Always a pleasure. I feel like I should go with you—ride shotgun."

"Much as I'd love that, Hugh and the kids would probably like to have you here. I envy what you have Meg. When you need someone to hold your hand as you walk into a room full of people you don't know, you have Hugh. I'd love to know someone was always in my corner like that. Anyway, I suppose the message in all of this is that I need to solve my problems for myself. I've been ducking them for a long time."

"Call me after the Awards."

"I will."

"Are you going to contact your folks?"

Rebecca grimaced. "Not sure."

Chapter 14

The Grand Ballroom at the Ritz-Carlton had an old world elegance, deep green velvet draperies framing the floor to ceiling windows, elaborate crown molding, and parquet floors that echoed the click of the women's high heels. The room was crowded with round tables, each set for six people. White tablecloths, off-white china, ecru napkins, and vibrant purple centerpieces as accents. While the guests were choosing where to sit, waiters in starched white jackets circled the room, placing baskets of crusty rolls on the tables and filling the water glasses from silver pitchers.

At the last minute, Olivia had invited Emily to accompany her to New York because Kurt had backed out in favor of participating in the annual Palm Desert golf tournament his college fraternity sponsored. Olivia hated attending functions like Elgin alone and, since she hadn't heard from Rebecca, she called Emily. "I know I was hard on you about Jake Hannigan, but would you like to come to New York with me? My treat."

Surprised by Liv's off-hand apology—Liv wasn't given to apologizing—Emily accepted. Perhaps she'd finally get to meet Rebecca Sawyer, though Liv said she had no idea whether Rebecca would show up. The trip would at least take Emily's mind off the fact that she hadn't heard from Jake for several days—six actually. The CNN footage of the protests in Tunisia frightened her. Jake was probably much too close to what was happening over there.

For the first time in a year and a half, Emily let herself feel something for a man and then—zap—he ended up in North Africa. A *déjà vu* situation she could have done without. She seemed destined to be attracted to men who—for ostensibly good reasons—went to dangerous places. In comparison to reporting the revolt in Tunisia, the Rebecca Sawyer mystery must now seem irrelevant. *Perhaps I'm not relevant either.*

She and Olivia arrived at the ballroom early because Liv wanted to sit at a table with a good view of the podium. An expectant buzz was running through the room. Liv seemed to know everyone, chatting with guests at other tables, working the room as though she were running for political office. Emily stayed at the table, content to watch the crowd. The other four chairs at their table were occupied by some of Samuel Stone's family. She'd introduced herself, but they weren't interested in conversation. Stone himself was seated at an adjacent table with more family members.

Not until the salads were being served did Olivia return to the table. "A very good turnout," she pointed out a couple of high-profile authors. "And most of the big publishing firms have people here. Kurt should have come; he's much better at networking than I am." Just then, Olivia looked up to see the sixtyish, rather distinguished man heading in her direction. Under her breath, "Oh shit."

Emily followed her gaze. "Who is it?"

"A movie producer. Nate Pullman. Have you heard of him?"

Emily shook her head.

"He wants to turn *Spring Farm* into a movie."

Nate stopped beside Olivia's chair. "Mrs. Bennett, Olivia. Good evening."

Olivia stood up. "Nate. I didn't expect to see you here." She turned toward Emily. "This is Emily Gerrard; she works for me."

Worked, Emily silently corrected, *worked.*

He extended his hand. "Ms. Gerrard. I recognize you from the picture in the *Twenty-First Century* article. You've been publicizing *Spring Farm.*"

Before Emily could reply, Olivia answered for her, a hint that this man was making Liv nervous. "Yes, she has. Are you here because of the article?"

He ignored her question in favor of his own. "Is *she* coming?"

"I have no idea. I haven't heard from her since the article came out."

Their conversation was interrupted by the high-pitched screech of the podium microphone as a woman in black silk slacks and a brilliant red tunic tried to get the audience's attention. Nate murmured, "Nice to meet you," in Emily's direction and walked back to the table where he was sitting with a dark-haired woman young enough to be his daughter or even his granddaughter. Noting Olivia's scowl, Emily didn't ask about his reference to Rebecca Sawyer. Clearly, he knew her or about her.

The microphone stopped screeching. "Ladies and gentlemen, welcome to the thirty-fifth annual Marvin Elgin Awards."

Nate Pullman would not ordinarily take the time to attend a book award banquet—the Oscars or Golden Globes perhaps—but after reading the article revealing that Rebecca Sawyer was the author of *Spring Farm,* he knew he needed to get a ticket. He suspected that this Rebecca Sawyer could be his goddaughter. The dates of the Kelley Jordan novels loosely coincided with the years Rebecca had been off everyone's radar. He now understood why Kurt Bennett was stonewalling on the film negotiations. Rebecca was probably the one refusing his offer.

At the last minute, he bought a second ticket for Sophia Maio. If Rebecca did come, he wanted to introduce Sophia, who would be perfect as Harriet. Perhaps meeting Sophia would help persuade Rebecca to sell him the movie rights. He'd been tempted to call Peter Kingston to see if he'd read the article but decided not to meddle in the Kingston family wars. His business was with Becca, and his relationship with her had always been better than her relationship with her parents.

The evening's program began with a rambling twenty-minute talk by the previous year's non-fiction winner, who had written a memoir about his return to Viet Nam twenty years after the fall of Saigon. It was almost nine o'clock when the first award—for the children's book category—was given. Next, the one for poetry, followed by non-fiction.

Seated at a table in the back of the ballroom, Rebecca had given up trying to eat her dinner; her nerves were turning her stomach over and over. She hadn't planned on being late for the ceremony, but her plane landed an hour late; then her cab was trapped in traffic for half an hour. Luckily, she'd reserved a room at the Ritz-Carlton so she was able to change her clothes quickly and come downstairs to the ceremony. When she presented her invitation at the banquet room door, the young woman screening the guests located her name tag—Kelley Jordan, *Spring Farm*—told her the main course was just now being served, and suggested she sit at the table just inside the door. Rebecca slipped into one of the vacant seats. Only two other people were at the table, probably late arrivals also. At least, if she lost, she had an easy escape route.

The ceremony seemed interminable. Someone should have edited the keynote speaker's material. Rebecca's anxiety level was rising steadily. Thank goodness the waitress had left a full carafe of wine on the table. Rebecca had already drunk three glasses.

"And now," the lady in the red tunic intoned, "Nora Templeton, last year's winner for her wonderful novel, *High Expectations*, will present the 2010 award for fiction."

A slightly overweight brunette probably in her forties stepped up to the podium and leaned into the microphone, "Good evening everyone." Thankfully, her remarks were brief and far more interesting than the keynote speech. Then she read the list of nominees, briefly detailing the subject of each book and the c.v. for each author. By the time Templeton had finished the preliminaries, Rebecca had almost stopped breathing. Until this moment, she hadn't understood just how badly she wanted to win this award. The winner," Nora Templeton's voice seemed very far away, "of the 2010 award for fiction is *Spring Farm*, written by Kelley Jordan, published by Bennett Books."

Rebecca wasn't certain she'd heard correctly. Perhaps she'd had too much wine. What if the winner was really one of the other authors and she walked up there to make a fool of herself? But when the man seated across from her smiled, "Congratulations," she knew it was real.

The world tipped over.

She'd won.

The man leaned forward, "You should go to the stage; they're waiting for you," and pointed to where Templeton was standing, holding a plaque that undoubtedly belonged to Rebecca.

Hesitantly, she made the circuitous journey to the stage, weaving through the tables, aware that all eyes were on her. The applause was for her. Terror and joy competed for her attention; her legs felt like they might give way as she climbed the three shallow steps to the podium. She hadn't faced this many people since *Mandy* had won the People's Choice Award in 1996; then, however, she had shared the stage with the other cast members. Tonight she was on her own, the audience blurring in front of her. She was on the verge of crying just when she was expected to say something gracious and sensible. Unwilling to tempt fate by being too prepared, she hadn't written an acceptance speech.

She reached for the plaque, polished silver on a dark wood base, and in desperation pulled out Mandy's smile—always useful in emergencies. "I'm so glad you liked the book." She inhaled deeply, "Since I do all my own research and most of the editing, I don't have a list of people to thank." There was no reason to thank her parents, who had never understood her interest in writing, or Alex who, through no fault of his own, didn't know what she was writing. She truly had done *Spring Farm* all alone.

On her way to the stage, she had caught sight of Liv and, according to the picture in Hannigan's article, Emily Gerrard. "However, my publisher, who took a chance on my first book, is here, Olivia Bennett," Olivia stood briefly, "and next to her is Emily Gerrard, who has done the publicity for this book." Stunned at being acknowledged, Emily stayed in her seat.

Clutching the plaque to her, Rebecca added, "When I begin a book, I have a destination in mind, but, in my wildest dreams, I didn't imagine this destination. Thank you so much for this honor." As the applause began again, she looked out over the audience and suddenly saw Nate Pullman sitting at one of the tables in the center of the room, smiling at her, giving her a thumbs up.

Nate.

Her Kingston childhood rose up to meet her. And she hadn't even left the stage.

Olivia was waiting at the bottom of the stairs. She kissed Rebecca on both cheeks, "Congratulations, you did it." She turned to include Emily, "Becca, this is Emily Gerrard."

Rebecca met the steady gaze of her alter ego. They hugged briefly, though Rebecca was never quite sure whether strangers should be hugged or not.

Emily didn't seem to mind. "I'm glad to finally meet you." The smile that welcomed the groups attending the readings spread itself over Rebecca, and she smiled back. "Congratulations on winning."

"Thank you."

"Becca," Olivia interrupted, "there's a media meet and greet in the foyer right now."

Rebecca felt her heart jump. *Reporters. Questions. Damn and double damn.* So far the evening had gone smoothly. Now the potholes were showing up.

Olivia took note of her expression. "Better to get it over with in a controlled setting. Sidestepping will only raise flags."

"The flags are already raised. Nate Pullman's here."

"I know. He came by the table earlier."

The ballroom was clearing out fast, a few people stopping to congratulate her.

Olivia kept consulting her watch. "Becca, avoiding the media will only make them more curious. Emily and I will stay with you. Do you want to talk to Nate first?"

"I have no choice. He's standing by the door." She handed the plaque to Olivia. "Hang on to this, would you?" and headed toward Nate, still tall, always ramrod straight. He looked older, his hair almost white. As she got closer, she could see his eyes smiling at her, the same "Uncle" Nate of her childhood.

He spread his arms and folded her against him. "Hi Baby." He kissed her cheek. "Where've you been?"

Tears were threatening. For the first time in years, she felt comforted. Cherished. She was five again and they were at Disneyland, eating cotton candy and choosing which rides to go on.

She fought to keep her voice steady. "Here and there. I was with Megan for Christmas."

Nate held Rebecca by the shoulders, studying her. *What is he looking for?* "It's a wonderful book. It deserved to win."

"And you want it." Why did she always have to be so direct? He didn't deserve that. She should have simply said *thank you.*

"Yes, I do." He turned to the young woman beside him. "Becca, this is Sophia Maio. I wanted you to meet her. She'll be the perfect Harriet." Rebecca shook the young woman's hand but wasn't going to get caught in the trap Nate had laid.

"How did you know I was the author?"

"I read the article in *Twenty-First Century* and listened to my gut." He grinned. "You've been hiding out."

She shrugged. "I have my reasons."

"I know."

Olivia stopped beside them. "We need to be outside in a minute or two."

Rebecca nodded. If anyone from the media had seen Nate hugging her, she was definitely outed.

He kissed her cheek. "I'll let you go. Where are you staying?"

"Here."

"Can we talk tomorrow sometime?"

She dodged the question. "I don't know what my schedule is."

He pulled out a business card and wrote his cell number on the back. "Call after you've had your morning coffee."

Perhaps. Perhaps not.

In the foyer, the winning poet and his agent were sitting at a table in front of eleven or twelve reporters and cameramen, answering questions. Watching and listening to the reporters, Rebecca felt her mouth go dry, felt lightheaded though that could be the result of consuming more wine than food. What would they ask? Would the truth of her past be exposed? Terror, years in the making, exploded into a million icy pinpricks. When she was sixteen, she'd had her first panic attack. Though she hadn't had one in years, she recognized the symptoms. Taking a few steps forward, she stopped beside Emily. "Will you sit at the table with me when it's my turn?"

Puzzled by Rebecca's request, Emily asked, "Shouldn't Liv go with you?"

Rebecca shook her head. "Please." Her eyes filled.

"Sure, no problem."

"Are you good at thinking on your feet?"

"Actually, yes." Answering questions for Kelley Jordan and answering questions about her own work at story swaps had taught her to accept criticism and defend her work. Critiques always tested Emily's courage, making her rethink what she wanted from a story.

Rebecca was the last interview. By the time she and Emily were seated behind the table, the other winners had left. Only the reporters and the Elgin executives remained.

Before the questions began, Rebecca introduced Emily. "Ms. Gerrard has been doing the public readings of *Spring Farm*."

One or two flash attachments went off and then the questions came.

How does it feel to win?

You've used Kelley Jordan as your pen name. Will you continue to use that name?

What are you working on now?

How did you get the idea for Spring Farm?

Is Harriet autobiographical?

She answered each inquiry as honestly as she could, struggling to calm her breathing. With each question, the knot in her stomach loosened slightly. Maybe she was going to dodge the bullet she'd been expecting. Then, from the back of the group, a woman—probably in her late twenties—raised her hand. "Is it true that Nathan Pullman is interested in filming your book?"

"Yes he is."

"I saw you hug him as you left the banquet room. Are you connected to him in a personal way?"

Under the table, Rebecca reached for Emily's hand to still the trembling that was flooding through her. "Yes." Rebecca was fairly sure the woman already knew the answer; somehow she knew who Rebecca was. Maybe she'd been a teenage fan of the show.

"How?"

Everything will change.

Everything I've become will revert to who I was.

The three-word reply came slowly, painfully.

"He's my godfather."

"Ms. Jordan—or Sawyer—when I was a teenager, I was a big fan of the TV show called *Mandy*. Are you Mandy? Are you actually Rebecca Kingston?"

Suddenly, the room was eerily silent. The young woman's question caught everyone's attention.

That long-dreaded question was going to force Rebecca to splice the separate pieces of herself together. To be truthful about who she was. Momentarily, she considered the advisability of saying *No*—but lying would only make matters worse. It was one thing to hide who she was; another to flat out lie.

Before she answered, she leaned toward Emily and whispered, "Come with me."

Then Rebecca stood up and looked directly at the woman who'd asked the question.

"Yes. Yes, I am."

Instantly, voices shouted questions and cameras went into over-drive. Rebecca instinctively shielded her eyes against the flashes. As a child, she'd hated the bright spots that stayed in her vision after the flash attachments went off. She'd wanted to win, wanted this award. The price was exposure.

A second later, still holding Emily's hand, Rebecca hurried into the lobby, heading for the row of elevators.

Bewildered, Emily let herself be pulled into a waiting elevator. Once the doors closed, Rebecca let go of Emily's hand. "Sorry. There was no time to explain." Her face was grayish, her eyes sunken. It was hard to know whether it was exhaustion or some larger terror that had erased the smiling face that had graciously thanked the audience for liking her book. Something in the way Rebecca had asked Emily to come with her had touched Emily's heart. This talented, famous, beautiful woman was in the midst of an emotional crisis. Emily knew what those kinds of crises felt like, though she'd trained herself not to revisit the months after Patrick's death. Visits to that searing emptiness always dropped her into a black hole that took days to climb out of, leaving her shaken and hollow. What she felt at those moments was what she saw on Rebecca's face.

Once in Rebecca's room, Emily remained standing, uncertain what her role was yet sensing she was needed. Rebecca dropped the plaque and her purse on the bed and slipped out of her blackstrap heels. "I'm going to order something from Room Service. I drank more than I ate. I'm wobbly. Do you want something?"

"Maybe some decaf."

Rebecca nodded and put in the order.

In an alcove near the windows, there were two comfortable chairs and a small table. Emily chose one of the chairs and waited to see what came next. For months, she'd wanted to meet Kelley Jordan and now—unexpectedly—she was sitting in Rebecca Kingston's hotel room.

Chapter 15

Emily had fallen into an Alice in Wonderland rabbit hole. One moment she was in the banquet room with Liv, now she was watching Rebecca devour a BLT and a pile of French fries slathered in catsup.

Her mind was still adjusting to the Rebecca Kingston revelation. She remembered *Mandy* but had been in college at the height of its popularity. Emily kept expecting Rebecca to say something but, so far, she'd only asked whether Emily wanted some of the French fries.

What Emily really wanted was to go back to her own hotel, several blocks away, to call her daughters before they went to sleep. It had been a very long day; she and Olivia had left San Francisco at dawn. She'd accepted Liv's invitation to attend the Awards, hoping she might finally get to meet Rebecca and, on Monday, while Liv was taking care of Bennett business, Emily would have time to visit the *Twenty-First Century* offices to ask how Jake was. He wasn't returning her calls.

But right now, it was time to jump-start some kind of conversation. The silence was awkward.

"I met Alex at your house in Oakhurst."

Rebecca had just picked up the last French fry; her hand stopped mid-air. "Alex? Alex Zimmermann?" She put the French fry in her mouth.

Emily nodded.

"What were you doing at my house?" Rebecca didn't sound angry, just curious.

"Jake, Jacob Hannigan, was leaving for Tunisia on assignment. He called me Christmas night and asked me to finish the research about you, to find you if I could. So my mother and I—we drove from Berkeley to Oakhurst one day. But of course you were gone." She stopped, fully aware she was babbling. "I'm sorry."

Licking the last of the greasy salt from her fingers, Rebecca studied this woman she'd unceremoniously dragged to her hotel room. Exactly why, she wasn't sure. An impulse. She needed someone, even someone she didn't know, to stay with her for a while in case the media came after her—which for once they hadn't. Maybe she was in some sort of shock. A reaction to winning—admittedly a hugely beautiful thing which had been quickly overshadowed by the reappearance of *Mandy*. At first, she'd thought the shakiness that had attacked her was lack of food, but she wasn't hungry anymore, and she still felt lighter than air. If she stood up, she might crumple into a heap on the floor.

"Sorry for what?"

"Invading your life."

Rebecca shrugged. "You're just the first of many. All kinds of people are going to be intruding. They believe it's their divine right to pry into my life. Tomorrow's headlines are already being written." Her voice was hard-edged. "They'll hound me, suck the life out of me until everything I was—everything I've become—will be—" she paused so long that Emily wondered if she was going to finish the thought—"dissected."

The word collided with the distress Rebecca had been holding in. Tears slid and slid down her cheeks. She almost never let anyone see her cry, yet she was dissolving in front of this stranger.

Not sure how to react, what to say, Emily simply reached across to take Rebecca's hand. They sat that way for half an hour until there were no more tears. Emily checked her watch; it was nearly midnight. "I need to make a phone call." She let go of Rebecca's hand and headed for the bathroom, shutting the door behind her.

When she returned, Rebecca had cleaned off the table and set the tray and dishes outside the door. Noticing Emily's rather tentative expression, "No worry, I'm not going over the edge—yet." Her slight smile was tinged with irony.

"Sorry. When I'm out of town, I always call my daughters before they go to bed."

Calmer now, Rebecca latched onto the new topic. "What're their names?"

"Claudia's almost ten. Cristyl just turned fourteen."

"Who stays with them?"

"My mother." Emily's voice broke just a little. "My husband died a year and a half ago." After all this time, she still choked up when she talked about Patrick. She worried she'd never be able to talk about him without tears.

Like the people you sit next to on airplanes, sometimes it's easier to tell them about yourself because you'll never see them again. For the next hour, Emily talked; Rebecca listened and asked questions, compassionate questions that showed genuine interest. She was curious about the Storytelling, about the girls. "Do you have pictures?"

Of course she had pictures. "Claudia's the tomboy, loves soccer. She seems to miss her father more than Cristyl does right now. Cristyl is busy finding ways to push my buttons. Last week it was wearing makeup. She's interested in a boy in her Algebra class, so I suppose dating arguments are next. My daughters aren't all that pleased about my seeing Jake."

"The guy who wrote the article?"

"Yes. I haven't known him long. When he began the article about you, he came to Miami where I was doing several signings." It felt good to talk about Jake, even though Rebecca might be angry about the article. There hadn't been anyone Emily could confide in. Certainly not her mother or Liv and, since Patrick's death, the women friends she'd had—mostly wives of couples they'd socialized with—were uncomfortable around her. Cautiously distant, as though widowhood might be contagious.

Sometime around one-thirty, the subject shifted from Jake to Alex.

"When I told him about *Spring Farm* and the other books you've written, he was shocked."

"Think how shocked he'll be when the Kingston part is revealed." Rebecca forced herself to make light of something that wasn't light at all.

"Seems like a nice guy; he was really worried about you."

"My bad. I was still annoyed about his leaving. He didn't dump me—we'd never committed to anything long term—but it felt like dumping. Skiing versus Becca, and I came in second."

Emily sighed. "I'd put myself in the same category, though Jake and I haven't known one another that long. He was almost killed in Gaza a few years ago, and now he's back in that part of the world, probably loving every risky minute. I'm undoubtedly going to be dumped for a by-line."

Monday afternoon, Alex picked up a discarded copy of *The San Francisco Chronicle* lying on the counter in the ski school office. He saw the picture first, then read the headline in the bottom right corner of the front page.

TV Icon Mandy Wins Elgin Fiction Award:
Teenage Star Surfaces after 7 Years

Mandy didn't mean anything to him, but he remembered Emily Gerrard mentioning the Elgin Awards, and there was no doubt that the picture was Becca. Her hair was longer than usual and she was wearing silver hoop earrings. He couldn't remember her wearing earrings in Oakhurst. A very sexy look.

He studied the picture; her mouth was a bit tight, her eyes looked tired. Becca's brief voice mail message from England had unnerved him, forcing him to examine his feelings for her. Not just the lustful ones—those were easy to figure out—but the other, dangerously emotional ones he'd successfully held at arm's length, afraid they would interfere with his getting back on skis. It had been six or seven weeks since he'd seen her. Not being with her had been harder than he'd expected.

She'd captured his interest the first day she came into his parents' store. He hadn't found much female companionship since returning to Oakhurst. It had been a long, dry spell.

Becca had an intriguing presence. A cross between confident and mysterious. When she returned to the store to pick up her skis, he invited her to have dinner with him the next evening. Nothing fancy—just BBQ at a hole-in-the-wall diner down the road in Coarsegold. They danced to jukebox music, drank beer, and then said a chaste good night at her front door. Not his usual style, but Oakhurst wasn't Europe and this was a mature woman—not one of the willing young things he usually hooked up with. She listened to him talk about his skiing, talked knowledgeably about European ski resorts but didn't offer anything much about herself. *I'm divorced and write for people who can't string two words together but have a tale to tell. The pay's good and I can take on as much or as little work as I want.* Unquestionably beautiful—that spun-gold hair was magnificent, brownish gold eyes, and a great figure. That first night she'd worn denim jeans, a sweater and a leather jacket. The jacket looked expensive. The jeans and sweater did not.

It was several weeks before they slept together but, in that time, they had been—figuratively—running toward each other, then backing away before the moment of impact. Neither quite sure about taking the next step. The first night they took that step, Becca had invited Alex over to try a new lasagna recipe. "It's an experiment. Promise you'll eat it, regardless."

An easy promise to fulfill in spite of the eggplant hiding in the sauce. To set the mood, he'd brought along a CD of Forties love songs. They danced and drank their way through a bottle of red wine, each acutely aware that tonight was finally the moment of impact.

The moment began with his hands unbuttoning her blouse, slipping it off her shoulders, letting it fall to the floor, expertly unhooking her bra, unzipping her jeans and slowly tugging them to her ankles so she could step out of them. His hands rested lightly at her waist. God, she was gorgeous, curved in all the right places.

Once all their clothing was on the floor, they resumed dancing, locked together in an exquisite foreplay, hands and mouths exploring, feet barely moving. When neither could wait a moment longer, they sank onto the rug in front of the fireplace, the flames reflected on the tangle of their bodies.

Remembering that night and so many others, Alex was beginning to realize he shouldn't have left Oakhurst the way he did.

The Chronicle's article introduced him to another Becca. Emily Gerrard had already told him about the novels and the Elgin nomination. Now Rebecca Sawyer had become someone named Rebecca Kingston, a famous teenage star with equally famous parents. Probably rich. Thus the leather jacket and the Lexus SUV she drove. Financially, and in many other ways, she had moved out of his league.

Yet she'd been living like any other single woman. Emptying her own trash, shoveling out her driveway after a snowstorm, taking the cats to the vet, cooking for him. He never would have guessed she had that kind of pedigree. Once, when he'd asked about her childhood, all she'd said was *I was rotten spoiled. You wouldn't have wanted to know me.* About high school, *I was home schooled. My parents traveled a lot.*

The article revisited her life, detailed her parents' careers, and made her reappearance sound like finding a long lost Renoir in someone's attic. There was no mention of her living in Oakhurst. Alex folded the paper back at A-16 where there was a photo of Becca with Emily and an older woman that the caption identified as Olivia Bennett. The lady who hadn't returned his phone call.

The ski school's brass bell broke through his thoughts. It was time to start the last class of the day—six preschoolers who had no fear of speed.

One of the many perks of having as much money as Peter Kingston had was employing a driver. No coping with traffic, either in Los Angeles or New York. His assistant made sure—based on each day's schedule—that a car and driver were always available. When Peter did drive himself, he preferred open country and two lane roads.

The trip from Malibu to his office in Santa Monica might take only fifteen minutes or, in heavy traffic, half an hour. In that time, he typically scanned the front page of the *Los Angeles Times* and the entertainment section, waiting to read the rest of the paper, as well as *Variety*, at his office while he drank his morning coffee—black and strong—and treated himself to a powdered sugar donut. Hillary would fuss about the donut if she knew. But she was on location in Florida.

As the car pulled out of the driveway, he unfolded the paper and saw a headline similar to the one in *The Chronicle*, his daughter's photo beneath. He read through the first part of the article, turned to A-12, and stopped reading when the article began reviewing her childhood and his own career. Those parts he knew. By heart. What he didn't know about was the Elgin Award and *Spring Farm*.

Closing his eyes, he leaned back, letting the full force of the news sink in. Though he hadn't seen her for nearly seven years, she occasionally called, never revealing anything personal. *I don't want you and mother to worry about me. I'm okay.* Birthday cards and Christmas gifts had UK postmarks, Megan's fine hand.

He and Hillary had made irreparable mistakes with Becca, though Hillary didn't think so. His wife was never much good at admitting she just might be wrong. Ask any director she'd worked with. For Peter, however, that stubbornness was part of her charm and he'd learned to work around it. Becca however did not find her mother's belief that everyone should want to be an actor in the least bit charming.

Though nothing in the article mentioned where Becca was currently living, Peter had known about Oakhurst for several years. Two years after her divorce from David—Hill had always called him David the Dull—he'd hired a private investigator who had reported her address and phone numbers. But Peter hadn't used the information and hadn't risked telling Hillary because she would have driven to Oakhurst and delivered one of her emotional monologues. She was going to be furious when she found out he'd known where Becca was.

He understood why his daughter kept her distance. It wasn't that she didn't love them. It was simply that she couldn't cope with the attention that their careers and hers received. Even though she'd been born into their lifestyle, it wasn't in her genetic makeup to tolerate it. A changeling forced to walk in footsteps that did not fit her personality. Not until she defied them and canceled *Mandy*, did he truly pay attention to what she wanted but, by then, it was too late to put Humpty Dumpty together again. Clearly, two high-profile careers weren't the best qualification for raising a happy child.

And so he hadn't visited Oakhurst, though he knew exactly where it was and how long it would take to drive there. It was hard not to go. He missed his daughter, but he owed Becca her privacy. Now that she was front-page news, some enterprising reporter would eventually uncover Oakhurst.

As soon as he got to the office, he asked his assistant to call a bookstore and have copies of all of Becca's books delivered. He had some reading to do. Then he put in a call to his wife. He needed to tell her about their daughter before someone else did.

Chapter 16

Rebecca's Tuesday afternoon flight from San Francisco into Fresno was rough, buffeted by west winds pushing yesterday's storm over the mountains. The storm hadn't been cold enough to bring snow so at least the roads would be clear. For a few hours, she could concentrate on simple things like driving, buying cat food and food for herself. It felt as though she'd been gone for a decade or two instead of weeks.

Retrieving her SUV from the long stay lot, she tossed her suitcase and carryon in the back and prayed the engine would start. Three weeks in freezing temperatures might have finished off the battery, but it turned over on the second try. All the practical matters that Rebecca Kingston had never had to deal with—cleared roads, car batteries, and cat food—these were the things Rebecca Sawyer took comfort in. Since Sunday, she'd been living in Rebecca Kingston's shadow. Of course the odds were that the shadow would follow her to Oakhurst.

In the years she'd been living in the Sierra foothills, Rebecca always loved driving into their beauty, but today she was afraid of what she would find. Were reporters camped out at her house? Had they been interviewing the townspeople about her? Had someone mentioned her relationship with Alex? Had Alex read the newspaper stories? If only he were still working at the store, she could stop by to enjoy his smile, feel his hand at the back of her neck as he kissed her. But, just like her privacy, Alex was history. The only things that remained were her house, the cats, and her work.

As she left the generic strip developments on the northern edge of Fresno and began the gradual climb into the Digger Pine forest, she struggled against the creeping sense of unease that had begun in the Ritz-Carlton hotel lobby well before dawn. A couple of reporters had been lying in wait when she checked out.

The cab that the concierge had called for her was already at the curb. As she pulled her suitcase across the lobby, the male reporter called, "Rebecca Kingston, Mandy—we'd like a word with you." *She hated being called Mandy.* The man was probably in his late twenties, the woman older—both looked like they were in need of sleep. They'd probably been on the *Mandy* night shift.

"Hey Rebecca, we need a word with you." They followed her onto the sidewalk where the cab was waiting. "How do you feel about winning the Elgin?" Because the woman was physically violating Rebecca's space, she instinctively backed away as she signaled the waiting cab driver to put her bags into the trunk. At that moment, the woman snapped Rebecca's picture.

"Are you going to resume acting?"

"Will you see your parents?"

"Do you have a boyfriend?"

The questions pummeled her, leaving invisible bruises. Thankfully, the cabbie put himself between Rebecca and the reporters, held the door open, then quickly closed it. Undeterred, the woman knocked at the window. "Where are you going? Home? Where do you live now?"

To escape the woman's face pressed against the window, Rebecca slid to the center of the back seat. As the cab pulled away from the hotel, the cabbie asked "Which airport?"

Rebecca's mouth was so dry she could hardly answer, "JFK. American."

It was nearly dark when she pushed a shopping cart into Raley's Supermarket and headed for the pet food aisle, then the deli counter. After the day she'd had, she didn't feel like cooking.

"Hi Rebecca, what can I get for you?" The petite, dark-haired girl—a year or two out of high school—was holding a cardboard container in one hand and a plastic scoop in the other.

"Hi Audrey. A pint of coleslaw, a pint of your German potato salad, and a roast chicken." Enough for several days, in case her house was under siege.

"Sure thing," Audrey opened the sliding glass panel behind the display case. "I saw all the stuff about you on *Entertainment Tonight*. They showed pictures of you with your parents and clips from your TV show. I'd never have guessed you were such a famous star."

Rebecca's fingers tightened on the cart handle as her breathing quickened. *Don't panic. Don't panic. She doesn't mean any harm.*

Audrey seemed unaware Rebecca hadn't responded or that she was frowning. "I told my boyfriend that you come in here all the time—just like a regular person. He was really impressed that I know you." She handed the packages over the counter. "Anything else?"

"No—that's it, thanks." Rebecca hurried away, grateful the girl hadn't forced her into more conversation. She added milk, bread, cereal, and two bottles of white wine to the cart. As she went through the checkout line, she realized she was instinctively keeping her head down, hoping she wouldn't meet anyone else she knew. She usually enjoyed having casual conversations with other shoppers, especially after a day alone, writing. Today, however, she felt like a fugitive.

Just as she'd feared, everything was different.

Because Olivia Bennett never flew Economy, Emily was sitting in Business Class. Wider seats, more leg room, and food service. Once the plane was in the air, Olivia opened her laptop and began pecking at the keyboard, leaving Emily free to sift through the details of the last two days and make sense out of her part in them.

When she'd arrived at *Twenty-First Century's* offices early Monday afternoon, she was led to Maxwell Adam's office even though she had no appointment. "Ms. Gerrard, Emily, please sit down. What can I do for you?" He seemed preoccupied but his smile was genuine. Perhaps Jake had told Max about her or he remembered her name from the article.

"I wondered if you know whether Jake Hannigan is all right. I called here last week, but the person I talked to wouldn't give me any information. Jake isn't answering his phone, and CNN is showing the protests in Tunis. Is he in the middle of all that?" She knew she was talking too fast.

As she was talking, Max was anxiously shifting papers around on his desk, as though he'd lost something, and drinking from an oversized coffee cup that said *Frazzled Editor*. She wasn't sure he was actually listening to her until "Yes, he's in the thick of it and doing some of his best reporting. Just a second." Max turned to the computer monitor on his desk, typed for a few seconds and then the printer on the console behind his desk clicked on. "The only communication I get from him is by e-mail. This is a copy of the story he filed yesterday." He handed her the pages from the printer. "As far as I know, he's okay. Tunisia's been eager to have reporters help get its story out, so he's reasonably safe. I suspect his phone isn't working. He's been using the Internet connections at the Al Jezeera office in Tunis to file his stories."

As she was leaving, Max promised to e-mail Jake that she was concerned, though whether Jake would actually get the message was problematic. She gave Max her business card with her cell number and e-mail address.

The conversation with Max eased Emily's worry about Jake, but only a little. Jake was in the midst of the turmoil—safe for the moment—but being there was potentially dangerous. Max had mentioned the possibility that this revolt in Tunisia could have a domino effect, spilling into other countries in the region. Which could mean Jake wouldn't be back any time soon because he'd want to be where the action was, and Max would want him there.

She was well acquainted with the knot of fear that had taken up residence in her stomach—the same knot she always had when Patrick was on one of his overseas trips. As attracted as she was to Jake, as wonderful as their time in Chicago had been, she didn't know if she could face another loss. Neither she nor the girls needed to have their lives destroyed again. Before she got in any deeper, she probably should end the relationship. She told herself it was better to be alone than worried all the time, but she wasn't listening all that closely.

The time she'd spent with Rebecca was much less troubling than her meeting with Max. Surprisingly, she and Rebecca had connected easily and before Emily returned to her own hotel room at 2:30 Monday morning, they'd agreed to spend Monday afternoon together.

While Emily went to the *Twenty-First Century* offices, Rebecca, wearing a knit cap that covered her hair and the glasses she didn't need, waited at a nearby coffee shop, reading about herself in the papers.

Later, they played tourist, walking a few blocks to the ferry that crossed to Liberty Island. They didn't bother with tickets to the museum or the statue itself, content to walk the perimeter of the island, enjoying the views of New York City. Back in Manhattan, they stopped at a deli for an early dinner. "I do miss good deli." Rebecca was adding spicy mustard to her thick Reuben sandwich. "Whenever I was in New York with my folks, we sent out for deli several times a week. Of course, it's better to actually eat in the restaurant itself but, if we'd done that in those days, we'd have been mobbed."

"That bad?"

"It wasn't always the media. Once someone recognized either my parents or me, we'd have to sign autographs. When I was little, all that staring scared me, and I'd end up in tears. When I was older, it just made me feel like I was a freak." Rebecca briefly closed her eyes. "There was never any peace. And once I began doing TV, the whole feeding-frenzy thing escalated. The public thought that I belonged to them and they deserved to know everything about me. What I ate for breakfast, which of my co-stars was the best kisser, did I have PMS. I was always afraid someone would rip my clothes off as a souvenir. My parents cope, sort of, but I never got used to the attention."

"That's why you're wearing the hat and glasses?"

"Yeah. Mandy's trademark was my long hair—a dead give away. Once the show was off the air, I cut it and that helped. I was tempted to dye my hair, but it's really the only color that works with my fair skin. The glasses are useful too. Sunglasses are even better. In the last few years, I've been recognized a few times but not as often as ten years ago. I hope your connection with me doesn't send the media after you and your daughters."

"I'm not very interesting."

"That's only your perception. Your role as Kelley Jordan makes you fair game."

"No one has bothered us today."

"Mostly because we're bundled up in scarves and hats and because the concierge at my hotel called to warn me there were reporters hanging around the lobby. I tipped a bellboy to take me out through the kitchen."

"Good heavens. I never thought to check whether anyone was in the lobby of my hotel." Emily was new at this game. "What time is your flight tomorrow?"

"Seven o'clock. Yours?"

"Nine. Liv is anxious to get back."

"Since *Spring Farm* won, she's probably doubled the print run on the paperback edition and is preparing a new ad campaign."

Emily grinned. "You know her pretty well."

"Oh yeah. Liv's been good to me, helped me stay out of the limelight but, on balance, I've also made their company a lot of money."

Over coffee and dessert, they shared phone numbers and e-mail addresses. "Let's not lose touch. I'd love to see one of your Storytelling performances. Do you have a schedule?"

Emily reached for the small planner she always carried, flattered that Rebecca was interested. "I have several school dates this month. Martin Luther King's birthday is this weekend. Next month, I have a few for Presidents Day. The history programs for the elementary schools are my bread and butter right now. I also have a booking in San Diego in March at the University of San Diego. For adults, not kids. Then not much until the Ojai festival in May."

"Send me the date and time for San Diego. I promise to come in disguise. Since you aren't working for Liv anymore, will you have to find another job?"

Emily sighed. She'd been trying to ignore the money problem until after the Awards. "Afraid so. I put in applications at a couple of local libraries. I minored in Library Science in college, but libraries have been hit with the state's budget cuts, so I don't hold out much hope. Worse comes to worst, I'll be back waiting tables. When Pat was doing his residency, my waitressing job paid the rent."

At the entrance to Emily's hotel, Rebecca put her hand on Emily's arm. "Thank you for letting me monopolize your day. I've enjoyed getting to know you."

Emily smiled. "My pleasure. I only wish we didn't live so far apart."

"Me too," Rebecca hugged her. "Be safe."

As Rebecca approached her driveway, she saw a green VW Bug parked by the mailbox. Hoping reporters would not yet know what kind of car she drove, she sped past her house and down to Trudy's, her heart racing. How did these vultures track people down so quickly? Had they also set up shop at Emily's? Hopefully, they didn't know about Alex—yet.

Trudy's small cedar shingle house was at the end of the road. As Rebecca pulled into the driveway, Trudy was filling a wheelbarrow with split logs from a stack at the side of the house. Seeing Rebecca, she straightened and came toward the car. In her sixties, her hair still a rich brown, Trudy was the prototype of a nineteenth century pioneer woman: raw-boned, self sufficient, and down to earth. Rebecca had tried to fit a Trudy character into *Spring Farm* but hadn't found the right spot for her.

Rebecca got out of the car and leaned against it. "Hey, stranger, want some help?"

"Nah, keeps me in shape."

"Thanks for looking after the house and the cats. Everything okay?"

"Matilda's eyes are running again, but it's probably the cold weather. I cleaned 'em up. Otherwise, they're all good. Just lonesome for you."

"Do I owe you for anything?"

"No, there's some money left. I put milk and dried food out this morning. They're probably waiting for their dinner, but I wanted to get the wood box filled first. You should have called ahead so I could turn the heat up in your house." She removed the heavy leather gloves she was wearing. "Let me get your mail." A few minutes later she returned with a cardboard box. "Is there still a car parked in front of your house? It was there when I came back from town this afternoon."

Assuming Trudy had read the papers, "Undoubtedly a reporter waiting to pounce."

"If you need some protection, I'll bring my 22."

Rebecca laughed. "That would provide an interesting headline. *Mandy's Neighbor Shoots Paparazzi.*"

"Bet you'd like to shoot them."

"You've got that right." At least Trudy was taking Rebecca's new identity in stride.

Chapter 17

Miracle of miracles, the green car was gone when Rebecca returned from Trudy's, so she pulled straight into the garage and closed the door. Her stalker had either gone for dinner or decided she wasn't coming home tonight. But there was tomorrow—and all the other tomorrows.

Giving one reporter an interview seldom made the rest of them disappear. Instead, they multiplied, all clamoring for their ten minutes of time. Having a press conference was only a little better but required *people* to make the arrangements and then keep the hordes from devouring the victim. Having lived beneath the publicity radar for seven years, Rebecca no longer had *people*, though Liv might want to arrange something to promote the book. The trouble was—once you were news and had poked your head above ground—you would be fielding all sorts of requests for interviews from the print media and TV talk shows. The last thing she needed was to be on Letterman or Oprah.

There was, however, always the possibility that Megan's theory might be right. Perhaps Rebecca had blown her childhood traumas way out of proportion, hiding all this time for no reason. *Might* was the operative word, but she was in no mood to let down her guard. Even if the media stayed out of her way, the people in Oakhurst would undoubtedly treat her differently now. She'd stopped being Becca Sawyer and had once again become a curiosity.

Her writing was already taking a beating. She'd lost a month of work—more actually. Writing required peace of mind and peaceful surroundings—neither of which she'd had since Alex left. The scrambled state of her brain confirmed the wisdom of her previous hermit lifestyle. Going off the grid had, however, worked only so long. Now she had to figure out what the next chapter of her life would be. Books were much easier to plan than lives.

She spent much of the evening on the sectional, all three cats vying for her attention. Around eleven, she dragged herself to the shower then crawled into bed, the cats tucked in beside her.

She didn't listen to the messages on her answering machine until the next morning. In addition to the usual sales pitches, there were the six messages Alex had left during the week she'd promised to visit him: "You're scaring me, Bec. Are you okay?" Two from Liv: "Are you attending the Awards? I need to know." One from Karen: "Where are you?" The last one was from Alex yesterday afternoon: "Are you back home? I'm driving down on Friday for my mother's sixtieth birthday celebration. I'll check in afterwards."

Alex.

He sounded the same. But so much had changed since November, *same* wasn't possible.

It took most of the day to sort through three weeks of mail. Trash in one pile, bills in another, and a miscellaneous pile that she needed to take a closer look at. Her accountant had already sent the preliminary IRS forms. There must be 1099 statements in the stacks somewhere. She focused on business matters first—paying bills and looking for last year's tax receipts. In between, there was laundry to do, as well as her personal e-mails and the entries on the *Spring Farm* website to read. Usually, she answered all the questions and comments on the website—Liv believed the personal touch was good for sales—but whatever had been posted on the site since Sunday might not be the kinds of comments she had answers for. Too many places in Rebecca's life were now available for all to see and pick over like scavengers. Thank God she'd never gone on Facebook.

She'd promised to call Megan and she should check with Emily.

Today at least, she was safe.

Olivia hadn't expected there'd be so many fires to put out. As soon as she walked into her office on Wednesday, Ashley handed her a mug of tea, not the usual china cup on a saucer. "You should look at the *Spring Farm* website. It's a nightmare. I know Kelley, I mean Rebecca, answers those comments, but you should read what's on there."

Olivia never responded well to the word *should* and certainly not from Ashley. "Give me the abridged version." The tea was so hot it had instantly scalded her tongue. Not a good omen.

"Most of the comments are from women who attended one of Emily's readings and are upset because Emily wasn't the real author and so they don't have the real signature. The word fraud is being tossed around.

"Others say they will only buy the books if they're signed by Rebecca Kingston in a bookstore, in person. No substitutions. A few more are diehard *Mandy* fans, full of nostalgia, and a few are fans of the other authors nominated by Elgin, complaining that their favorite author was robbed. Those were to be expected, I suppose. Only a handful offered congratulations on the award."

Olivia felt a headache coming on. "What else?"

"Your husband wants to revisit the Nate Pullman offer, and one of the producers at *20/20* is requesting an interview with Kelley, sorry Rebecca, while the story is *hot*. His word, not mine."

"And."

"That's all, so far."

Fortunately, headache or no headache, Olivia was good at prioritizing under pressure. "Set up a meeting with marketing—earliest possible. I want to know where they are on publicizing the *Spring Farm* paperback before I talk to *20/20*. Let's put Kurt off until those two are done." *He would not be happy about being third in line.* "I'll talk to Rebecca about the website later."

Ashley nodded and hurried back to her desk. Olivia reached for the bottle of aspirin she kept in her desk drawer and took two, washing them down with the tea, which was considerably cooler now. All things considered, nothing Ashley mentioned was earth shaking, but one never knew just how far angry readers would go.

Now that Bennett Books was no longer keeping Rebecca's secret, many things would actually be easier, and sales of *Spring Farm* were going to be phenomenal. Kurt would certainly be pleased about that.

The next two days, the VW, driven by a twenty-something male, showed up at Rebecca's around ten o'clock, disappeared at noon, returned at three, and stayed until five or six in the evening. His predictable schedule gave Rebecca time to sneak into town early Friday morning. He hadn't trespassed on her property or varied his schedule. He could easily have parked somewhere along the road into town, followed her, and tried to interview her once she was in public space, but he hadn't. Probably new at stalking. And where were the others? Maybe she was only worth one reporter's time. The irony of that made her laugh out loud, sending Matilda scurrying from the room.

Thursday afternoon, a reporter followed Emily as she was walking to the BART station near her house, shouting, "How long have you known Rebecca Kingston? Are you friends?"

Not used to ignoring someone who was speaking to her, "One week. Not exactly."

"Why were you passing yourself off as Kelley Jordan?"

"It was a job."

When he raised a camera and pointed it in her direction, she ducked into the Postal Annex outlet she was in front of and asked the clerk whether it was okay to leave through the back door. Now she knew what Rebecca was talking about.

Just the immediate family celebrated Mae Zimmermann's birthday. Randy and his wife Carol, their two boys, and Alex. Carol, whose cooking skills had never quite measured up to her mother-in-law's standards, made reservations at the Cookhouse and bought a cake at the Sweet Dreams Bakery. Normally, Alex would have invited Becca—but this wasn't *normally*. He knew his parents were curious about the news, but he needed to talk to Becca first. She certainly wouldn't appreciate being interrogated by his mother. And Mae specialized in interrogation.

He called Becca a little before nine, keeping his voice more upbeat than he felt. "Hi—it's me. Sorry to be so late."

"This isn't late." *Well maybe too late to salvage our relationship, but not too late for a drink.*

Rebecca had given their meeting considerable thought. Wrongs were scattered everywhere.

Not warning her he was leaving until the last minute.

Not letting him know where she was at Christmas.

Not telling him who she really was.

There was probably no going back to the way they'd been. In truth, she wasn't sure she wanted to and wasn't sure they could or should go forward with a relationship built on the assumption that neither was committing to anything more than sex and companionship. No baring their souls, no long term plans. Rather like renting a house instead of buying. Easy to pack up and move on.

Alex already had.

And in a bizarre turn of events, she was being forced to revisit her past. Moving on in reverse.

"Can we go someplace for a drink? The Pines at Bass Lake maybe." The green car had disappeared at six.

"Sure. I'll pick you up."

"Why don't I meet you there." Safer that way. If he came to her place, they'd undoubtedly end up in bed, such was the chemistry between them. Not a good idea right now. She was an emotional wreck. Confronting what was happening to her was exposing tender places in her memory that she'd been refusing to touch for years.

"Twenty minutes?"

When she arrived, Alex was already in the bar at a table near the door. A bottle of beer for himself and a glass of white wine for her. He kissed her cheek and helped her out of her heavy jacket. His eyes tried to tease her and failed. He was deeply tanned from the ski slopes—his hair longer than he'd worn it when he was working in the store.

"I like your hair longer." She felt first-date tentative.

"My cool look and it keeps the sun off the back of my neck."

"Suits you." Sitting across from him, unsure how to talk to him, she sipped the wine and waited. They'd never been very good at talking about personal things—the *really* personal things. And men, well, men never did the whole talking thing especially well, preferring to skate on the surface. So they talked about non-essentials.

"How was the party?"

"SOP. Mom going on about how wonderful it was to have someone else do the cooking, Dad talking store business, bragging about how quickly Jorge is learning the business, my brother trying to keep the boys in check, and Carol pretending we were all having a good time. Which, I suppose, we were. Mom asked three times why I hadn't brought you."

"And you said?"

"That you'd just flown in from the East Coast and were tired."

"Mostly true. Thanks."

"I didn't think you'd want to face her questions."

"No. The paparazzi are easier." The invisible elephant made its entrance. "I assume you've seen a newspaper?"

"Yeah, but even before I read the article, I accidentally met Emily Gerrard at your house; she told me about Elgin and what kinds of books you really wrote."

"Emily said you'd come looking for me."

"I bought your book."

Rebecca almost said *you never read books* but thought better of it. "Have you read it?"

"Not all of it. I like the way you describe things, and I'm at the point where I'm curious about what will happen. The weird part is I keep trying to find you in it."

"I wasn't writing about myself." *No one but Megan and her parents would know that some of the father/daughter stuff was pretty close to true.*

"It's a good read."

"Can't ask for more than that. How's the skiing?"

"Terrific. Biggest snowpack in years."

"Do you like teaching? I know you did it when you were younger."

"Yes and no. It lets me ski as much as I want, but telling students the same things over and over, class after class, gets monotonous. Fortunately, the people I work with are great."

"Party time?" A loaded question she was pretty sure she knew the answer to.

"A drink or two after we shut down for the day, nothing else." He held her eyes intently, making sure she heard his answer, "And if you're wondering about girls—women—no." When had he discarded his preference for one night stands? Perhaps as soon as he met Becca. When Alex first arrived in Squaw Valley, Jay had kidded him about becoming a monk. *Have you sworn off sex? Where's the Alex of old?*

Ashamed of what she'd been imagining, Rebecca whispered, "Sorry."

"Becca, I was really worried about you when you didn't show up and I couldn't reach you."

She sighed. "Things from my past were chasing me—still are. Running for the nearest exit has always been my weapon of choice. My friend Megan lives south of London. That's where I was."

"You never mentioned her."

"Let's face it, I didn't mention a lot of things." *Might as well start dealing with the elephant.* "Megan's an American. She was my high school tutor on the TV set. She's married to an Englishman and has two kids. Probably my best friend."

"Dad said a reporter's been sniffing around, asking about you. A young guy—drives a green VW."

"The same one that's been parked in front of my house. So far, I've eluded him, but I suspect my time is running out. You'd better scurry back to the mountains before he catches up with you."

"That won't save me. Dad overheard Jorge being naively honest—telling the reporter I was your boyfriend."

She groaned. "I can see the supermarket tabloids now. *Ski Instructor and ex TV Star Share Oakhurst Love Nest.*"

"The attention will die down."

"Don't count on it." She finished her wine.

"More?"

She shook her head, "I don't need a DUI to spice up the news. Decaf please."

Rebecca watched as Alex walked to the bar, appreciating his smooth stride, bordering on graceful. The result of dodging slalom poles. He'd lost some weight since Thanksgiving. She caught herself remembering his touch, the way he spooned her in his sleep and, in spite of having resolved not to sleep with him tonight, she was tempted to ask him to come home with her.

He returned with two cups of coffee.

"Did Jorge tell the reporter anything else?"

"Jorge doesn't know anything else to tell. I suspect the reporter's gone up and down the street looking for tidbits. Have you talked to Karen?"

"No."

"She always loves to tell what she knows."

Rebecca smiled ruefully. "Bet you never thought that knowing me could get you into the tabloids."

"Been there on my own once or twice in Europe. Why didn't you tell me?" His voice was gentle.

Her throat threatened to close against tears. "Fear. The media are only part of it. The real problem is that strangers come up to celebrities on the street, stare at us in restaurants, astonished that we actually eat food. Though they won't mean to, people here will treat me differently because, all of a sudden, I'm not who they thought I was. They'll get uncomfortable, like I'm some sort of curiosity." A few tears escaped her throat and moved into her eyes. "It was so nice to just be like everyone else."

"You've never been like everyone else." Until that moment he hadn't realized how true it was. She was classy, smart, down to earth, sexy.

And he loved her.

"There's nothing special about me—I write fairly well—and I don't mind people recognizing that, but everything else is nothing but an accident of birth. You aren't your parents either; you don't want to work in their store. I don't want to live in Hillary and Peter's world. Same thing."

She had a point.

"Hey Becca, Alex."

They turned to see Karen approaching, carrying a bottle of beer. "I didn't see you guys come in." She pulled a chair from an adjacent table and sat down. "I thought tonight was your mother's birthday shindig." There weren't many secrets in Oakhurst.

"It's over. The kids have a hockey game in the morning."

She turned to Rebecca. "Did you go?" As much as Rebecca enjoyed Karen's company, her directness often set Rebecca back on her heels.

"No, I just got home." *A small lie.*

"Probably best. It must be hard to have people asking you all sorts of questions."

Questions Karen was undoubtedly dying to ask—and ultimately would. "I was so surprised—you winning an important prize like that. I see that the bookstore has a big display of your books. Local celebrity and all that. Are you going to have a signing?"

"Not that I know of." Rebecca's voice slid into snarky, but Karen didn't notice.

"I had no idea I was having coffee with a celebrity every Monday. I'd love to meet your parents sometime. Your mother was so amazing in *Temptation.*"

"Hey! Karen," a male voice shouted across the room, "if you want a ride home, come on."

"Oops. I came with Cal. See you on Monday as usual? I have a million questions."

Rebecca was close to telling Karen where she could take her questions, but Alex, reading her thoughts, shook his head at her.

"Sure, see you there."

Once Karen was out of earshot, "Don't burn your bridges, Bec, until you're sure you want to. She's just being Karen."

"I rest my case about people's reactions." Rebecca drank the last of the decaf. "Do you go back north tomorrow?"

"Yeah—early."

"Are you staying with your parents?"

"Yes."

"Just as well, I'm a neurotic mess right now."

"No problem." *He hoped he sounded convincing.*

"It's gotten complicated."

"Yeah, I guess it has." *He never had done complication particularly well.*

Outside the bar, he kissed her—slowly, sensuously. "I miss you, Bec. I miss us. And I don't give a damn who you were." *At least he was pretty sure he didn't.*

For a moment, she leaned her forehead against his, wishing she could sink into his arms and let everything else disappear for one night. But he would still leave in the morning and she'd be alone, facing herself and all the baggage that had caught up with her.

"Will you come north sometime?"

Reaching up, she kissed his lips lightly, by-passing the invitation. "Be safe."

She saved her tears until she got home, not exactly certain what she was crying about. There were so many reasons.

Chapter 18

Since her scenes in *A Matter of Trust* were finished, Hillary Wallingford lost no time getting a flight to Los Angeles—first class, of course. Peter's information about Becca had been rather superficial, so she sent Mikaela, her publicist, out to buy whatever newspapers were available. She needed to be prepared to answer the paparazzi's questions. Most assuredly there would be questions. By the time she and Mikaela boarded the flight to Los Angeles, she'd graciously given several interviews to the local reporters who had descended on the movie set.

"Do you know where your daughter is living?

No. *She was trying to throw us off by having Megan forward the mail.*

Rumor has it she lives in Oakhurst, California.

I don't know where that is. *Though Peter had admitted on the phone he'd known for some time where Becca was.*

When's the last time you had contact with her?

We talk on the phone every few months. *Maybe ten minutes.*

Would you say you and your daughter are estranged?

No. *Actually yes. She can't deal with the attention our lifestyle creates so she keeps her distance. I've given up trying to understand.*

Did you know she was such an important author?

She's always wanted to write. *Why, I can't imagine.*

Why didn't she continue acting?

She didn't like it or the media attention." *No secret there.*

Once they landed at LAX, Mikaela called Peter's driver, who was parked nearby, telling him to collect them at the arrivals curb. For once, no one in the airport recognized Hillary. The media in Florida had not picked up on her return to L.A. Unlike her daughter, Hillary rather enjoyed her celebrity status. Having fans recognize her and the media shout questions validated her work. And she craved that validation. Always had. In first grade, she'd reveled in the applause of her family and classmates after she recited a poem she'd learned.

Such a good memory for her age.

You can understand every word.

So she memorized more poems and auditioned for every school play. When she was twelve, she begged for acting lessons and, after high school graduation, was accepted at the Pasadena Playhouse. Two years later, when it closed its drama department, she and Trisha Ford headed for New York. After a month of making the rounds, Hillary landed a small part in an off Broadway play directed by Peter Kingston, an actor who was rapidly making a name for himself as a director. A very handsome man.

And, as Hillary loved to explain, *the rest is history.*

By the end of the play's run, Peter and Hillary were living together. When his next play, in which Hillary had a supporting role, was being turned into a movie, Peter flew to Hollywood to oversee the project while Hillary finished the New York run. Another actress played her role in the film—in Hillary's view *not nearly as well.* As soon as the play closed, Hillary hurried to the West Coast to put an end to rumors that Peter was being pursued by a voluptuous blonde actress. Several weeks later, she and Peter eloped to Las Vegas, effectively taking him off the market.

For the first eight years of their marriage, they worked in films—sometimes separately and sometimes together, on Broadway and in London's West End, spending as much time with each other as their careers permitted. The glamorous golden couple. Early on, they'd agreed not to have children. No sense complicating what was already a complicated lifestyle.

Rebecca had not been planned.

When Hillary's pregnancy could no longer be camouflaged by Portia's costumes, she reluctantly turned her role in a West End production of *The Merchant of Venice* over to her understudy, but Hillary had no intention of being a stay-at-home mom. For the first few weeks of Rebecca's life, Hillary followed the new mother script—getting up for two o'clock feedings and changing diapers. But as soon as she could get into the costumes, she was back on stage. Though she loved Rebecca, loved showing her off and having people comment on how much Rebecca looked like her, arm's length mothering suited her better. If Hillary went on location, Rebecca and the current nanny accompanied her. Rebecca celebrated her third birthday backstage at the George Gershwin Theater in New York. Her fourth was spent with both parents in Spain where Hillary was appearing in Peter's latest film.

Rebecca's phone rang at 8 a.m. on Sunday. As soon as she heard her father's voice—he still had the deep, resonant voice of a stage actor—she felt a peculiar blend of pleasure and panic.

"Becca darling, I hope you don't mind my calling so early."

Breathe deeply. "Of course not. How are you?"

"Good. You?"

"Okay." No sense explaining to anyone—certainly not her father—how many ways her life was not okay, perversely rearranging itself without so much as a by-your-leave. Yesterday Liv had called twice. The first time to give Rebecca the release date on the paperback edition of *Spring Farm* and tell her that the Oakhurst bookstore and three other stores in the Bay Area were requesting readings and signings.

"I'll think about it."

"The perfect time for a signing in Oakhurst would be next week when the paperback edition comes out."

There is no perfect time.

Firmer this time, "I said I'd think about it." Probably no chance of getting Emily to fill in. That charade was over.

The second call from Liv was about *20/20's* request for a joint interview with Emily. "No."

"It'll lay lots of questions to rest. Great PR."

"I doubt Emily wants to be involved." *I don't want to be involved either.*

As though Rebecca hadn't answered, "They need an answer soon." Liv hung up before Rebecca could say *No* again.

And now her father was on the phone, asking whether he and her mother could visit. The prospect of having them in Oakhurst, in her house, was daunting. "Just for the day. We'll fly into Fresno, then drive up. My friend Brad is always looking for an excuse to log some flying time. We'd really like to see you, see where you live."

"Well—" There seemed to be no way to stop her discarded self from being resurrected.

"We'll keep a low profile. I'll put a sack over your mother's head and I'll wear my fake Groucho nose and glasses."

In spite of herself, Rebecca laughed. "At least cut holes in the sack so she can see where she's going." She'd forgotten her father's humor. One of her good memories. "When?"

"Saturday after next. Does that work for you?"

Enough time to prepare answers for their questions, clean the house, decide what to feed them. More than enough time to freak out. "That's fine. Do you have my address?"

"I do."

Of course he did. He also had her phone number. "Call me when you get to Fresno. The drive from there will take you an hour."

"Promise you won't run away."

It was a moment before she committed herself. "Promise."

She was fresh out of places to run anyway.

Rebecca spent the rest of the morning in the yard, raking leaves and pine needles into piles, then stuffing everything into trash bags. Physical labor worked off some of the stress her father's phone call had created. She could picture their visit—complimenting her house, petting the cats, asking about her writing. She would ask about her mother's new movie, her father's next project—and when those topics petered out, the discomfort would set in because they were strangers. Some families could talk about the past, about this or that nostalgic event, but the past was a dangerous topic mostly because Rebecca would get angry. If Hillary reminisced about Rebecca's first movie in Spain, Rebecca would remember how she'd hated doing it, and Peter would end up playing referee. Rebecca was not really looking forward to their arrival.

Karen had cancelled their Monday morning coffee date and rescheduled for Wednesday. Something about a termite inspection at the gallery. Wednesday morning, Rebecca was already at their regular booth when Karen arrived with a copy of *The Enquirer*. She handed it to Rebecca, "Something to read while I get my coffee. You're on page three."

Beneath the headline ***The Secret Life of Rebecca Kingston,*** by Tim Collier, was one of the pictures snapped at the Elgin Awards and a picture of her house—with Tinker sitting in the driveway, scowling at the photographer. At the end of the article was a rather attractive picture of Oakhurst's business district.

Collier briefly described Oakhurst, its proximity to Yosemite, the population and demographic make up. He'd obviously visited the local

Chamber of Commerce. He'd also interviewed several people: Karen, Jorge, the vet she took the cats to, the woman who owned the bookstore, and the bartender at Bass Lake. So he'd followed her after all. Thank God he hadn't taken a picture of Alex kissing her in the parking lot, though perhaps he was saving that one for a second article. Collier identified Alex as her lover, listing his skiing achievements in a sidebar that included a picture of him with his skis balanced jauntily on his shoulder. Sexy pose. Sexy guy.

She really missed him.

When Karen returned to the table with a double something or other in one hand and an almond biscotti in the other, Rebecca gave her the all-purpose Mandy smile, determined not to let Karen or the article get to her—in public anyway. "Pretty flimsy stuff. My life here isn't tabloid material. Fortunately, he hasn't learned to lie with innuendo."

"Good picture of you."

"From the award ceremony."

"The picture of Alex must be three or four years old. Is he still here?"

Rebecca shook her head. "You got quoted a lot."

"And accurately too. Please note I only said nice things. Didn't mention all the times you've been late for coffee. He didn't quote you."

"He never talked to me. Just sat in his car on stake out."

"Did Alex know about—all this?"

"My dark past? No."

"What did he say? How does he feel about—everything? Are you two still a couple?"

Karen had missed her calling. She should have been a prosecuting attorney or a reporter. Rather than walk out of the coffee shop, Rebecca countered, "Can we not talk about this? I've been gone nearly a month. What's been going on? How was your Christmas?"

Reluctantly, Karen gave in to Rebecca's request. "I've had better holidays. I spent the day with my ex-mother-in-law."

"Which one?"

"Sally, the one that lives in Mariposa. Where were you over the holidays?"

"In England, visiting an old friend. What's been happening in town?"

"Let's see—Bill Jessop broke his leg skiing over Christmas. He's on crutches," and for the next half hour, Rebecca was spared Karen's questions.

Instead of going straight home, Rebecca headed for the post office—ostensibly to get stamps but actually to look at the bookstore's window display. Sure enough, all three Kelley Jordan novels and a poster with her picture filled the window.

Local Author Wins Elgin Award:
Our very own Rebecca Kingston Sawyer/Kelley Jordan

She lingered at the window a moment too long. "Hi, Becca." The store's owner, Dee Dee Applegate was standing in the doorway. "What do you think of the display?"

"Very nice."

"My son Mickey did the poster. He's studying computer graphics in college. I talked to your publisher about you doing a signing. Did she tell you?"

At the rear of the shop, two women who'd been looking at cookbooks were now quite openly staring at Rebecca, making the back of her neck tingle with irritation. "Yes, but right now isn't . . . ."

"Oh but the paperback will be available this Saturday. It's a perfect time." Dee Dee's eyes were almost dancing in anticipation. "Please say you will. Everyone's so excited that we have a celebrity living here."

Rebecca was about to try her *I'm no different than I was a month ago* line but decided it wasn't worth the effort. If she refused the signing, she might be labeled a snob—too good for the likes of Oakhurst. If, however, she accepted, she'd have to sign and smile and answer questions. Play celebrity.

A special kind of purgatory.

"Please say yes. And could you do a reading?"

"I don't think . . . ."

"Then just a signing. I'll contact Mrs. Bennett to make sure we have plenty of paperbacks here in time. Two hours, Saturday afternoon. Would one o'clock be okay?"

Rebecca now understood the concept of being steamrolled. "Just this one time. Two hours, no longer." Driving home, she realized she should also have stipulated no press.

The only good thing—the green car hadn't shown up since last Saturday.

Alex had always had a restless, impatient energy that was perfect for racing around slalom poles and sprinting to the finish line. Not so perfect for teaching beginning skiers who often spent more time in the snow than on it and invariably lost a ski pole at just the wrong time. It was hard to stay calm when, for the tenth time, a skier had fallen while practicing turns. It took every bit of his self-control to calmly repeat, "Put your weight on the outside ski. Try again. The outside ski, not the inside ski."

He taught three two-hour classes every day except Friday, but neither his head nor his heart was enjoying any of it. The sense of being in the wrong place doing the wrong thing had been prowling around his thoughts since Christmas. When he arrived in November, he'd believed that being back on skis would be infinitely better than working in his parents' store. The trouble with that theory was that, somehow, skiing had now become a job. How had that happened? All he'd ever wanted to do was ski—never really explored any other way of making a living. He was 30, had saved a little money but was still something of a transient, living on the edge of society. No roots, few possessions other than top-of-the-line ski gear, and only casual friends like Jay. Three or four years ago, those edges were exciting, and he was proud of not being tied down, of not living the nine to five, wife and 2.5 children existence.

But now that he'd gotten what he thought he wanted, he didn't want it. Alex Zimmermann, the hotshot skier who was popular with the ladies, had always dodged living in the real world. So he didn't know how to do anything else except sell sports equipment. Even more startling, his time with Becca had made trolling the après ski scene unacceptable. The great escape was falling apart.

His general sense of dissatisfaction extended even to food. He was sick and tired of eating out or heating up TV dinners in the microwave, so he bought the *How to Cook for One* cookbook, a few pots and pans and decided to teach himself to cook. Unfortunately, cooking made him think of Becca. She loved experimenting with new recipes, humming to herself as she worked.

So many things reminded him of Becca.

Chapter 19

Emily was now officially worried about her finances. The job market for thirty-eight year old single mothers, whose only full time job had been waiting tables twelve years ago, was almost non-existent. Libraries were laying off employees, not hiring them, the waiting list for becoming a teacher's aide was depressingly long, and working in any kind of pre-school required college courses she hadn't taken. Spending time and money to qualify wouldn't help her current need for more money.

Each night, after the girls were in bed, she sat at the kitchen table figuring and refiguring the household expenses. Her mother paid for their food; Emily paid for everything else. The loss of the monthly check from Bennett Books had cut Emily's income in half. She'd been sending out feelers for more Storytelling gigs but had added only two weeks at the end of February in a local YMCA after-school program, teaching children to create and present their own stories. Not enough money to fill the gap.

She felt like everything in her life had come to a screeching halt. Still no contact from Jake or from Max about Jake. She went from worrying about him to finding it hard to believe he'd really been in her life. Not the time to fall for a guy on the other side of the world.

Without question, the call from Liv was a godsend. "Becca has actually agreed to a signing this Saturday but refused to give a reading. Will you do it? Your usual fee, of course, and expenses." Not waiting for Emily to respond, "We'll drive over Friday afternoon. I need to deliver a trunk load of the paperback editions, oversee the publicity, and make sure Rebecca goes through with the signing. Please say yes." Liv was close to giddy, not her usual businesslike self. Making book deliveries surely wasn't part of her job description.

Accepting the job was easy. Any extra cash was welcome, and Emily could perhaps spend some time with Rebecca.

"Good, good. I need to talk to the owner about posters and other publicity. I'll pick you up at your place around one o'clock tomorrow."

Emily lost no time calling Rebecca to warn her that Liv was planning more than just a local signing. "Maybe I shouldn't have agreed. I played right into her hand."

"Not your fault. I'm the one that caved in to the bookstore owner. It was one of those *rock and a hard spot* situations. And I suppose now that the Rebecca Kingston story has hit the news, Liv feels she deserves to get some mileage and profit out of the secret she's been keeping. Tell you what—plan to stay with me Friday night. Though Liv thinks she's slumming at the motel, she'll prefer staying there than at my house. She hates my cats and they're none too fond of her."

Friday, Olivia and Emily arrived in Oakhurst just before the bookstore closed at six. Olivia supervised while Dee Dee and her son unloaded the boxes of books into the display area.

Emily called Rebecca. "We're at the bookstore."

"I'm on my way."

Liv was giving the bookstore her full attention, showing Dee Dee where the podium and table should be placed. "Do you have a microphone?"

Dee Dee nodded.

"Did you call the local paper—what's it called?"

"The *Sierra Star*. Yes, they'll have someone here tomorrow. The posters are ready. Mickey," she turned toward her son, "distributed them yesterday." She held one up for Olivia's approval.

"Okay then—we're set. I called the *Fresno Bee* and had the information posted on our *Spring Farm* website. We should have a terrific turn out."

Emily was relieved when Dee Dee invited Olivia out for dinner. Four plus hours in a car with Liv was enough for one day. Rebecca's arrival was perfectly timed. She briefly made nice with Dee Dee and Liv, loaded Emily's overnight bag into the Lexus, and the two of them made their escape.

"Let's stop for pizza and go out to my place. Dee Dee can pick Liv's brain about books and publishing, and Liv won't have to confront my cats."

"Liv is rather high maintenance. Three days in New York seemed more like ten and this afternoon was interminable."

"Dee Dee will be very impressed by Liv. A great match. I don't even want to think about tomorrow. I could kick myself for agreeing to the signing. What's your favorite pizza?"

"Anything but pineapple and ham."

"Noted. How about prosciutto and mushrooms and olives?"

"Sounds good. Thin crust?"

"Sure. What do you want to drink?"

"Beer. But wine's okay too."

"Done. Girls night in."

Forty minutes later they were at Rebecca's, all three cats waiting impatiently at the door. "Sorry babies. I know. Dinner is late."

Emily slipped out of her shoes and followed Rebecca into the kitchen, admiring the comfortable feel of the house. "You have so much space. My house is too small for four people. Since my mother moved in, the girls have to share a room. Never put a ten year old and a teenager entering puberty in a 12' x 14' room."

"Is it the house you and your husband lived in?"

"No. Ours was larger, had a great yard, and was in a slightly better neighborhood. I couldn't make the mortgage payments on my own, so I downsized and was able to keep some cash. That money and Pat's life insurance is the only way we're surviving. The house I bought a year ago has about 1,300 square feet, and the lot is really narrow. But even this mortgage is pushing me. Especially since I'm no longer pretending to be you."

"I trust Liv is paying you for tomorrow."

"Yes. But it won't be long before I'm going to have to find a job waiting tables."

Leaving the cats to their dinner, Rebecca carried the pizza and paper plates into the living room, Emily bringing the beer and wine. "If Liv had come back here, we'd have to eat properly at the table. I doubt pizza on paper plates is her style."

"She doesn't know what she's missing."

Just like the night after the Awards, they talked until nearly two in the morning, Rebecca filling Emily in on the locals' reactions to her celebrity status, Emily describing her one encounter with the reporter. "Fortunately only that one."

"I'm hoping the whole media thing will eventually die out, but I doubt I'll ever lose my paranoia."

"If you hadn't been hiding all those years, would you have lived differently?"

Rebecca swirled the wine left in her glass and considered the question. "Not sure. I definitely would be writing. I love that. Maybe let my hair grow and give up fake glasses."

"Nothing else?"

"I'd probably have been honest with Alex." The truth of that caught her by surprise.

"What about your parents? I can't imagine not staying in contact with my mother."

"I'd have let them come visit or met them on neutral territory. Going to visit them in Malibu or New York would have attracted too much attention."

"Did you see your parents when you were married?"

"Oh yes. David loved being able to tell his clients, *my in-laws, Peter Kingston and Hillary Wallingford, are staying with us this weekend.* He and his parents quickly snagged bragging rights to my childhood. I got married to have a life that kept me away from the hoopla that followed my parents around. Instead, David pushed me back into their lives."

"You didn't notice that problem before you got married?"

"Sadly no. I was so focused on trying not to be who I was that I missed his fixation with who I was. David's not a bad guy. Very social register and very linear. Always straightening pictures, even in restaurants, making sure the checkbook balanced to the penny. He's remarried to a Vassar girl with an acceptable East Coast pedigree and has two little boys."

"How has Alex reacted to your Kingston identity?"

"I've only seen him once for a drink, and we mostly avoided the subject. We've always avoided difficult subjects. I think he feels a little guilty about the way he took off to Squaw Valley. So any guilt I might have about not telling him about myself is pretty much matched by his. We tiptoed around each other."

"Do you love him?"

Rebecca closed her eyes for a minute, then "I didn't know I did until he was gone. We were so busy not committing to one another I missed the fact that I was committed. In many ways, we're good together. He doesn't straighten pictures, loves my cats," she inhaled, "and he makes me happy." There—she'd said it out loud. Happy.

"I know about happiness. Pat always made me happy even when we were thousands of miles apart."

"Jake?"

"Not sure about long term happy. I've spent very little time with him. My daughters come first right now. I don't know how his job and my life can possibly fit together."

"Same here. Skiing is a seasonal thing. Not a job for any kind of settled existence. And I like being here—settled. Alex doesn't like working for his parents, and I don't blame him. It's hard being under your parents' control at his age."

Rebecca survived Saturday's signing with only minimum damage to her nervous system. Not as scary as she'd imagined but intense, nonetheless. On their way into town, Emily coached Rebecca on the tricks of signing. How to keep her hand and arm from cramping up, to ask the name of person the message should be written to, and how to keep the line moving when someone wanted to talk too long.

Instead of pushing through the crowd squashed into Oakhurst Books, they entered through the shop's back door. Rebecca peered around the shelves at the crowd, half of whom were standing. "Okay, now I'm nervous."

"No need. They'll tell you how much they like your work, thank you for signing their book—that's pretty much it."

"But if they bring up—well, you know."

"Sidestep whatever you don't want to answer. You have control. And I'll have your back."

"Thanks. I mean it. No one has had my back for a very long time."

Emily hugged her, then made her way to the podium, a new paperback copy of *Spring Farm* in hand. She adjusted the microphone and smiled the smile that had captivated Jake that first day in Miami. "Good afternoon. Thank you for coming. My name is Emily Gerrard. I'm going to read from the fourth chapter of *Spring Farm*. This is the morning Harriet and her physician father . . . ."

Emily's voice didn't get in the way of the words. Just enough inflection. From where she was sitting, Rebecca could watch the faces of the women in the audience. Alex's mother was in the front row, a paperback copy on her lap.

The actual signing took longer than Rebecca had imagined; one woman wanted to talk about the story, another how Rebecca had come up with the idea. Her actually being there in person seemed to matter to them. Connecting with her fans—even briefly—was surprisingly fun. A high school girl had two copies of the book, "One should say to Ann, that's my mother. She couldn't come today because she had a doctor's appointment. And my name is Stella. I've read your other two books." Rebecca began writing. At Liv's request she was signing each book *Kelley Jordan/Rebecca Kingston*. Stella thanked her profusely. "Someday I want to be a writer too."

A red haired woman carrying a squirming boy hadn't bought a book. She just wanted to talk to Rebecca. "Ms Kingston, I'm so glad to meet you. I grew up watching *Mandy*. Are you going back to acting?" That was the only time Mandy's name came up and, for once in her life, Rebecca didn't care. When the baby began to cry, the woman moved on.

A gray haired woman wearing Levis and a yellow Yosemite sweatshirt laid *Spring Farm* and Rebecca's first two books on the table, "Please sign all of these. I love your work. I've always wanted to write. Could we meet for coffee sometime? I work for Dee Dee every Friday and Saturday." Rebecca promised to come by the shop.

At one point, Karen was in front of her, "I couldn't miss your coming out party," and later Alex's mother couldn't resist asking, "Are you back for good or are you moving to Los Angeles?"

Rebecca smiled, signed the book and simply said, "I'm glad you came, Mae."

What was meant to be ninety minutes of signing stretched to two and a half hours. Rebecca's hand was aching. The tension in her neck would probably turn into a headache by evening. Several times, she was aware of camera flashes, whether from the attendees or one of the reporters she didn't know.

When there was no one else waiting, Dee Dee and Mickey began putting the chairs away, moving the table back to the front window.

Olivia had Mickey load the extra boxes of books into her car and went to tell Emily they needed to leave. She'd promised Kurt she'd be home tonight. "A total of 118 books—not a bad afternoon for a small town. The newspaper publicity and word of mouth will boost early sales. The woman from the *Fresno Bee* got some terrific pictures. I'm hoping other newspapers pick them up. Becca, have you given any thought to the *20/20* interview?"

"I already told you no."

Liv scowled. "Come on Emily, we need to get on the road. I'll keep in touch, Becca."

Emily hugged Rebecca and hurried after Liv.

For Rebecca, the highlight afternoon had been how much she'd enjoyed talking to her fans.

Chapter 20

The day after the signing, Rebecca took down the *Spring Farm* website, not telling Liv until the deed was done. Since Kelley Jordan's real identity had been splashed all over the tabloids and *Entertainment Tonight*, the site was no longer an author/reader forum. It was inundated with questions about Rebecca Kingston Sawyer's personal life. Those kinds of invasive questions were precisely the reason she'd walked away from all things Kingston, including her parents.

The parents who were about to appear on her doorstep.

Other than cooking for Alex, she'd done very little entertaining in this house, never purchased good dishes or silverware. She was still using the plain white Corelle she'd bought at the Target in Fresno the year she moved in. If she hadn't been so nervous about Peter and Hillary being in her house, she'd have laughed at the absurdity of her trying to impress them. Clearly, she was being victimized by the genetic code that makes women obsess about cleaning their houses, shop for new placemats, and fret about the menu whenever company is coming. On Wednesday, she made herself stop cleaning and move on to buying new placemats and dishes, squeezing in a haircut and manicure. With every passing day, the fretting escalated. She wanted her parents to see that—all by herself—she'd built a life. Her kind of life. Separate from theirs. To her, they weren't the famous golden couple with Tony Awards and Oscar nominations; they were simply the parents who loved her without understanding her. She needed them to appreciate her Oakhurst life, but the odds of that happening were low.

When Emily called her early that Saturday morning, Rebecca was close to being a basket case.

"What time will they arrive?"

"Maybe ten or eleven. A friend of theirs keeps a plane at the Torrance airport. He's flying them to Fresno. Then they'll drive up here."

"Nervous?"

"Big time. How was the drive back with Liv?"

"Fast. She was so wound up over the success of the signing, she never let the needle fall below seventy-five."

"That's Liv. Thanks for coming." Rebecca had sincerely enjoyed their time together.

"The signing was interesting, to say the least. I never had to deal with that kind of frenzy when I was signing books for you."

"According to Liv's latest phone call, bookstores all over the country are clamoring for the *Spring Farm* duo. Clamoring might be an exaggeration."

"Are we going on the road?"

"Not on your life."

"Probably wise. All that clamoring would be exhausting. By the way, I finally got a call from Max, Jake's boss."

"Is Jake okay?"

"Yes, he's been in Cairo since the Egyptians took to the streets. Out of one frying pan into another."

"So he's not coming home?"

"Probably not anytime soon. Max did say that Jake's been trying to replace his phone. Perhaps then I'll be able to talk to him."

"Have you decided what you're going to tell him?"

"That this whole long distance thing isn't for me."

Rebecca was glad Emily hadn't asked what she was going to do about Alex. Her answer wouldn't have been so definite.

Ten minutes later, Rebecca's cell rang again. Thinking it was Emily calling back, "Did you forget something?"

"No." A man's voice, "Is this Rebecca Kingston?"

Assuming it was a reporter, her voice sharpened, "How did you get this number?"

"From Peter Kingston. Are you his daughter Rebecca?"

Something in the man's voice made her say "Yes. Who is this?"

"Lt. Ray Jovic, LAPD."

Time stretched and stretched, then snapped. Her lips began trembling. "What's happened?"

"Your parents have been in an automobile accident. You're needed in L.A. as soon as you can make travel arrangements."

Later, she could only recall the words *accident* and *405 Freeway.* Though she could hear the officer's voice, she couldn't process the words. "I don't understand." Jovic repeated the information. "Your father's being taken to UCLA Medical Center."

"My mother?"

There was a log pause. "Your mother and the driver died at the scene."

Blunt. Brutal. No punches pulled. No euphemisms or *I'm sorry for your loss.*

The moment cried out for softer words, a gentler tone. No one should hear this kind of information on the phone.

From a stranger.

The trembling traveled to her hands. Eventually, all she could hear was a dial tone. Somehow, she must have had the strength to call the Fresno airport because a flight confirmation number was written on a post-it. 1:30 p.m.

There were no words for what she was feeling. She'd never confronted death up close and personal. Only intellectually, on paper. Killing off a character to fit a plotline, trying—not always successfully—to describe the agony of those left behind. In *Spring Farm,* when Harriet's mother died, Rebecca had described Harriet as hysterical, inconsolable for weeks.

But Rebecca didn't feel hysterical. Instead, an icy energy sent her in search of her suitcase. Because she was pretty sure she shouldn't be driving, she called Trudy and then went looking for the business card Nate had given her in New York. His personal cell number was scrawled on the back. She left a message on his voice mail, stumbling over the words that explained what had happened, asking him to meet her at the hospital—if he was in town. Suddenly, she was five again and he was holding her hand as they waited in line at the Jungle Cruise. She needed that hand now.

The half hour flight to LAX was too short and too long. Her mind was everywhere at once as though she'd drunk gallons of coffee. She kept trying to remember where her mother's brothers were living, where her cousins were, wondering what her father's injuries were. Surely she wouldn't lose him too. All those years she'd stayed away from her parents, convinced she didn't need them, didn't want to be part of their lives. Now she would never be even the smallest part of her mother's life. What she'd been hiding from didn't exist any more.

Be very, very careful what you think you want.

When the taxi dropped her at the hospital's emergency entrance, Nate was leaning against the building, hands in the pockets of his windbreaker, his face taut, eyes sunken. He and her parents had been friends for forty years. Hillary had introduced him to his first wife, a gorgeous French actress named Lia. Rebecca pulled the suitcase to where he stood, let go of the handle, and stepped into his embrace, grateful for the comfort of his voice. The adrenaline that had been propelling her ever since the phone call drained away. She closed her eyes and let herself believe, for just an instant, she was safe, that everything was all right. A few minutes later, she realized she hadn't been listening to what Nate was telling her. "Say that again."

"Peter, he's in surgery but he'll recover. Lots of broken parts but nothing life-threatening. He was in the back seat. Hillary was riding alongside the driver."

Her mother's chronic motion sickness.

"They told you?"

"I said I was Peter's brother. Don't give me away." She couldn't see his face, but she sensed he was trying to be upbeat. "Let's go inside. The ever-vigilant members of the paparazzi squad who have access to police scanners will find their way here soon. I'm surprised they aren't here already. Thankfully, the hospital won't let them inside."

He pulled her suitcase through the automatic door and stayed with her while she navigated the bureaucratic nightmare of forms and questions. She had no idea about her father's medical insurance or power of attorney, about whether there was a specific mortuary the hospital should contact. Though Rebecca was the appropriate next of kin, people unrelated to her parents knew more about them than she did.

In frustration, "I don't have the names or phone numbers of their staff or their lawyers." *I don't know much of anything about my parents' lives.*

The woman behind the counter was equally frustrated with what Rebecca didn't know. "I'll call Social Services."

Eventually, a social worker brought her mother's bulging Coach handbag—always Hillary's label of choice—to the waiting room. Rebecca reached a hand toward it, then couldn't touch it. That purse had always been off-limits to everyone but Hillary. "I can't," she whispered. "She never lets—."

Lets

The present tense.

Her mother would never again be present tense. "She never let—." Even using past tense, Rebecca couldn't finish the sentence.

Nate moved the purse onto his lap, searching for a cell phone or a planner with numbers and names that would put them in contact with someone who could answer the questions the hospital was asking. Rebecca watched him from what seemed like a great distance, remembering when she was three or four and had been scolded for emptying Hillary's purse onto the living room floor, opening the lipsticks, turning the pages of the planner she carried.

"Bec," Nate was studying Hillary's phone, "What's Mikaela's last name?"

"Who's Mikaela?"

"Her publicist. Here it is, Mikaela Hirsch." He punched the speed dial and waited. "Hello, is this Mikaela?" He stood up and walked away so Rebecca couldn't hear him explain that Hillary was dead. Thoughtful. Odd that Nate had never stayed married. Two divorces and no children.

"Mikaela's coming." Rebecca looked up and saw tears on his cheeks. "She's contacting the lawyers." Rebecca reached for the phone and scrolled through Hillary's contact list. Not until numbers ten and eleven did she find her uncles' names. At some point they would need to know. Preferably before Hillary's death made the nightly news. Undoubtedly Rebecca's job, but right now she couldn't imagine how she could tell them that their baby sister was gone.

By the time Miklaela showed up with the necessary paperwork, Rebecca and Nate had been sent to a waiting room on the third floor. *When Mr. Kingston is out of surgery, the doctors will find you."*

Mikaela was older than Rebecca had imagined—maybe in her late forties—streaked ash blonde hair pulled into a ponytail, no make-up. They shook hands. "Sorry to be so long. I had to track the paralegal down, then get her to fax all the information. Also the name of the funeral home where your parents made preliminary arrangements several years ago." She slipped out of the long khaki trench coat that covered an expensive sweat suit. "I was at the gym when you called. I just can't believe," she cleared her throat, "well, who should I give this information to?"

Rebecca walked her downstairs to talk to the impatient and probably overworked clerk on the first floor, then hurried back to the oppressive waiting room that was saturated with the angst of all those who had sat here before, dreading what a doctor or nurse would tell them. She felt as though a giant boulder had settled in her soul. Unexpectedly, she found herself mentally rewriting the chapter about Harriet's grief. The last few hours had taught Rebecca how badly she'd missed the emotional mark. Grief wasn't hysterical; it was a cold, dispassionate vacuum that was letting her function without feeling.

An hour later Nate was standing over her. "I brought you a sandwich and coffee."

She stared stupidly at the sack with SUBWAY printed on the side. "I thought you and Mikaela were in the cafeteria."

He frowned. "Seriously unappetizing food. We ate at the Subway across the street and shared some ideas about what needs to be done, if you agree of course."

Rebecca unwrapped the roast beef sandwich. It didn't look especially appetizing either. She reached for the coffee.

"Cream, right?"

She nodded, touched that he remembered.

He sat beside her, "Please eat, Bec."

"Not hungry."

"Please." His hand lightly rubbed the hollow between her shoulder blades.

She tried a few bites, then put the sandwich down. The boulder was taking up too much space in her stomach.

"What did you two talk about?"

"Preparing a statement for the media. The bloodhounds are camped outside. We used a side entrance to get back in. Mikaela's in the cafeteria writing it up and trying to contact the LAPD about the specifics of the accident. Fortunately, she's used to handling situations like this, but it's hard on her too. She and Hill had become friends."

When Mikaela walked out of the hospital to face the reporters, she forced herself to look into the camera lights without flinching. This wasn't the first time she'd faced cameras and the relentless questions from the press. PR was her job. She read from the single sheet of paper in her hand, her voice not as steady as it would normally be.

"This morning at 9:17, Producer/Director Peter Kingston and his wife actress Hillary Wallingford were involved in an automobile accident. The car they were riding in was exiting the 405 Freeway onto Crenshaw

Boulevard when a pick-up truck going sixty miles an hour ran a red light and hit their car on the passenger side. The driver of the car and Hillary Wallingford were killed instantly. Peter Kingston is presently undergoing surgery for his injuries. He's expected to recover. Funeral arrangements for Ms. Wallingford are pending." She looked up. "That's all for now, thank you."

Ignoring the shouted questions—*What about the other driver, is Mandy with her father, what will happen to the movie Hillary was filming*—Mikaela escaped into the hospital. When she found her way to the waiting room, two doctors were talking to Rebecca and Nate. She waited in the doorway until the conversation ended. "Rebecca? Good news, I hope."

"Yes." She turned to Nate, "You'll explain better."

He kept his arm around Rebecca's shoulders. "The surgeon set Peter's shoulder and collarbone. He had a collapsed lung, which has been re-inflated. Several broken ribs, a ruptured spleen. They'll bring him to ICU shortly. He was very lucky. The car was totaled. How'd the statement go?"

"I simply read it and walked away. Otherwise, they'd still be throwing questions at me. For the present, I'll try to manage the information but, as you know, it'll soon be beyond our control. A story as big as this will take on a life of its own."

"Thanks Mikaela. I couldn't have done it." Rebecca reached for her jacket and purse. "I want to be in ICU when they bring him down."

Nate pulled up the zipper on his windbreaker and took his car keys from the pocket. "Call when you're ready to leave. I'll come back and take you to my place. I don't want you to be alone."

Chapter 21

Hillary Wallingford's death was the lead story on the eleven o'clock newscast that Eldin Zimmermann was watching while eating a bowl of strawberry ice cream. He hit the mute button on the remote and called Alex.

The first words out of Alex's mouth were "What's wrong?" His father seldom called, certainly not this late.

"Do you have cable up there?"

"Sure."

"Turn on the news. Becca's mother, Hillary what's-her-name, died in an automobile crash this morning."

Alex was already searching for the remote. "You and mom okay?"

Brusquely, "Of course. You worry too much." Eldin hung up and rinsed out the bowl, hiding it in the dishwasher. Ice cream was not on his post heart attack diet.

Alex tuned into CNN just as a tall blonde woman in a long coat was reading a prepared statement to cameramen pushing to get the best shot and reporters holding digital recorders in her face. He watched until the channel started running clips of Hillary's movies and then called Becca's cell. When he didn't get an answer, he risked calling Trudy.

"It's late," she grumbled.

"Were you asleep?"

"No."

"Tell me about Becca."

"I took her to the airport just before noon. I assume you're watching the news about her parents?"

"My father called to tell me what happened. How was she?"

"Exercising superhuman control but her eyes were hurting."

"Sorry to bother you."

"It's okay," she admitted, "I'm worried about her too."

For most of the night, he vacillated between taking a couple days off to fly to L.A. to make sure she was okay or staying clear of her other life, the one she'd hidden from him and everyone else. Perhaps she wouldn't want him calling attention to their relationship, wouldn't have time for him in the midst of this tragedy. When they met at Bass Lake, she'd been afraid the reporter hanging around Oakhurst would link them. Was her fear for him or herself? He was learning that he didn't know Becca as well as he thought he did. But then he'd never been good at really knowing any of the women he'd slept with. Not something he was especially proud of.

By the time he went to sleep, he was no closer to a decision. Since he still felt guilty about accepting Jay's job offer without telling her until the last minute, he wasn't in any position to ask why she'd never told him about her other life. In truth, he didn't care about that life, didn't care whether she was famous or had famous parents. He cared about the Becca who loved her cats, took long walks, and had let him stack ski magazines in her bedroom.

In the dim light of the ICU, the myriad of wires and tubes connecting Peter Kingston to various monitoring machines made him look like the fragile captive of some alien culture. At regular intervals, nurses checked the equipment, asked Rebecca whether she needed anything, and continued their rounds. She was afraid to take her eyes off him, afraid he might die too. Afraid that all of this was essentially her fault.

If she hadn't been hiding from her parents and everything else in her other life.

If they hadn't been on their way to Oakhurst to visit her.

If she'd been brave enough to visit them instead.

Then, Hillary would still be alive and Peter would have been on the golf course this morning, instead of riding in a car that had been reduced to scrap metal.

All of this pain because she'd been so small-hearted, so selfish and yes cowardly. All these years, she'd blamed them for foisting the family business on her, blamed them for the way she'd had to secretly rebuild her life. But if she were brutality honest with herself, her paranoia was not really their fault. It was hers.

And there was no way to undo this tragedy.

Peter's head felt like it was wrapped in some sort of fluffy cloth that muffled sounds and feeling. In spite of the cloth, however, he knew Hillary was dead. Nothing could soften that blistering, irrevocable fact. But where was the despair? There was only an odd absence of—everything. A chemically induced limbo.

When he woke again, the cloth was thinner, the pain creeping closer. Not the pain of the accident. This other pain was deep and indefinite, nothing pills or drips could reach.

So beautiful, his Hillary.

So powerful a presence in the world, in his world. From the moment she walked into that audition in New York forty years ago, he'd been a man possessed.

He treasured and tolerated her moods, her laughter, loved the way she dramatized everything. For her, life was meant to be lived boldly. When she'd followed him to Los Angeles, letting him know, in no uncertain terms, that she loved him and intended to marry him, he felt as if he'd won the prize of prizes—and never seriously looked at another woman.

Of course, living and working with her was frequently explosive and exasperating. Two creative temperaments in close quarters. Ultimately, they'd learned how far an argument could go before real damage was done. They trusted each other's artistic instincts, knew that each of their careers depended on the other person's support. Now he'd lost that support. He wasn't sure he wanted to live in a world without her.

Sensing there was someone else was in the room, he experimented with opening his eyes, managing just a slit of light. Becca was sitting in a chair, her head tipped back, asleep.

Rebecca was walking along an empty beach, skirting the waves that were polishing the sand, the ocean's foam sharply cold on her bare feet. As a child, she loved walking with her mother on the beach at Malibu. It was one of the few activities they shared. Peter preferred walking on a golf course. Hillary would often rehearse her lines for an upcoming movie or play—shouting them over the roar of the ocean.

Softly, "Becca."

She looked around for the source of the whisper, but the beach was still empty.

"Becca, please wake up."

Her father was looking straight at her.

Awake.

Alive.

"You were smiling. What was the dream?"

"A beach." She sat forward, "I was walking."

"With your mother?" His voice wavered.

She shook her head. "Alone."

He closed his eyes for a moment, understanding.

"I'm so sorry Daddy."

"I know."

"Who told you—about mother?"

"I overheard the paramedics say *two dead*. Since I was still alive—" Tears collected in his eyes, quietly spilling onto his cheeks. She'd never seen him cry before.

Though she wanted to hold his hand, wanted to comfort him, she was afraid to disturb the tube attached to the back of his hand, so she just rested her cheek on the bed rail, wondering when it would be okay for her to cry.

As soon as he slipped back into a medicated sleep, she walked into the corridor and called Nate. "I'm ready to leave. Can you come get me?"

Nate Pullman's luxurious condo was in a gated complex atop the Hollywood Hills. His guestroom had an enormous window overlooking the quilt of lights in the city below, but Rebecca was in no mood to appreciate the view. Still functioning on autopilot, she dug through her duffle suitcase, hoping she'd packed a nightgown, then stood under the shower's pulsing heat, finally letting the sobs come, salted tears mingling with the steaming water.

When the water began to cool, she dried off, slipped into the nightgown and, without turning the lights on, curled under the covers, staring out at what remained of the night. In another hour or two, dawn would outline the city and the world would move into another day. A day her mother would never see. A day her father would have to live through without his wife. But at least he was alive.

Giving in to exhaustion, she fell asleep just as the birds began their morning songs.

Before Alex went to work the next morning, he tried Becca's cell but only got her voice mail. In frustration, he called Olivia Bennett, praying she wouldn't ignore him this time.

"Olivia Bennett." All business.

"This is Alex Zimmermann, Becca's—friend."

"I know who you are. How can I help you?"

"Do you have a phone number, other than her cell, that I could use to reach her? I've been trying since last night."

The line was quiet. He hoped she wouldn't hang up.

"Try this number." She read it so quickly he had to ask her to repeat it because he hadn't caught the area code.

"Whose is it?"

"Nate Pullman's. He's her godfather and a friend of her parents. He might know where she is."

"Thanks."

"If you talk to her, give her my condolences."

He hadn't expected that. Perhaps Olivia Bennett was human after all.

Rebecca woke reluctantly, willing herself to open her eyes. Nate's guestroom was filled with sunshine. Rain would better suit her mood. Closing her eyes against the full force of what had happened yesterday, she lay still, wondering whether she was going to cry again. When she didn't, she forced herself out of bed. She needed to go back to the hospital. Needed to make sure her father was okay.

Nate was in the kitchen, fixing coffee.

"Hi, Baby. I'm making a fresh pot. I finished off the first one by myself." He looked as though he hadn't slept. "Do you want cereal? Actually, it's all I have."

"Cereal's fine." She put her arms around him. "Thank you for letting me stay here last night."

"Did you sleep?"

"About dawn. What time is it? I can't seem to locate my watch."

"Close to eleven."

"I need to get to the hospital."

"I checked with the nurses' station earlier. Peter's doing well. They're going to move him to a private room today. And he ate some breakfast, or what passes for breakfast in those places." Nate set the box of Cheerios, a bowl and a spoon in front of her. "I only have one percent milk."

"I'm not really hungry, but I probably need to eat something."

"You got a phone call this morning, someone named Alex Zimmermann. He wants you to call him."

Alex had tracked her down. How nice. But right now, nice was more than she could handle. Nice made the tears come.

"Who is he?"

"Friend."

"Boyfriend?"

"Until last November."

"Because?"

"He's a skier, won two World Cup races a few years ago. He was working in his parents' sporting goods store in Oakhurst until his father's health improved. Now he's moved to Squaw Valley."

"I see."

"We both kept the doors open. No harm, no foul." *But when he left, there had been harm she hadn't expected.*

"You should call him back. He sounded very worried about you."

"I will, tonight, when he's done working. He's a ski instructor."

"And Mikaela called an hour ago. As soon as you're ready, she'll pick you up and take you to the hospital. Paparazzi are everywhere. She'll run interference."

"I want to stay at the house tonight. Then I can use one of the cars if I need to go somewhere."

"I don't think—"

"Putting it off won't make going there any easier."

He changed the subject. "Mikaela wants to talk to you and Peter about the service for your mother."

Her throat tightening, Rebecca concentrated on the unappetizing yellowish circles floating in the milk.

"It has to be done, Baby. According to Mikaela, Hillary left fairly specific instructions about the service." He smiled, "Your mother's in control to the last, not trusting others to design her final performance."

"It'll be a media circus." Instantly, her stomach knotted. She pushed the bowl away.

"No doubt. She'll be sorry to have missed it. Hillary loved a good media circus, especially if she was center stage."

When the coffee was ready, he poured her a cup. "Even though it's Sunday, I have to go over to my office. I want to reschedule some meetings. Then I'll come to the hospital."

"You don't need—"

"Yes I do. I want to see Peter and hear what Mikaela says about the service. I loved her too, you know."

Pouring some of the one percent milk into her coffee, "May I have Mikaela's number?"

At the northern end of the Pacific Coast Highway, the Kingston house sat on a low rise above the beach. By Hollywood standards, not a pretentious house, just under four thousand square feet. Split level, cream-colored stucco, red tile roof, and floor to ceiling wall to wall windows along the ocean side. A small apartment above the garage for the live-in housekeeper and cook, currently a woman named Selena Jiminez. A great house for entertaining. As Mikaela's car approached the wrought iron gate set into the block wall separating the front yard from the highway, she activated the electronic opener so the gate slid open. As soon as the car was in the driveway, the gate automatically slid shut.

"No paparazzi. We're lucky." Mikaela went ahead to punch the keys on the security pad alongside the door while Rebecca wrestled her bag from the trunk.

In the front hall, Mikaela was fiddling with the thermostat. "The house is freezing. I had no idea you'd want to stay here so soon. I told Selena to close everything up and go stay with her sister in Huntington Beach. She's inconsolable."

"I can manage." *I've been living without servants for a long time.*

"Let's see if there's food in the refrigerator."

Rebecca followed her to the enormous kitchen, clinically clean with every possible stainless steel appliance. A kitchen Hillary entered only to give instructions.

Mikalea peered into the refrigerator. "Looks like leftovers of one kind or another. A dozen eggs, half a loaf of bread." She opened the freezer. "More to choose from in here. You won't starve. Do you know how to cook?"

"Rather well, actually."

Mikaela smiled slightly, "You didn't learn from Hillary."

"Of course not." *From my mother I learned how to deliver a line and how to ignore the camera while I was delivering that line.* "Why don't you tell Selena to take the week off. I'd just as soon not have someone hovering. Do you know where the extra car keys are kept?" Hillary was the only one who had regularly driven herself. Peter's car seldom saw the light of day.

Once Mikaela left, Rebecca walked onto the deck overlooking the beach. The sun was barely touching the horizon, pale orange streaks skimming across the water. She slipped out of her shoes and stepped onto the sand, icy without the sun to heat it. Retreating to the steps, she sat down to watch the sun do its daily disappearing act. The breeze smelled of her childhood, seaweed and wet sand seasoned with ocean salt. The last two days had been two centuries, as though she'd time-traveled back to a self she thought she'd escaped. And here she was. In her parents' house.

Rebecca had spent most of the afternoon in Peter's hospital room. He was more alert today, his color better. It took Mikaela a couple hours to go through all of Hillary's wishes for the service; then she and Nate had gone off to start making arrangements, checking the availability of the church Hillary attended once or twice a year, and contacting friends Hillary specifically wanted to take part in the ceremony. It was no surprise she wanted to be cremated. *I don't want anyone looking at my corpse or putting me in a satin-lined casket. I'm claustrophobic.* She'd listed the music and named the soloist she preferred. In addition to two favorite Psalms, she'd chosen three readings from her favorite Shakespearean roles and Elizabeth Bishop's poem "Conversation." The only thing she didn't specify was who would give the eulogy.

With more than an element of truth, Nate suggested "Maybe she really wanted to deliver it herself."

That made Peter smile. "Trisha Ford should do the Shakespeare."

When it was too cold to stay on the steps any longer. Rebecca faced the reality of an empty house. She couldn't remember whether she'd ever been alone here. The silence followed her as she wandered through the rooms. If she were in Oakhurst, she'd be feeding the cats, closing the shutters against the night, deciding what to fix for dinner. But tonight she wasn't hungry, hadn't been since the phone call yesterday. Reading a book was out of the question; she seemed to have lost all power of concentration. And she was afraid to turn on the TV for fear there'd be some sort of special on her mother's life and career.

Exhausted by the events of the last two days, she pulled her suitcase upstairs, past her parents' room—too soon to look inside—and entered her old room. It faced the ocean, the sliding glass doors opening onto a narrow balcony. Rebecca hadn't been in this room since she and David had spent Christmas with her parents nine years ago. Since then, the room had been redecorated in grays, whites and shades of violet. Nothing of Rebecca's childhood was visible. Only fair. More than once, she'd made it quite clear she didn't consider this her home.

She stretched out on the bed, intending to be there only a few moments, and was immediately asleep.

Chapter 22

Alex waited two days. When Rebecca didn't return his call, he tried her cell again—and again. Not sure whether he should be worried or annoyed, he tried Nate Pullman's number.

"Sorry, Becca's not here. She's at the house in Malibu." *As though Alex should know whose house that was.*

"Would you mind giving me the number? She's still not returning my messages on her cell. I know this is a hard time, but I'd really like to talk to her."

"No problem." Nate read off the number. "I don't think she should be alone at the house. She won't even let Selena come back to take care of her."

And who was Selena? "Thanks. Do you know anything about her mother's funeral?"

"A memorial service will be on the twenty-third. Her father will be out of the hospital by then."

"How is he?"

"Recovering, physically at least. He'll go home in a few days with a nurse to help."

"Where will the service be?"

"The Santa Monica Congregational Church. 10 a.m. It's by invitation only. If you give me your address, I'll see that you get one."

A different world where he needed an invitation to attend a memorial service. Alex gave Nate his address and cell number. "I've given up any hope she'll return my calls."

"She's always had a mind of her own."

A quality Alex had only experienced in its milder forms. The first time was the stand off about where the cat door should be. Not until he proved to her—using her copy of the original house plans—that knocking a hole in the kitchen wall would compromise the pipes going to the laundry did she agree to let him put it in the studio. That mini war had lasted a week. Then he'd been rather amused.

But she had never before ignored his calls. When he hadn't been able to reach her at Christmas, it was because her phone wouldn't work in England.

This silence was different.

The morning of Hillary Wallingford's memorial service, the skies over Los Angeles opened up, flooding streets and turning the freeway system into an adult version of bumper cars. Not a good introduction to the city.

Alex found his way to the church only because he'd borrowed his father's GPS. Left to his own navigational skills, he was fairly certain he'd have arrived late or not at all. In the mountains, he seldom got lost. Cities were a different matter altogether. Yesterday, he'd driven from Squaw Valley to Oakhurst; this morning, he left before dawn to drive to a city he had successfully avoided all of his life. Though he was uncomfortably aware she might no longer be the Becca he'd known, he needed to see her. Needed to know whether she was beyond his reach.

Since he didn't own a dark suit, he was wearing gray slacks and a short sleeved white shirt under a dark green sweater. The yellow slicker, part of his search and rescue gear, was definitely not formal enough. Hopefully there would be some place to leave it at the church.

But before he could get into the church, he needed a parking space. The church lot was jammed, as were the surrounding streets. He ended up parking three blocks away, arriving at the church entrance just as the service was starting. TV camera crews and reporters crowded under golf umbrellas and makeshift tarps, claiming ownership of the sidewalk outside the church. The rain had discouraged a massive fan turnout.

Alex handed the invitation Nate had sent him to the woman guarding the door. Taking note of his dripping slicker, she pointed to a row of coat hooks on the wall behind her and whispered, "The only seats left are upstairs," and pointed to a wrought-iron circular stairway.

Alex hung up the slicker and took the stairs two at a time. The seats in the choir loft were steep enough to give him a good view of the front of the church. He easily spotted Becca's bright hair. The man in the wheelchair next to her aisle seat was undoubtedly her father. Alex stared at the top of her head—all he could do from that distance—willing her to feel his eyes, but she didn't turn around.

Though a black-robed minister led the audience in prayer and read several Bible passages, the rest of the service was more about theater than religion. A remarkable blend of laughter and pathos. Behind the altar was a wall-mounted flat screen TV continuously showing pictures of Hillary Wallingford; several shots included Becca when she was young, living in that other world she never talked about. Alex was struggling to blend the Becca of that world with the Becca he knew.

In addition to the woman who read the Shakespearean passages, thirteen or fourteen people walked to the podium to share personal memories of Hillary. A famous actor whose name Alex couldn't remember recounted anecdotes about the first movie he and Hillary made together. One of her brothers laughed about helping her put on plays in the back yard of their childhood home. There was a Broadway director and a woman who always did Hillary's make-up on the movie sets. In the midst of so many high profile people, Alex felt insignificant. This was definitely not Oakhurst or Squaw Valley.

The last speaker was Becca. Alex sat forward, trying to see her face more clearly, but he was too far away. She adjusted the microphone and looked at the audience. Outwardly, she seemed composed but, when she spoke, Alex could tell by the raggedness of her voice that she was deeply tired. One of the personal things he knew about her—among all the other things he didn't know.

"My father has asked me to read his remarks for him."

Peter Kingston's brief tribute to his wife was a love letter, at once tender, poignant and gently amusing. How was Becca able to read it without faltering? But of course she'd been trained to perform in all sorts of situations. He kept forgetting that she'd been an actress.

When she finished reading, she carefully folded the sheet of paper. "Hillary Wallingford never needed a compass to find her way in this world. She was her own compass. All of you are here today to honor the power of that compass. Thank you for coming to say goodbye to—my mother."

Hearing the crack in her voice, tears sprang to his eyes. Becca had always seemed so sure of herself, confident in who she was and what she was doing—as though she too had a compass. Today she seemed lonely and terribly sad.

He stayed in his seat until the choir loft had emptied, watching Becca and Peter Kingston accept people's condolences. Joining the line to tell Becca how sorry he was would be too public a reunion. He wanted to be alone with her, to hold her. But that probably wasn't going to happen, certainly not in the church.

Half an hour later as Alex was retrieving his jacket, a man's voice asked, "Are you Becca's friend?" The voice belonged to a distinguished man in an expensive gray silk suit, carrying a golf umbrella.

"Yes." Alex extended his hand.

"Nate Pullman. Did you find a seat?"

"Upstairs."

"Have you spoken to Becca?"

"No."

"The family, Peter's nephews and Hill's brothers and their families, are going back to the house. Would you like to come?"

"Will it be okay with Becca and her father?"

"Actually, I don't know, but I could use a ride to the house and that way you won't get lost. I came with Mikaela, Hillary's publicist. She'll be busy for a while throwing fresh meat to the press. I try to skip those kinds of experiences whenever I can."

Nate stepped outside, checked that Alex was behind him, then walked briskly through the knot of reporters, ignoring the shouts of *Mr. Pullman, how was the service? How's Peter Kingston?* As Alex was following Nate, he heard someone ask *Who's that guy in the yellow jacket?*

Once they were clear, Nate opened the umbrella. "Which way to your car?"

Alex pointed to the right. "Three blocks. Before we drive very far, I'll need to stop for gas."

When Rebecca and her father exited the church, the flashbulbs and shouted questions assaulted them. She pushed his chair straight ahead, not caring whether she hit one or two of these vultures. Serve them right. Peter's car was waiting at the curb; her uncles helped her father from the chair into the passenger seat, storing the wheelchair in the trunk. Rebecca slid into the back seat and quickly slammed the door. Thirty-two years old and she still couldn't tolerate the boorish behavior of people who fed off others' lives. When she was a teenager, their antics frightened her. Today she was simply angry. This wasn't about news. It was about interfering in the lives of people who were hurting. As the car pulled away, she looked out the rear window; her uncles were hurrying back into the church. Neither of them had ever had to face the kind of chaos their sister's sudden death had unleashed.

Chapter 23

In spite of the hollow ache in her stomach, Rebecca had endured the receiving line at the church, calmly accepting all the *I'm so sorrys* from people she knew and didn't know. Actors, directors, writers. People who had worked with and admired her mother. *You are so lucky to have had such an amazing woman as your mother.* Rebecca couldn't think of an appropriate answer. She'd never seen herself as lucky to be Hillary's daughter. Quite the opposite. Today, however, was perhaps not the right time to be honest about those feelings or examine them. Today was all about surviving.

The logistics of honoring the dead were wearing on her nerves. Thank God for Selena and the catering service Mikaela had hired. At least the relatives and their families had something to eat. As soon as everyone was back at the house, Peter thanked them for coming, excused himself, and went upstairs to rest, leaving Rebecca to entertain people she barely knew.

Peter was now able to walk short distances unaided and climb the stairs to the guest room, but he adamantly refused to enter the room he'd shared with Hillary. A nurse came to the house in the morning to help him shower and dress; another came after dinner to check on his medications and get him into bed. This was the first day he'd left the house. In fact, most days he didn't come downstairs, preferring to sit on the balcony watching the waves—regardless of the weather. He ate what was placed before him and answered questions briefly or not at all. To save him the effort of facing the paparazzi stationed outside the house, his doctor had come out to Malibu twice since Peter had been released from the hospital.

Once he came home, the reality of Hillary being gone—not just on location or shopping in New York—had driven him into a distracted depression that Rebecca didn't know how to deal with. Because there were no current projects in the pipeline, the staff at Kingston Productions was adrift, hoping Peter would soon be back. So far he showed no interest in anything but the ocean.

Today's service had used up whatever emotional reserve Rebecca possessed. When she faced the crowd of mourners in the church, it was all she could do to keep from crying at the sweetness of Peter's farewell words. Her parents' love for each other had never faded. Remarkable in the entertainment world. She should be proud of that but, for most of her life, she'd been so busy blaming them for what they hadn't done for her—or what she thought she lacked—that she couldn't see who they were. Or who she was.

At this point, Rebecca just wanted to stand in the shower and cry, but Peter's exit was forcing her to make small talk with aunts, uncles and cousins she hadn't seen in a decade. Of course, it wasn't their fault that she hadn't had contact with them. Her Uncle John, a retired high school history teacher who lived in Bakersfield, had driven to Los Angeles with his wife Sharon and their youngest son Steven, a struggling artist who had struggled back home two years ago and was still waiting for the world to appreciate his talent. Her Uncle Theo owned a car dealership in Long Beach and was in the midst of a nasty divorce from his second wife; he'd come with his daughter Pearl, her husband and twin daughters, both of whom bore an unsettling resemblance to Hillary. Since Rebecca hadn't seen Peter's nephews since she was eight, she was having trouble keeping their names straight.

Around two o'clock the rain finally stopped, encouraging a watery sun to sneak under the clouds stretched along the horizon. When Mikaela found her in the kitchen, Rebecca was pouring herself more coffee. "Nate's here."

"Thank goodness. Maybe he can find something to talk to them about. I'm out of ideas."

"He brought someone named Alex."

Alex.

Even though she'd ignored his messages, he was here.

She wiped at the sudden tears that came unbidden. "Would you ask him to come out here?"

"Sure. Great looking guy, by the way."

She probably looked a wreck. Eyes swollen, mascara smeared. But then Alex had seen her look far worse during her ten-day bout with the flu last September.

He hesitated just inside the doorway, his unruly hair damp from the rain. "Hi Bec."

The Mandy smile failed her, so she simply walked the few feet between them and leaned into him, feeling his arms close around her.

"You don't mind that I came? You didn't answer my calls."

Her "No" was muffled into his sweater. "This has been hard; I just didn't, couldn't—"

"It's okay," he kissed the top of her head. "Can we go for a walk on the beach?"

"They'll come after us."

"They?"

"The paparazzi."

"A patio then? Some fresh air would feel good. It's stopped raining." Without answering, she led him onto the deck partially covered so the cushioned chairs were almost dry.

Alex pulled two of the chairs side by side. "Will you be warm enough?"

She nodded. "How did you get here?"

"I had Nate's phone number. He sent me an invitation to the service." He took her hand.

"You were there? Where? I didn't see you."

"I was late and sat in the choir loft." He turned her hand over and pressed his lips into the palm. "You were so brave—to read your father's words. And what you said about your mother's compass was perfect."

Tears again. It had been that way all day. "I stayed away too long. I didn't get to tell her goodbye. They were coming to visit me." Soft sobs blurred her words. "In a way, I'm responsible for them being in that car on their way to the airport." She finally gave voice to the guilt that had been following her around since that fateful phone call. "I can't undo that."

"Bec, it's not your fault." His words probably couldn't touch her guilt.

They talked in choppy, unconnected phrases. He wanted to tell her how much he'd missed her—that he wanted to help her, protect her—but she was intent on telling him the scattered memories of all the days since the accident. She couldn't seem to stop talking. Now was clearly not the time to reveal what was in his heart.

From the moment he'd entered this elegant house, he'd been confronted with the vast difference between his life and the life Rebecca had come from. Though the outside of the house wasn't elaborate, the luxury inside was overwhelming. Marble floors, museum quality paintings, a white leather sectional in front of an enormous, wall-mounted flat screen. So different from the cluttered comfort of his parents' house, the upholstery that was worn, the rugs that had seen too many pets. The Kingston world was light years away from the Zimmermann world.

Alex had always known Becca made more money than he did. That difference hadn't bothered him when they were in Oakhurst. But now that he was in the midst of her past life, the differences seemed insurmountable. He had little to recommend him—a high school diploma, no career, and very little money. Compared to the Kingstons, he was a drifter with nothing to bring to the relationship. A couple of medals, a handful of newspaper clippings. And love.

A chilling wind drove them inside about the time Hillary's family was leaving. Rebecca let them hug her, tried to say all the right things to them, but there really were no right things. She walked them to the door—how unfair not to be able to leave the house for fear of cameras and questions—and thanked them for coming. So odd. She had family but she felt, even with Peter upstairs, alone. In need of a compass of her own.

Selena began clearing the dishes, storing the leftovers in the refrigerator. "I'll take care of all this. Will you be needing me this evening?" Grief was written on her face. Selena had attended the funeral, then hurried back to the house to prepare for the guests. She'd worked for Hillary and Peter for five years, living above the garage, saving most of what she earned to send to her daughter, who was attending the University of Texas on a partial scholarship.

"No. Thanks for your help today, Selena." Rebecca wasn't accustomed to having someone wait on her anymore. She'd never acquired the art of telling someone to do the tasks she could easily do.

Nate was sitting in the family room, watching CNN and drinking Peter's scotch. Once upon a time, the room had simply contained a television set and an elaborate sound system. Now it had something called a home entertainment center that dominated an entire wall.

Rebecca sat beside Nate. "Did the service make the news?"

"I haven't seen anything yet. But it'll probably be on *Entertainment Tonight*. Their truck was at the church."

"Are the reporters still outside?"

"Of course. They're hoping for a shot at you, but they'll have to settle for Mikaela. She's out there right now, feeding them trivia while trying to shoo them away."

Alex was puzzled. "What more can they want?"

"Crumbs. And if there are no crumbs, they'll invent them." Nate finished the scotch. "Alex, why don't you come home with me tonight. If you stay here, they'll decide you and Becca are secretly married and she's pregnant with triplets. Page one tomorrow."

Rebecca was grateful Nate was offering Alex a place to stay. As pleased as she was to see him, she recognized a new, uneasy distance between them. These three months had dragged her back into a world she'd never wanted to revisit. A world she was afraid she might not be able to escape a second time because now her father needed her.

At the door, she let Alex pull her close. "Are you going north tomorrow?"

"I don't have to. I can stay another day." He'd need to call Jay. "Could we have lunch tomorrow?"

She frowned. "Going out to eat could get complicated."

Once again Nate stepped in. "Why don't I bring him here. I'll be the smoke screen. Let them think he's a friend of mine. I'd like to spend time with Peter, even if he won't talk to me. I'm pretty good at monologues. Selena can whip up something."

Alex saw the wisdom in Nate's suggestion. "Becca? Okay with you?"

"Sure."

He brushed her lips lightly and followed Nate outside, carrying his yellow slicker, averting his eyes to avoid the flashbulbs. He was beginning to understand Becca's paranoia about the media.

In the age of social networking and 24/7 news bulletins, no one has any secrets. As soon as Alex arrived at the Kingston house, research into the identity of the man in the yellow slicker began. He'd been at the memorial service, left with Nathan Pullman, and visited the Kingston house where only close friends and family had gathered. They had a new bone to chew on.

The answers came in time for the next day's edition because the first *Enquirer* article about Rebecca's Oakhurst life had already indentified Alex, and Tim Collier had thoroughly researched Alex's backstory. On the front page was a picture of Alex, who did not look entirely sober, dancing with a sexy blonde in what appeared to be a bar. The headline read *World Cup Don Juan Is Rebecca Kingston's Secret Lover.*

Just in case one of Mikaela's clients needed her help, each morning the staff checked the tabloids. She called Nate at nine. "You might want to pick up a copy of *The Enquirer* before you go out to Malibu. Alex is today's cover story."

Since Alex was still asleep, Nate drove to the 7-11 on North La Brea, buying the *L.A. Times* and several tabloids. Becca was not going to be happy. For years, she'd purposely kept away from this kind of exploitation and now her boyfriend was being fed to the lions.

By the time Nate returned to the condo, Alex had showered and helped himself to the coffee. Nate laid *The Enquirer* in front of him, "Trouble."

Alex saw the photo of himself with Gracie Henderson. "How did they dig up that shot?" Gracie had been one of the ski team trainers who, at one time or another, had slept with a large percentage of the males on the tour. Her promiscuity was something of a team joke. Almost a rite of passage for the new guys. During his first year on the tour, Alex had slept with her a couple of times. Embarrassed, he read the article through, conscious of Nate watching him. Unfortunately, the facts were pretty much correct. In addition to listing many of the women he'd been linked to, there was his Lake Placid arrest for being drunk and disorderly and, in Austria, he'd spent two days in police custody after a bar room brawl. That time, he'd nearly been tossed off the team.

Alex forced himself to meet Nate's gaze. "It's accurate." The chickens had picked today to come home to roost.

Nate grinned. "So we can't sue for libel?"

"Hell no. That's who I was. If my folks hadn't needed me at the store, I'd probably still be trying to compete on and off the slopes."

"Does Becca know the details?"

She will now. "Until recently, neither of us was particularly honest about our past lives but, since I met Becca, there hasn't been anyone else." He hoped Nate believed him—more important that Becca would believe him.

"We'd better get over to the house. The pressure from the media is going to be even worse than it was yesterday, and you're the new victim."

As they hurried past the paparazzi, the shouting was hard to ignore.

Hey Alex, tell us about life on the ski team.

A new girl every night?

How long have you known Mandy?
What's she like in bed?

When he and Nate finally reached the safety of the porch, Selena already had the door open for them. For lunch, she'd made chicken burritos. There was beer and, if they wanted dessert, ice cream in the freezer. She left the burritos in the warming oven so they could eat whenever they were ready.

Nate took plates for himself and Peter upstairs. Rebecca and Alex were in the family room, Rebecca reading the article while Alex waited nervously for her reaction. She looked exhausted, dark circles beneath her eyes. When she finished, she tossed the paper aside, "So now you're grist for their mill. Sorry. If I'd known you were coming yesterday, I'd have warned you to stay away. It'll be this way until they find someone else to harass. These people enjoy blowing everything out of proportion."

"Becca, they haven't blown anything out of proportion. It's mostly true. Actually I'm surprised they missed my two-week engagement to one of the women on the German ski team. A downhiller named Ingrid. Once both of us came to our senses, we unengaged ourselves. The European press had a field day with that one. So you see, I'm no stranger to making the front page."

"A colorful past." *A little more colorful than she'd imagined.*

"Nothing to brag about. It's a glamorous environment with plenty of temptations. In those days, I was easily tempted." *Not anymore.*

Rebecca was too exhausted to be seriously upset about the article. She hadn't slept more than two or three hours a night since she'd returned to the Malibu house. Too much to worry about. Worry about Peter, about her own ability to withstand the public thirst for information about the Kingston tragedy, worry about the cats and her own house, about her writing, which had been on hiatus for the last four months. Hillary's death, however, made her earlier "worries" about attending the Elgin Awards and Alex leaving seem childishly insignificant. She kept coming back to the fact that her safe life in Oakhurst had cost Hillary hers. A *quid pro quo* of sorts. The logical side of Rebecca knew she hadn't directly caused Hillary's death, but her emotional side refused to pay attention.

In the last few days, she'd made several difficult decisions. She must stay with her father for a while, if necessary even help out at his production company until he was ready to resume control. She owed him that—probably more.

And then there was Alex.

It was time for her to get off the fence and admit the timing for them was wrong—maybe it always had been. Though they'd agreed that either one could walk away tomorrow or the next day, all the while she'd been falling in love with him without realizing it. She'd never before been *in love*. Never felt this way about David, hadn't been entirely sure this *was* love until she saw Alex standing in the kitchen doorway yesterday and felt the comfort of his arms, heard his voice.

But she was trapped in her old life and he had a skiing life.

"Becca?" His hand on her arm jolted her into the present. "A penny—"

"I'm going to close the house in Oakhurst for the time being."

"And move here?"

She could hear the disappointment in his voice. This world was not Alex's world. She nodded, "As corny as it sounds, my father needs me. How long I don't know." Alex hadn't moved. "You stayed at the store two years to help your folks."

"I understand." He did. Yet understanding and acceptance were not the same. He also remembered how difficult it was to leave skiing and go to work with his family. A simultaneously familiar and foreign environment. Returning to Oakhurst had cost him his independence and his pride because he was reduced to living their life, not his own. And now his skiing life wasn't what he'd expected it would be. Teaching wasn't all that satisfying. Bottom line, he didn't know what to do with the rest of his life. Listening to Becca, it looked like whatever his life was going to be, she wouldn't be part of it.

She laid out the reasons for her decision.

He listened. Listening was all he had to offer. He felt helpless in the face of her distress.

"I'm glad you've been able to go back to skiing. It gives me hope that this won't last forever." She stood and walked to where he was sitting. "Thanks so much for coming, but I'm really bone tired; I can't think about anything today." Her kiss was clearly meant as goodbye. He watched her climb the steps away from him.

As difficult as all this was for Becca right now, he hadn't expected her to shut the door on him. He'd come to help if he could. For a fraction of a second, he was tempted to feel sorry for himself until he remembered how many times he'd shut that same door on other women. It was his turn to be left behind.

Later, Nate found him alone in the family room. "Selena certainly makes terrific burritos."

It was then Alex realized he and Becca hadn't eaten lunch.

The day Becca kissed him goodbye at her father's house, Alex drove straight to Squaw Valley and gave Jay two weeks' notice. He had no idea what he was going to do, no idea whether he was able to do anything but ski or work in his parents' store. It was depressing to discover that he was entering his thirties with nothing much to put on a resume. High school kids had more work qualifications than he did.

He needed direction. If he ever wanted something permanent with Becca—or anyone, he had to acquire a grown up life of some kind. Unfortunately, by the time he had direction, Becca would probably have recovered and moved on. She was a beautiful, talented woman, who had lived among the rich and famous—was famous in her own right. He'd been so busy not wanting to settle down, not wanting to commit to anything but a ski slope that he'd screwed up the relationship with the one woman he couldn't get out of his head. That she might wait for him was a long shot.

Since the owner of the condo wouldn't be moving back to Squaw Valley until May, Alex decided to stay put and enroll in a block of short session business classes at the Tahoe campus of Sierra College. To pay the rent, he found a bartending job in Tahoe City.

Only Jay, who had the wisdom not to ask questions, knew what Alex was doing. Not why he was doing it.

Chapter 24

Since January, Jake Hannigan had been surrounded by chaos. Though technically he was observing and reporting what he observed, it was impossible not to be caught up in the passion and violence of what the media was calling the Arab Spring. But having a front row seat on history was taking a toll on him. Judging from the way his Levi's fit, he'd lost about ten pounds, and he was having trouble sleeping whenever he found the time and a place to lie down. The breakpoint, however, was his leg. The throbbing pain had finally become so bad that he was limping all the time, wishing he had a cane to take the pressure off. Occasionally, other reporters had a few aspirin to spare, but he really needed a stronger painkiller. He ultimately had to admit he needed medical treatment that he couldn't get in the midst of all the shouting, rock throwing, and gunfire.

These months had been a journalist's dream come true. The stories he'd been filing were some of the best writing he'd ever done, and Max was making noises about a promotion, certainly a raise. A long way from Jake's days of free-lancing. Besides the *Twenty-First Century* articles, he'd been keeping detailed, personal journals that he never let out of his sight, sometimes carrying them inside his shirt for safekeeping. He was recording what he saw and felt, as well as human-interest stories of those who were gambling everything for a chance at a better, freer life. The seeds of a book.

But first he had to get rid of the pain.

It took Max three weeks to send Turner Booth, an eager young reporter with two good legs to replace Jake. Booth caught up with him in Benghazi, Libya, on a day when rebels, crowded into dusty pickups, were pushing to the west. Jake had only twenty-four hours to show Booth how and where to file his stories and introduce him to the other reporters who would have to provide him with additional survival skills. The following day, Jake caught a ride into Egypt and, after two nights sleeping in the Cairo airport, snagged a seat on a flight to New York.

Three weeks later, he was in surgery so the doctors could repair his leg—once again. After a month in rehab, he was fitted for a lightweight leg brace, and Max and the doctors lost no time grounding him. No more uprisings. The surgeon was firm: *Next time, we might not be able to put you back together.*

While Jake was recovering, Max studied the journals Jake had been keeping and, with his permission, showed them to a friend at M-1 Publishing. By the time Jake reported to work, Max had good news.

"A book now?" Jake was dumbstruck. "Before we know how all those rebellions will play out? Seems premature." *But encouraging.*

"Hot topic. They're interested in your up close and personal look at the beginning of the uprisings in Tunisia and Egypt. The ending will be someone else's story. You were there; you talked to the people on the streets, to other reporters. Who better to do this?"

"How long do I have to think about it?"

"A few days. The offer won't keep."

"I'll get back to you." He needed time to absorb this sudden career shift. He'd seen the possibility of a book as some far off project. Instead, it was sitting on his doorstep.

"How's the leg?"

"Better but not as good as before. By the end of the day, I usually need to use the cane." He eased himself out of the chair, careful not to put too much pressure on the leg too quickly. He was tired of moving like an old man.

"Did you ever get in touch with the woman you met while you were working on the Elgin article? Emily something-or-other. She came to see me in January."

"No. Using someone's phone for a personal call or the e-mail at Al Jezeera just didn't seem right, and finding a new phone was out of the question."

"So you don't know how that story turned out?"

"Been a bit busy, Max."

"It's interesting. Go online and catch up."

Jake hated to admit to himself or Max that he'd been more interested in the uprisings he was covering than keeping in touch with Emily. If memory served, he'd made a similar mistake with Darlene. He seemed incapable of keeping a relationship alive while he was chasing stories in foreign countries. Though Darlene had claimed he wasn't much better at a relationship when he was in the States. When he was in North Africa, he'd often thought about Emily, but slowing down to figure out how to stay in contact got in the way of the compelling, day-to-day stories on the streets. And since he'd been back in the States, he hadn't known quite how to resurrect what began last winter, and so he did nothing. By now, she could be seeing someone else, a possibility that was oddly upsetting.

Before he left the building, he gathered up back issues of *Twenty-First Century* and headed for his apartment. He had research to do. He googled Kelley Jordan and Rebecca Sawyer, then was linked to Rebecca Kingston and finally Hillary Wallingford's death. After reading fifteen or sixteen articles on line, he had the bare bones of the story. If this were a movie plot, critics would have dismissed the storyline as implausible. The puzzle about *Spring Farm's* author had more pieces than he'd imagined when he told Max there was more to the story. At least he'd been right.

The next day, he googled the words *Ojai* and *storytelling*. The Ojai home page showed that the festival Emily had told him about had been May 5th through the 8th. He was too late to see her perform, to surprise her and perhaps rekindle their chemistry. Once again, bad timing.

Not wanting to risk losing the possibility of a book deal, he made an appointment at M-1 to meet Max's editor friend and, after discussing the project for two days, signed a contract, collected a rather handsome advance, and asked Max for a leave of absence from *Twenty-First Century.* "I need some down time." An element of truth. Actually, he needed to talk to Emily face to face.

Max agreed to a month.

Before Jake analyzed the Emily issue to death, he bought a Monday afternoon plane ticket to San Francisco and spent the weekend making copies of his journals, over-nighting the originals to Max for safekeeping, then buying a new laptop so he could begin fleshing out his approach for the book.

Tuesday morning, Jake rang Emily's doorbell in Berkeley. It took Mildred McGee a second or two to recognize him. "Jake. My goodness, what a surprise."

"Perhaps I should have called first." *But he'd wanted to surprise Emily.*

"Not a problem. It's just that Emily isn't here. This is one of her weeks in Los Angeles. She flew down to L.A. Sunday night. Come in, please."

"What's she doing in Los Angeles?" He'd been right. She moved on without him. *A boyfriend?*

"Coffee?"

"Sure." He followed her into the kitchen, perching himself on one of the stools at the kitchen counter.

Noticing the brace, she asked, "Were you injured over there? Emily watched the news every night, wondering if you were in all that fighting. She was worried about you."

That information cheered him a little.

"It's an old injury that I aggravated by thinking I could run and jump like a teenager. The brace may be a permanent part of my wardrobe, but fortunately I still have my leg. What's Emily doing in L.A.?"

Mildred set a mug of steaming coffee in front of him. "Cream or sugar?"

"Black's fine. I got used to drinking it that way over there."

"How much do you know about the Rebecca Kingston story?"

"Just the basics. Rebecca Sawyer is actually Rebecca Kingston, Hillary Wallingford was Rebecca's mother, and *Spring Farm* won the Elgin. Why is Emily in Los Angeles?"

"In January, Olivia Bennett invited Em to attend the Elgin Awards with her. Rebecca and Emily hit it off and, once they returned to California, they kept in touch. There's a lot of drama in all of what happened with Rebecca's mother, but the short version is that Rebecca needs help sorting through her mother's papers and pictures—a painful process since Rebecca and her mother were never close and her father has been too distraught to be much help. So Peter Kingston is paying Emily to come to L.A. every other week until she and Rebecca get Hillary's papers ready for the biographer. All sorts of publishers are chomping at the bit to do the biography."

"Would I be interrupting if I went to Los Angeles?"

Mildred's gray eyes were evaluating him. He was sixteen again, facing the parents of a girl he wanted to take to a high school dance.

"I don't imagine it's a problem." Her words sounded surer than the tone of her voice. "But don't play games with her, Jake. You already disappeared once."

He wanted to argue that a job assignment wasn't disappearing, but this was probably not a battle worth fighting right now.

"No games. I promise."

She wrote down the Malibu address.

The last couple of months had convinced Rebecca that her past had never really gone away; it had simply been lying in wait, ready to devour the present.

Though she'd known that attending the Awards could change her life, she hadn't imagined how much; and with the wisdom of hindsight, she was pretty sure she should have stayed in England another week to avoid that pivotal question: *Are you Mandy?*

It was entirely possible she was being punished for having run away from her childhood. Now, four incredibly long months after the accident, she was still living with Peter, who was healing physically but was still depressed, unwilling to return to work. When his doctor insisted he start getting some exercise, he grudgingly returned to his golf club though his injured shoulder wasn't helping his game. A step at a time, he and Rebecca were finding small ways to reconnect, occasionally playing Cribbage, a game he'd taught her the Christmas they were in Vermont, and watching baseball games.

By early May, the daily paparazzi stakeout had pretty much ended, though Rebecca often had the feeling that there was a car following her when she went shopping or to her father's office in Santa Monica. She was acting as a liaison between her father and his staff, bringing him documents and checks that needed to be signed and scripts his staff saw as possible projects. He skimmed them and sent them back to the office without comment. Kingston Productions was at a standstill. Two employees had already told Rebecca they were worried that Peter would never come back and had begun bringing their resumes up to date.

Rebecca was at a standstill too. Waiting for her father to come back to life, waiting to return to Oakhurst. Liv called every ten days or so, asking how Rebecca was getting along, how her father was. The subtext was, of course, when are you going back to work on the next book? If Liv had asked outright, Rebecca could only have answered *I don't know.* She kept making notes and creating timelines for the plot, but she wasn't writing.

She had no idea what to do about her life. At the end of March, she'd driven up to Oakhurst to put a forward on her mail and telephone, and give Trudy a substantial check to cover the care of the cats. If Rebecca took them to Malibu, they'd be restricted to the house because of the traffic. They'd hate that. She told herself they were happier in familiar surroundings, but she missed them. Missed everything about her home. With every passing day, she feared she'd never be able to return. Oakhurst had been the only place she'd ever been completely comfortable. Of course, part of that *at home* feeling had involved Alex. Maybe Oakhurst wouldn't feel the same now that he was out of her life.

She packed up what she needed for the book, knowing she probably wouldn't be able to concentrate on it now that she'd begun to sort through her mother's papers and personal effects. With Peter's blessing, Mikaela was fielding book offers for Hillary's biography, looking for the right author. But first, Rebecca needed to organize as much of the tangible information as possible. Peter had turned over his own papers and letters to her but wasn't willing to get involved.

"On top of everything else," Rebecca confided to Emily the first week they worked together, "my father is talking about selling this house. If he does put it on the market, there'll be even more stuff to go through. They lived here thirty years."

"Rather soon for him to be making major decisions."

"Maybe, but everything in this place reminds him of my mother. He may do better starting over."

Rebecca was beginning to realize that the picture she'd always had of her mother was incomplete—based only on what a daughter, a child really, thought she knew. Rebecca had been self-righteously comfortable seeing Hillary as the flamboyant, self-centered woman whose career mattered more than her family, than her daughter. But sifting through Hillary's personal effects was giving Rebecca a clearer picture of the young Hillary. So far, she had spent nearly five weeks, three of them with Emily, sorting through family pictures, letters, scripts marked in Hillary's careless scrawl, *turn here, laugh softly*, and publicity clippings that had never made it into a scrapbook. Organizing any kind of paperwork was never one of Hillary's strengths. Rebecca discovered boxes of memorabilia hidden in back of almost every closet, in the garage and, amazingly, under the king-sized bed her parents had shared. Who would have believed that the glamorous, talented Hillary Wallingford kept her press clippings and theater programs beneath her bed?

Before she went to sleep at night, Rebecca was reading the first of Hillary's diaries, being introduced to the day-to-day life of the young Hillary. Eager. Optimistic. Insecure. A Hillary Rebecca had never imagined. The first diary began when Hillary was eighteen, newly enrolled at the Pasadena Playhouse: *Every day is electric. The teachers and other students make me want to be the best actress I can be. But sometimes I'm afraid I'm in over my head. The competition is fierce. I couldn't bear it if I were asked to leave because I'm not good enough.*

Early on, Hillary made friends with another new student, Trisha Ford, willowy, jet-black hair, funny and a fantastic mimic. *She can do any accent they throw at her. I'm so envious. I struggle with accents.*

Hillary had been envious of another's ability! Amazing! Rebecca just might have liked her mother at eighteen. Searching through the photos in the 1960s stacks that Emily had been working on, Rebecca had found a snapshot of Hillary and Trisha sitting on a porch step—maybe in Manhattan—smoking cigarettes. Hillary had always abhorred smoking, had threatened Rebecca with permanent house arrest if she caught her smoking anything. Something else to be amazed about.

The second diary, begun two years later just after the Playhouse closed, revealed that same anxious Hillary, devastated because she wouldn't be able to finish her studies at the Playhouse. *I don't know what to do. Trisha wants us to go to New York, just like that. I've talked to my father. He agreed to give me the same amount of money he'd have paid for my tuition. It's a giant step from L.A. to New York. I'm terrified.*

That diary covered her first months in New York and ended the day she auditioned for Peter's play. *Mr. Kingston is gorgeous, charismatic. I read badly because I knew he was looking at me, but he was probably only listening to me read, not looking at me LIKE THAT. I've been in my room crying ever since I came home. Such a terrific chance and I threw it away because an incredibly sexy man was conducting the audition.*

The rest of that diary was blank. The name of the play was *Second Circle*. In the one scrapbook that Hillary had kept during those first years as a working actress were her newspaper reviews. In the one for *Second Circle*, Hillary's performance received three sentences. *Ingenue Hillary Wallingford makes her first Broadway appearance. Her role as a vapid teenager doesn't begin to show off her considerable abilities. Keep an eye on this one.*

Chapter 25

The day Rebecca began reading Hillary's third diary, Peter announced he was closing down Kingston Productions, putting the Malibu house and the New York penthouse up for sale, and subletting a small apartment for himself in New York. All of this from the man who'd been hibernating for months, wanting no part of the world around him.

Unable to think of an appropriate response to his sudden rush to redo his life, Rebecca went for a walk on the beach, returning an hour later to confront her father, who was calmly eating a meatloaf sandwich at the kitchen table. "Why?"

"I'm not interested in directing movies right now. Since there's nothing in the pipeline that I have to finish, it's a good time to quit. I'll give my staff a month's notice and good recommendations. Nate already wants to hire my office manager since his is moving to Seattle to get married. As for the house and penthouse, too many memories and too much upkeep. Like Thoreau, I crave simplicity."

The past Rebecca had so carefully avoided was disappearing, a person and a house at a time. The irony of that wasn't lost on her. No longer was there much to run away from, except of course the media.

"What will you do in New York?"

"I've been offered a part in an off Broadway revival of *Death of a Salesman.*"

How had she missed all of this activity? "Which part?" Not that the role mattered but she couldn't think of anything else to ask.

"Charley. I've always admired his closing speech in The Requiem."

"When?" She couldn't seem to get past the Why, What, When questions.

"Rehearsals start in August. Bec, my decision isn't just because of your mother," his voice wavered a little, "though all of this upheaval has been a catalyst. I've missed acting for a long time and, during a conversation with Emily, I mentioned that I wanted to go back to acting. Her reply was *why don't you see if there's a part you could play?* And there was."

"But all the way across the country!" The thought of having him so far away was unsettling. She'd just begun getting reacquainted with him.

"That's what airplanes are for, darling child. You've spent all these months holding my hand, and I appreciate everything you've done, but it's time for me to find a new life and for you to go back to yours."

"Not sure it's there anymore." *I don't know where I belong or who I want to be.* She'd been so sure she didn't need her parents or anything from her past. Now she was afraid of not having some of that past. Hard to get it right.

"Your home is there, your writing."

"Well, yes."

"So?"

"I'm not sure it's enough." She was tempted to add *because Alex isn't there and I have no idea where he is.* When he'd come looking for her, wanting to help, she'd turned him away. What had she been so afraid of?

Being with her father and Nate had forced her to rethink her childhood. When she'd seen Nate in New York, held her father's hand in the hospital, and spoken at the memorial service, that hidden self came racing back. Memory by memory, she'd been dragging the fragments of yesterday to the surface to understand what yesterday's child hadn't understood.

The memory of Nate holding her hand, explaining that her parents had entrusted her fifth birthday to him. She'd been waiting to be five for a very long time. But five probably didn't matter to her parents. They'd already had a lot of fives. Her heart had been disappointed. Didn't they love her enough?

Then there was the memory of being in that first movie, Peter showing her where to stand, where to look as she said her lines. Three takes and he was satisfied, smiling as she walked toward his embrace. "You did well."

Later, both parents quizzed her. *Would you like to have other parts?*

Her *Not really* hadn't made an impression because, three months later, she was appearing in a London play with Hillary. The cold vastness of the theatre where hundreds of people were watching her never stopped being frightening. Thankfully, the play ran only three months.

On a warm Wednesday morning, Jake showed up at the Malibu house unannounced. Selena led him to the deck where Rebecca was drinking coffee and making to do lists on her computer. She enjoyed working outside in the morning before the afternoon sun bore down on the west side of the house.

Selena's voice cut into her thoughts. "Rebecca, a Mr. Hannigan is here to see Emily."

Shading her eyes, Rebecca looked up at the man who had started her on this journey, taking note of his height and deep tan. "I finally get to meet the man who set all of this in motion."

"Should I leave or apologize?"

He was direct. She liked that. "Neither. Please sit down. Selena would you bring more coffee for us? I've let mine go cold."

Selena nodded and, in the quiet way she accomplished everything, was back almost immediately with a tray. "I've brought some of my warm cinnamon bread, just in case you're hungry." She smiled at Jake and disappeared.

He poured coffee from the thermal carafe into the empty cup and added coffee to Rebecca's. "Cream?"

"Thanks."

Sipping at the strong coffee, Jake debated how to begin the conversation. He wasn't entirely sure of his footing with this beautiful, accomplished woman who was taking his measure. For that matter, he wasn't sure of his footing with Emily either. It was going to be a difficult day. "The Elgin article certainly took on a life of its own."

"Hard to argue that. It certainly changed my life."

"I didn't intend—"

She immediately regretted her remark. "Sorry, I'm not angry at you. You simply did your job too well. People like me, who reinvent themselves and then keep their pasts a secret, are inviting discovery at some point. If not you, it would have been someone else. I always knew Mandy would catch up with me. At least I no longer have to be on guard. Hiding from the past is hard work."

"Congratulations on winning the fiction prize."

"Thank you. Winning meant a lot to me, but it's gotten lost in all of—this." She added more cream to her coffee. "And now you've come looking for Emily."

"Yes. As soon as I got released from rehab," he pointed at his leg, "the orthopedic kind not the drug kind, I headed for Berkeley. Mildred told me Emily was with you. I wanted to surprise her."

Alex had done the same thing the day of Hillary's memorial. What was it about men that they couldn't warn a woman they were coming?

"Emily thinks you're still in Libya or one of those other countries."

"I came back to have surgery on my leg." He poured himself more coffee. "My days of covering uprisings are over. I didn't want to see her until I was put back together again. The only way her mother would give me this address was if I promised I would not play fast and loose with Em's life and go running off to some other foreign land. Mildred McGee is a tough negotiator."

"I've never met her."

"She's actually a nice lady, just looking out for her daughter's welfare."

"Em came to help me with my mother's memorabilia. She's also spent hours and hours with my father and really helped bring him out of his depression. While the rest of us were tiptoeing around his grief, Emily met it head-on because she'd been in his shoes. No platitudes or feel good speeches. Over these weeks, they've become friends. He even lets her win at Cribbage. Me he beats."

"She's a special person."

Emily had spent the morning shopping for cardboard boxes. Somehow, it seemed wrong to have to pay for flattened cardboard that had to be folded into boxes instead of going to the back doors of grocery stores to collect boxes tossed into the alley the way she used to whenever she and Pat moved. Today, those discarded boxes were crushed before they reached the alley and sent to the recycling plant to be turned into the flattened cardboard she'd just purchased. There was definitely a Storytelling piece hiding in this absurdity.

She parked Hillary's car alongside the strange car in the driveway. Perhaps Peter had company. The trunk could be emptied of its pristine cardboard later. Letting herself in the front door, she walked through the living room and out to the deck, looking for Rebecca. Instead, she found Jake drinking coffee and watching the waves. Tanned, handsome, smiling cautiously, a little grayer at the temples, a brace on his left leg.

Jake.

Here.

With no advance warning.

Her hair was windblown, probably standing on end, her lipstick long gone; she was dressed in khaki shorts and a much-washed red t-shirt. This was not the way she'd imagined their reunion. Actually, she'd almost given up on the possibility of a reunion. For months, she'd mentally rehearsed sensible, slightly snarky speeches that included the line *Long distances make for poor relationships.* At the end of the speech, she planned to cut him loose.

"Hi Em." Looking a trifle uneasy, he stood up but didn't move toward her. Just as well because her bones tended to melt whenever he got close to her, touched her, his fingers igniting her skin. This moment shouldn't involve melting. At least he was alive and still standing on two legs. Those prayers had been answered. The answer to the other prayer was pending.

"Where's Becca?"

"Upstairs, being discreet." He noticed Emily wasn't wearing her wedding ring. His heart lifted.

"So you two have met?"

He smiled slightly, "And she didn't hit me."

"Not her style."

"What about you?"

"Not my style either, though you might deserve it."

He risked taking a step toward her but stopped when she moved back slightly.

"How did you know I was here?"

"I went to your house."

"Ah yes. My mother would give away state secrets if she knew any."

"I had to make several promises before she'd give me this address."

"Such as?"

"Not to ruin your life."

Rather sweet. "Oh."

"Can we sit down?"

"Sure." She took the chair farthest from the one he'd been sitting in. "How long have you been back?"

"Seven weeks or so." *And yes I should have called.*

"Your leg?" *Calling would have been nice.*

"Yeah. It finally rebelled and I—well I couldn't ignore it any longer. They operated on it again, sent me to rehab again, and figuratively revoked my passport."

"Are you in pain?"

"Sometimes. It's getting better, but the brace will probably stay awhile. I still need to resort to a cane. The good news is that I qualify for handicapped parking."

"Will you stay on at the magazine?"

"Yes, though I'm on leave for a month. My choice. I have a contract to turn the journals I kept into a book on the Arab uprisings."

"Congratulations."

"I might need someone to do readings," he gambled that humor would defuse the tension between them—and won.

"My voice isn't nearly deep enough. You're on your own."

He leaned forward, "I'm sorry I didn't stay in touch." *Sorry* probably wasn't enough.

That makes two of us. "Max said you didn't have a phone."

"I should have tried harder to find one." He *really* should have, instead of letting the excitement of chasing the story carry him away from her. She looked wonderful, her hair every which way, no make up, very sexy shorts and a t-shirt that said Berkeley Youth Soccer. He'd been careless, treating her as though she weren't important.

She was.

Emily met his eyes. "Yes, you should have. Did Max tell you I went to his office when I was in New York in January?"

"Not until I was back in New York."

"I had a feeling he wouldn't follow through."

"This is all my fault, not Max's." He gathered his courage, "Em, can we perhaps restart what we—started? Somehow?" Jake clasped the cup as though it would provide some sort of support in case she said no.

Her insides warmed at the thought of having him back in her life, but she was afraid to hope they could recapture what began before Jake went to Tunisia. "I don't know."

"What can I do to help you know?" He was choosing his words carefully. The slightest misstep on his part, and she would close the door. He was pretty sure he didn't want that to happen, but there were going to be a lot of hoops to jump through.

"Give me time." Surely that wasn't asking too much.

"Will you at least have dinner with me tonight? Since I'm here. Nothing fancy, someplace quiet so we can talk."

Emily considered his request. If she walked back into this relationship, everything had to be right—for her and the girls. For Jake too. At this moment, she couldn't see how two lives on two coasts would fit together. "I'll ask Peter for a restaurant recommendation. Seven o'clock."

It was entirely possible she wasn't going to be able to cut him loose. What had made her think she could?

Jake went in search of a motel room, registering for just one night. He didn't dare assume he'd be here longer. Then he took himself to a matinee to kill time and keep from worrying that tonight might be the last time he'd see Emily.

At seven o'clock, she opened the Kingston front door so quickly that he knew she'd been waiting for him in the hallway. She was wearing an ankle-length, filmy skirt of oranges and reds, and a white, spaghetti-strap top that showed off her shoulders, the curve of her neck. Memories of their days in Chicago washed over him. *Jacob, you've been the fool of fools.* Unfortunately, tonight was not going to end in the bedroom. Emily would keep him at arm's length until he could prove he wasn't going to run off to exotic places.

"Wow" was the best he could do.

"They're Becca's clothes. I didn't bring anything appropriate for a dinner date."

"I repeat Wow. Shall we go?" He resisted the urge to take her hand.

At Peter's suggestion, Emily had made a dinner reservation at Duke's. "It's not far. Peter said it's beachfront casual."

Hawaiian style architecture and a dining room close to the crashing Pacific waves. Profoundly romantic but romance wasn't supposed to be on the menu tonight. Until their drinks arrived, they let themselves be hypnotized by the waves that slid over the sand beneath the window, leaving a silvery shine. Neither was quite sure how to begin.

"Peter Kingston has good taste in restaurants."

"Peter has good taste in many things. He's a very nice man who's been through a lot in the last few months. When he moves to New York in August, I'll miss his company. I've been able to help him a little. Most people don't want to talk about what it's like to lose a spouse, but I've been there. Talking to him has also helped me get some perspective on my own experience. I thought I was past grieving, but I'm not sure anyone is ever completely free of it."

"You and Rebecca have become friends?"

"When I went to the Awards with Liv, Rebecca and I hit it off right away. She called a couple months ago just as I was about to take a waitressing job. After spending time here, I'm beginning to understand why Becca ran away from all the publicity. Peter takes that aspect in stride, but then he's not immediately recognizable since he's mostly been behind the camera."

Little by little, she was relaxing, so he felt safe asking, "How did your Ojai performance go? I didn't forget about it, but I was still in rehab and they frown on taking off in the middle of therapy."

"Ojai was wonderful. And fun. Actually, I thought I'd be more nervous than I was. Mom and the girls drove down; Rebecca loaned me her mother's car for the trip." It felt so good to be telling him all the things she'd been saving up.

"I'm sorry I missed it."

"I have the DVD of the whole festival if you'd like to watch it." Conversation with him was still easy.

"I'd love to." He inhaled carefully, "About Chicago, I didn't think it would be so long before we'd be together again."

For all those months, she'd longed to know how he felt about her, about them, but tonight she wasn't quite ready for the conversation to get personal—not that kind of personal. "Tell me about the uprisings. Where did you stay? What were your days like? Were you afraid?" She knew she was babbling.

"You're interviewing me again."

"I'm interested." Though she hadn't been able to share what he'd been through, she desperately needed to understand that part of his life, why risk-taking was so appealing. Being in the middle of dangerous situations had attracted Pat too, had killed him. If she could understand, then perhaps she and Jake might have a future. Might.

Sensing he needed to get this right, Jake played down the raw, ugly parts—the teenage boy brutally trampled in Tahrir Square when the Army tanks rolled in, the women wailing over his mangled body. The nondescript hotel that he and several other reporters stayed in; most nights he got only two or three hours of sleep, afraid he'd miss something important. It was tough to find food in a restaurant or a grocery store that might be open for an hour or two. Thus the lost weight. He tried to explain the yelling, always so much yelling. What it was like filing the stories, trying to find fresh notebooks when he had filled the ones he'd brought with him from home. Trying to get his clothes washed. The unglamorous side to battlefield reporting.

"Do you know some of those languages?"

"Not really, just enough to get in trouble." He recounted some of his verbal missteps. "I tried to find young people to interview or give me directions. They usually speak some English."

"Was it exciting, being there?"

He knew he had to be honest—she'd see through anything less. "Yes, because they were so committed to changing their country. The excitement in Tunisia and Egypt was energizing. Libya had a much darker energy. It felt like a war instead of a protest. More weapons."

"Will you go back? I mean if your leg improves. There are still countries that are struggling."

A loaded question. He was fairly sure she didn't want him to go back to dangerous places.

"I would," he saw her lips tighten slightly, "but I can't. My leg won't take any more punishment. I've accepted that." *Almost.*

She pushed. "But you would if you could."

"Yes." *And there went his hopes of reestablishing their relationship.*

"Why? I really need to understand your reasons. Then maybe I can understand why Pat kept going on medical missions." She probably shouldn't have brought Pat into the evening.

Jake needed to explain in simple, rational terms. He put his fork down and sat back. "I guess it's the physical rush of witnessing something so profoundly life changing. There's a beauty in those frightening, chaotic moments that defies explanation. As cliché as it sounds, you have to be there."

She nodded. "Were you scared?"

"Sometimes. I'd be a fool if I weren't."

She nodded again, not in agreement but acknowledging that she understood.

They took their time over coffee.

Emily filled him in on what the girls had been doing. "They're coming down with me for a week in July. Peter's having Selena clean out the room that he and Hillary shared since he's in one of the guest rooms and I'm in the other. They are so excited they're actually getting along with one another. Malibu, a movie director and an ex TV star."

"Your life has changed."

"It's been interesting work. I've enjoyed spending time with Becca and Peter."

The check came. Jake slipped a credit card into the folder and left it for the waiter.

"Is she writing?"

"Not that I know of. Too much else going on in her life."

A perfect segue. "Is there a lot going on in your life too?" *Are you dating someone?*

"Right now, yes. But once the work here is finished, probably in August, it's back to job hunting and the beginning of a new school year. For the girls."

"Storytelling?"

She shrugged. "Too early to tell whether Ojai will give me a chance at another festival. I have a series of tellings at a few elementary schools, but they don't pay all that well. I'm at the point of admitting that Storytelling is a lovely hobby but not a practical way to make a living."

Jake resisted telling her he would be happy to take care of her and the girls. He could support a family now that Darlene had remarried and there were no more alimony payments. But he was sure Emily was too independent to let money determine whether their relationship continued.

"I don't have to be back at the magazine until July. If I stay nearby, may I see you when you have free time?" Here would be better than trying to spend time with her and the girls in Berkeley. Right now, he didn't need to figure out how to make points with Cristyl and Claudia. If there was anything left between him and Emily, they needed time alone.

She searched his face, trying to read what he was thinking—well she actually did know what he was thinking and remembering because she was remembering Chicago too. In one of her conversations with Peter, she'd told him he needed to risk going out into the world again.

She took her own advice. "Yes."

"Good. Great." He was grinning foolishly. "I'd love to spend more time with you." Even though the girls would be with her for a week.

"Where will you stay?"

"Don't know." He hadn't really planned to stay in California, hadn't brought much in the way of clothes, but he had his laptop and the copies of his journals. A visit to an office supply store would provide whatever supplies he might need to start work on the book. It was warm enough that t-shirts and Levi's would be sufficient. All minor issues. She'd opened the door—just a crack.

Emily reached into her purse and found a pen. "Do you have a slip of paper? I'll give you my new cell number and the number at the Kingston house."

Chapter 26

Hiring Jeri Toland to write Hillary's biography was Mikaela's idea. "She's written three other biographies"—Mikaela listed the titles—"and she's got a good reputation for accuracy as well as a readable writing style. I know it may seem too soon to start on this project, but it's best to get the memories down before they're forgotten."

Peter agreed.

Once the contracts with the publisher were signed, Jeri began her interviews with Peter at the Malibu house. There would, of course, be follow-up questions as the book progressed. Her assistant, Angela, scheduled two weeks of interviews with Peter between 8 a.m. and noon, weekends included. Worried that the emotional stress would be too much for him, Rebecca asked to be present, but Jeri refused. "After each session, you can listen to the recording for that day—like the dailies for a movie."

"I'm only worried about his stamina, not about what he says."

Almost six feel tall with salt and pepper hair and a taste for colorful silk scarves, even in the heat, Jeri Toland was used to getting her way. "I'm afraid that, if you're in the room, he might hold back on what he says. It's imperative that he feels free to be honest."

"Keep in mind it's barely six months since the accident." Rebecca knew she was behaving like an over-protective parent. In the space of six months, she'd gone from avoiding her father to hovering, worrying that he wasn't eating enough, sleeping enough, or getting enough exercise.

Jeri countered with, "Peter trusts me. I'd appreciate it if you'd trust his judgment and mine."

Rebecca backed off.

This was Emily's last week organizing the data. Berkeley's schools would start next week, and she had to get home. She and Angela had spent hours boxing up Hillary's papers and photographs, shipping everything to Toland's Santa Barbara office. Putting together an accurate portrait of someone as complex as Hillary would take months of interviews with actors, directors, her friends, as well as researching all the articles and reviews over the last forty years. Rebecca was grateful she didn't have to do any more toward the project than she already had. She was full and running over with information about her mother.

Jeri's first session with Peter began with Hillary's all-important audition in New York. His voice was soft with memory. "She was wearing a pale pink cotton dress and flats. Her hair was long, pulled into a ponytail. She looked about sixteen—which was exactly what the part called for. She was terrified. Her hands were shaking so much I couldn't imagine how she was able to read the words on the pages."

"What was your initial opinion of her?"

"Her looks or the reading?" That sounded like her father. Perhaps there had been a hint of a smile. His sense of humor was gradually returning.

"Both. She was beautiful but in those days probably didn't realize just how beautiful. She was completely unaffected." *Rebecca found unaffected incredibly hard to imagine.* "Her reading, however, was ragged. If she hadn't been so stunning, I might have dismissed her after the first five minutes."

"So she got the part on looks rather than ability?"

"A little on looks, mostly on ability. Halfway through, I made her start the reading over, slow down, and get into the head of the girl she would be playing."

"Better?"

"Much better—she nailed it."

"And you too?"

"That took another month."

"Did she realize you were attracted to her on that first day?"

"Apparently. Later, she told me the way I was looking at her contributed to her nervousness."

"Love at first sight?"

"Close."

"You're older."

"Not that much. She was twenty; I was twenty-six. I was just beginning to direct off Broadway." He reminisced about the rehearsals, Hillary's first opening night.

As the session was ending, Jeri asked, "A great love?"

Silence.

Then a whispered "Yes."

More silence. "Not the cliché of two becoming one." He was having trouble with his voice. "Hill was always her own person. She came complete. None of that co-dependent crap, but there was never a day in forty years that we didn't talk. Even if we were on different continents. In those days, making an international call wasn't as easy as it is now. We always had separate identities but were completely connected. Both of us enjoyed the high drama of our disagreements about even the simplest of things, like what color to paint a room. There were some memorable arguments. I loved her penchant for delivering monologues when she was upset, striding around the room as if she were on stage. They were a delightful part of Hill even though I sometimes wanted to muzzle her. Rebecca, however, hated them."

"Married forty years. In your line of work, that's an enviable run."

As Rebecca listened to Peter's assessment of his marriage, she was brought face to face with the depth of his emotions. For the first time in her adult life, she felt a profound admiration for her parents. Not for their careers, but their ability to love so completely. She would give anything to know the kind of love that totally embraced another person—warts and all—committing to that person in a seamless joy, never questioning the wisdom of that commitment.

How terrible to have that swept away in a second.

Had she and Alex had that kind of closeness? She was pretty sure the answer was No. They'd been too afraid of anything remotely resembling commitment. For the briefest of moments, she wondered whether they should try to find that closeness.

During one session, Jeri asked, "What kind of mother was she? Rumor has it that she and Rebecca weren't close." Rebecca felt her stomach twist, not sure she wanted to hear his answer.

"They were always on different pages, had very different views of the world. Ultimately, it was just simpler for Becca to disappear from our day-to-day lives. She never liked all the attention from the media and the public. Though she wouldn't be happy to hear me say this, she's stubborn like her mother, minus the histrionics. Rebecca was determined to make her own life. I'm proud she had the courage to do that even though we didn't see each other for seven years."

He understood. She wondered whether her mother ever had.

Another question focused on the years her parents hadn't seen her. "She would call every so often—birthday cards and gifts came through her high school tutor Megan, who lives in England. Because we had no address for Becca, we called Megan once or twice a year to make sure Bec was okay."

Rebecca hadn't known that Megan was playing for both sides. She'd have to give her a hard time when Megan came over to New York in late September. "Did Hillary want children?"

"Not really. Her career—our careers—were demanding; she didn't think she would make a good mother."

"Did you want children?"

"I was more receptive to the idea than my wife was, but I could see her point."

"And then Rebecca was conceived," Jeri prompted.

"For the first three months, Hill suffered debilitating nausea every morning; nevertheless, by matinee time, she was somehow able to go on. When she finally was too big to hide behind Portia's skirts, she reluctantly turned the role over to her understudy. But as soon as Becca was four weeks old, Hill was back in Portia's costumes and Becca was backstage being cared for by our first nanny.

"Hillary loved Becca but not the idea of being a mother. Raising a child is a lot of work, and Hillary wasn't willing to give up her career to be a stay-at-home mother. Fortunately, we had some wonderful nannies, but Rebecca has always felt we neglected her, and there may be some truth in that."

"When Rebecca was older, did Hillary spend time with her?"

"Of course," he was instantly defensive, "she loved her. They particularly enjoyed walking on the beach."

Those walks would have been nicer if we'd talked instead of rehearsing her lines.

"But?"

"Potty training, parent/teacher conferences, math homework weren't on Hill's agenda."

They hadn't been on her father's agenda either.

When Peter's interviews ended, it was Rebecca's turn to face Jeri's questions. On the first morning, Rebecca brought along a cup of strong coffee for courage. She didn't want to make Hillary into some kind of a Mommie Dearest mother. Yet she couldn't lie.

Jeri surprised Rebecca by letting her choose the direction of that day's interview. "Tell me about being Hillary Wallingford's daughter."

Memories spilled into the room. Not since her sessions with the Milwaukee therapist after her divorce, had she shared her childhood with anyone.

"I didn't always see much of my mother. She worked long hours when she was in a play. I saw her at dinner sometimes, at least on Monday nights, but on the other nights I was in bed when she got home and at school when she woke up. I attended private elementary schools if we were in New York or California. In London, I had tutors. I was always trying to make new friends or remind old friends who I was."

"Tell me one of your best memories of Hillary."

That was easy. "She could read a bedtime story better than anyone, doing all the voices. She did a terrific Winnie the Pooh. I loved listening to her."

"One of your worst."

No contest. "When my father was pushing me to take the Mandy role, I called my mother to help me convince him to let me go to high school instead of doing a TV show. It was 7:30 in New York; she was due to go onstage and wouldn't take my call. She didn't return my call until the next afternoon. I felt like she'd turned her back on me."

After six days of Jeri's questions, Rebecca was emotionally drained. Eventually all the painful details of growing up Kingston would be read by thousands of people. A totally different kind of spotlight would be directed on Rebecca, not just one or two tabloid articles that would end up on the bottom of a birdcage by the third day. Hillary's biography would be a lifelong albatross, hiding in libraries and used bookstores, ready to be resurrected over and over. With her luck, it would be turned into a movie. And yes, she knew this shouldn't be about Rebecca Kingston—but old habits are hard to break.

Halfway through the final interview, Jeri shut off her digital recorder. "I promise not to use this, but I'm curious, "Do you want to have children of your own?"

Rebecca was taken aback. It took several minutes for her to answer. "When I was in my twenties, I would have said *No* because I didn't want to risk repeating my parents' mistakes. Today—a qualified yes. I'd like to see whether I could be a better parent, though that's not the best reason to bring a child into the world." She wondered whether Alex wanted children. They'd never discussed it.

Jeri turned the recorder on and continued her questions.

Peter flew to New York the day after Rebecca's last interview. She drove him to the airport in the rental car they'd been using since both his car and Hillary's had been sold. Because she didn't want to check large boxes on the plane to Fresno, Rebecca had shipped two Tiffany lamps and an original Monet to Oakhurst. The painting would look great in her studio. The rest of what remained in the Malibu house would be sold at auction. The whole process of getting rid of the externals of that life had been both sad and freeing.

Outside of airport security, they hugged. His going meant he was stronger but also meant she had to find a direction for herself. "Knock 'em dead."

He smiled, "I hope I still know how. This could be a humbling reminder that I'm not as young or capable as I think I am." More seriously, "For the first time in forty years, I won't have your mother to talk to about the play."

"I have faith in you."

"Faith is good. What about," he hesitated, "love?"

Rebecca was momentarily undone by the question, tears filling her eyes.

When she could answer, "Yes, love."

Chapter 27

When Megan arrived in New York in September, Rebecca flew cross-country to meet her. *Death of a Salesman* had opened the week before, and Rebecca was looking forward to seeing Peter as Charley. The Malibu house was in escrow for the second time. Even the wealthy were having trouble qualifying for loans. The New York penthouse was listed but hadn't sold yet, so Megan and Rebecca stayed there.

Peter was camped out in his spacious one-bedroom apartment overlooking the East River, gradually moving some of the furniture from the penthouse into his new place. The round oak table from the kitchen, a leather recliner, a couple of lamps. He bought a new double bed, then found striped brown and beige sheets and a matching down comforter at Macy's. Rebecca was amazed that he'd done the shopping himself. His post-Hillary life required new skills. He hadn't hired a housekeeper and was trying to clean and cook for himself. He actually seemed to be enjoying his simpler lifestyle.

Megan spent the first week of her visit with her own mother in Connecticut—"Otherwise, I'll be in deep trouble"—and the second with Rebecca.

"How long has it been since you were in the States?"

"Three years. I came back when my father passed on. I've been needing a break from the children and England. Don't misunderstand, I love my life but I get hungry for a real hamburger and American TV programs that start on the hour or half hour. I long to order French fries instead of chips and dessert instead of a pudding. And I miss driving on the right side of the road. There are just certain parts of your first twenty-five years that you can't entirely erase. Cultural fingerprints."

"Amen to that. I believed I could ignore everything from my childhood and my marriage. More the fool I."

"You were afraid."

"Still am, but I've had to confront a lot of my old life lately—well not David—but certainly my parents, Mandy, people recognizing me. God, I hate losing my privacy again."

"I haven't noticed it being a problem here."

"For the moment, I'm old news. Right after my mother's death, the paparazzi were everywhere. A few times, I was convinced they'd suffocate me. Since I moved back to Oakhurst, they've pretty much left me alone. Of course, Oakhurst is off the beaten path. A few reporters were tailing my father when he first got to New York but even that has stopped. By the way, he was able to get us tickets for tomorrow's matinee. Then we can all go to dinner before he has to be back at the theater for the evening performance."

Watching Peter play Willy Loman's next-door neighbor Charley, Rebecca almost forgot that he was her father, so complete was the transformation. Because acting had always been Hillary's forte, it was easy to forget that Peter's career had begun on the stage. Over dinner at a small Italian restaurant down the street from the theater, he regaled Megan and Rebecca with anecdotes about rehearsals. "The night after we opened, I exited on the wrong side of the stage. Such a rookie mistake."

From Megan, "Which do you like better, acting or directing?"

He considered the question for a moment, then "Split decision. With directing and producing, I was a nervous wreck for months in advance. Everything seemed to be my responsibility. But once the curtain went up or the film was in the can, my work was done, and I could let the stress go. In acting, the stress builds gradually, culminating on opening night, then sticks around. The best part is only being responsible for myself."

At 6:30, he signaled the waiter for the bill. "Stay and enjoy your wine and coffee." He kissed both of them on the cheek and hurried back to the theater to get into make-up.

"He seems to be handling his new life pretty well."

Rebecca had been thinking the same thing. "He's always loved New York. My mother was the beach person."

"Do you think he'll marry again?"

Rebecca shrugged. "Our new relationship hasn't reached the stage where we talk about such things."

"Would you mind if he did?"

"No," about that Rebecca was sure. "He let me stay in hiding all those years when he knew exactly where I was. I wouldn't presume to interfere in his life."

"Are you going to stay in Oakhurst?"

"I don't know where else to be right now."

"You haven't mentioned Alex since I've been here."

Alex.

"Nothing to mention. I haven't heard from him since the day after the memorial service when I pretty much shut down everything between us. My fault. And since I got home last month, I haven't had the nerve to go into his family's store to ask where he is."

"Why not?"

Rebecca pushed the wine glass away and reached for her coffee, cold by now. "No rational explanation."

"You don't want to seem like you're chasing him in case he isn't interested?"

"Maybe. More to the point, I don't feel like the Rebecca I was when we were sleeping together. He might not like this Rebecca." She closed her eyes for a moment. "People in hiding don't share themselves well. Can't. Maybe I've never shared myself with anyone. When it really matters, I don't know how."

"You share with me."

Rebecca smiled ruefully. "Because you force me to come out of hiding now and then."

"You trust me."

"Yeah, I guess."

"If you want Alex back in your life, you need to trust him—your father too."

"First, I have to find out who I am. All the bits and pieces of Kingston and Sawyer are mixed in with Mandy. Jake and Emily spent all that time searching for Kelley Jordan—who didn't even exist—and what they found was a person who's still hopelessly confused about herself. I honestly don't know whether I want to pick up where we left off. Alex has never been a settle down kind of guy. You're right. I'm afraid he won't want me. Equally perplexing, I can't seem to get any writing done. I just keep doing research, making notes and more notes, but I haven't moved beyond the three chapters I wrote last fall. Maybe I can only write when I'm avoiding my past and the outside world."

"I doubt that."

Rebecca gambled asking a question she'd been thinking about since her Christmas visit. "Meg, are you completely satisfied with what you're doing with your life? I mean, are the kids and Hugh enough?"

"Yes, but—"

"Ah the infamous but."

"My family makes me feel safe and loved. But sometimes I miss the Megan who planned to teach math and science. Nowadays, I'm mostly helping Nigel with his maths—math to you—and converting American recipe measurements into English measurements." Megan asked the waitress for more decaf. "I don't think it's possible to have everything all at once. Warmth and safety—and a career of some kind."

"How did you know, really know you wanted to marry Hugh and live in England? To leave your country and your life was courageous."

"It just seemed right. I didn't think about anything beyond wanting to spend my life with him. No deep analysis or questioning. No list of pros and cons. But I also believe that life is made up of discreet stages. This is my second life stage, and I assume that, when the kids leave home, there'll be a third stage. Remember the story of Lot's wife in the Bible? As they were fleeing the city, she looked back and turned into a pillar of salt. I think we're meant to keep our eyes forward. I don't often look back at my life here except maybe for my hamburger craving."

"And I keep looking back."

"In a way."

When they left the restaurant, it was drizzling. "Want to get a cab?"

Megan laughed. "I live in England. This isn't wet."

"I live in California. It's raining, you idiot." Rebecca stepped to the curb and raised her arm.

Chapter 28

The premiere of *A Matter of Trust* was at Grauman's Chinese. Most of the movers and shakers in Hollywood were anxious to see Hillary Wallingford's final performance before it went into general release, just in time for the holidays.

When Rebecca's late afternoon flight from Fresno landed at LAX, Peter was waiting at the baggage claim. "Darling child, thanks for coming. I know how you hate these affairs."

Hate was not a strong enough word. Not only was she worried about having to walk the red carpet with him, but she was also dreading watching her mother on the screen, uncertain she could keep her emotions in check. She kissed Peter's cheek, then pulled away to study his face. The months of grieving had left their mark. His hair was grayer, the lines at his eyes deeper, but his eyes were clear—almost smiling. Acting agreed with him. The ticket sales for the play were good enough that it would at least run into February.

Trying to keep her angst from ruining his good mood, "When did you get here?"

"This morning." He took the handle of her suitcase. "Let's find a cab. We're having dinner at Nate's."

"I know."

As Peter waved for a cab, "You've talked to him?"

"Daily."

Inside the cab, Peter gave the driver Nate's address and turned back to Rebecca. "Daily?"

"I sold him the rights to *Spring Farm*. It took a lot of calls to convince me." Her "child" was all grown up and about to leave home.

"He'll do a great job. Do you have oversight on the script?" His director side kicked in.

"If I choose to exercise it."

"Good girl. You should use it to make sure the film is as close to the book as possible."

Rebecca nodded absently, looking out the window at the gridlocked traffic on the 405 Freeway. L.A.'s not-so-delightful evening commute. Undoubtedly, it would be a while before they reached Nate's.

She had mixed feelings about *Spring Farm* becoming a movie even though she trusted Nate and had been impressed with the woman hired to write the screen adaptation. Nate had driven Delia Luzano to Oakhurst to meet Rebecca and finalize the details. Last year at this time, Rebecca would never have imagined she would be back in the movie world because of her writing. Potentially back in the spotlight. Her own doing this time. She reminded herself she'd faced the spotlight several times this year—would face it tomorrow—and had survived. The reminder, however, did nothing to calm her nerves about the premiere.

The last time Rebecca had attended a premiere, she was a college freshman on her Christmas break. It was the film that had ultimately won Peter an Oscar for best director. She'd been so proud of him. There was talk of Hillary being nominated, posthumously, for an Oscar. Sentiment was running high.

One thing Rebecca had learned this year was that people in the entertainment business had sincerely admired Hillary's talent and loved working with her—perhaps because her mother loved acting above all else. Her father loved his work too. It had defined both of them.

Having stayed at Nate's until almost midnight, both Rebecca and her father slept in the next morning. Since they didn't have to be at the theater until seven, Peter spent the afternoon at the Wilshire Country Club—*New York City doesn't do real golf courses*—where he still had a membership. Rebecca went shopping for shoes to wear with the pale green gown she'd worn to a Boston art gallery opening with David and his parents eight or nine years ago. Buying a new gown for the premiere seemed frivolous. She didn't plan on attending an event like this ever again, not even if *Spring Farm* had a premiere.

Promptly at 6:30, she met Peter in the hotel lobby. Since he'd brought only a small carryon for his two days in L.A., he'd rented a tux for the evening and had his hair trimmed. He'd been wearing it a bit scruffy for playing Charley. No question he was still drop-dead handsome.

He smiled, bowing ever-so-slightly, and kissed her hand. "You look lovely." He noticed that Rebecca was wearing the intricate pearl necklace that he'd given Hillary on their thirtieth anniversary. "She'd be pleased."

"I hope so." It had been a long time since she'd wanted to please her mother.

Nate had hired a limousine for the evening, picking Rebecca and Peter up at their hotel, then calling for Mikaela at her office. When they were still a mile or two from the theater, Rebecca could already see the searchlights arcing across the night and felt her stomach knot up. As the car stopped in front of Grauman's, valets opened the car doors and Rebecca found herself squinting into the blinding floodlights that lined the red carpet, trying to ignore the roar of voices. She should never have agreed to attend. She hadn't had a full-blown panic attack in years—but tonight just might bring one on. She grabbed Peter's hand. She was trembling, but not because she was cold.

In her ear, she heard her father whisper, "You can do this Bec. It's just noise. Look straight ahead and let me do the talking when we're stopped."

A bit lightheaded, she nodded, grateful he'd noticed her discomfort. The theater entrance looked miles away.

They'd walked just a few feet when an overly made up blonde in a tight fitting blue dress and three inch heels pointed a microphone at Peter. "Mr. Kingston, can you tell us what you're feeling tonight, seeing the final movie your wife made."

Instantly impatient with the question, Rebecca almost answered for him. *Just what do you think we're feeling? It's painful.*

Stupid woman.

Barely pausing, her father was more diplomatic, "We're eager to see the movie. I hear it's wonderful." Before the woman could ask something else or involve Rebecca, he had moved past, smiling and raising his hand to acknowledge the crowd behind the ropes. Peter Kingston hadn't lost his touch.

Not being red carpet material, Nate and Mikaela had gone in a side door and were waiting in the lobby where Rebecca paused, trying to catch her breath and calm her racing heart.

Set in the Florida Keys, *A Matter of Trust* was the story of a large family falling apart after the suspicious death of a child. Hillary played the family lawyer trying cover up the truth, ultimately disbarred for unethical conduct. Rebecca had expected to feel sad seeing her mother, still alive, on the screen. Instead, Hillary's performance held Rebecca in its grip. She wasn't watching her mother; she was watching an intriguing character, superbly portrayed. Definitely an Oscar performance.

When the credits began, Hillary's name was first. The audience instantly burst into applause and one-by-one, group-by-group, everyone in the theater stood up. Rebecca was sure her mother would have been delighted by this spontaneous gesture, relishing every minute. She would be smiling at those around her, raising her chin just a bit higher.

Enveloped in the emotion of that moment, Rebecca felt tears threatening. Her father, however, was smiling, his voice steady. "A magnificent performance. She'd be satisfied with her work."

As soon as Peter and Rebecca left the auditorium and entered the lobby, they were surrounded by congratulations from the audience: actors and actresses, directors, writers. Hillary's peers. Peter willingly shook all the hands offered to him, introducing Rebecca, "You remember my daughter." The names and faces were a blur to Rebecca, all of them praising her mother's portrayal. *Such a loss to the industry. You must be very proud. She certainly has my Oscar vote.*

Twenty minutes into the Hillary love fest, Mikaela rescued Rebecca, walking with her to the perimeter of the crowd, leaving Peter in the midst of the well-wishers.

"You okay?"

Gratefully, Rebecca leaned against the wall. "It's like being caught in a well-meaning tornado."

Mikaela laughed. "Well put. The adrenaline at one of these shindigs never ceases to amaze me. Peter copes without succumbing to it; your mother thrived on it."

"I've often wondered if I'm some sort of throwback to a hermit ancestor. I do not thrive on any of it. I'm exhausted."

The lobby gradually emptied, Nate and Peter walking out together, Mikaela and Rebecca a few steps behind.

While they'd been inside watching the film, the crowd had gotten bigger and noisier, yelling for autographs, sometimes screaming for no apparent reason. As soon as Rebecca was outside, four reporters descended on her. "Hey Rebecca—Mandy—give us a minute." Mikaela was expertly maneuvered aside as cameras, microphones and other recording devices were shoved at Rebecca, cutting off any hope of escape.

She made herself stand very still, willing herself to be calm. *Breathe deeply. Slowly. They probably won't kill you. Probably.*

Then, from deep in her memory, she recalled something her mother had told her when Rebecca had faced hordes of reporters at a press conference during *Mandy's* third season. "Pick out one reporter, one face, and make eye contact. Even though you're being deluged with questions from all of them, look at that one person as you give your answers. It'll steady you."

Confronted by this human wall, Rebecca had been trying to look over and beyond the heads in front of her, willing them to disappear. Now, deliberately, carefully, she lowered her eyes, focusing on a rotund, balding man holding a small digital recorder over his head—and began answering.

Yes, it's her best work.

I loved the movie.

The audience gave her a standing ovation. Very moving.

No. I have no desire to be an actress.

Yes, my book is being made into a movie.

When someone asked about Alex—*No comment.*

Yes, I do miss her.

During the questioning, Mikaela had gradually been working her way back to Rebecca. Gently taking her hand, Mikaela led her to the curb where the limousine was waiting, leaving a barrage of questions in their wake. Once inside, seatbelt fastened, Rebecca realized her heart wasn't pounding; she wasn't short of breath. She was calm. She had faced the enemy and lived. For those few minutes, it seemed as though her mother had been standing beside her. Even though Rebecca had probably been imagining Hillary's presence, it had made all the difference.

Peter turned around in his seat. "You all right?"

"Yes, I am. I actually am." Her shock was genuine.

I am.

Nate gave her his usual thumbs up. "Drinks at my place. We've had enough of crowds for one night."

Watching her interview on the 11 o'clock news, Rebecca was impressed with her poise under pressure—thanks to keeping her focus on the unknown reporter. She looked as though she faced reporters every day. Very different from a year ago when she'd fled to England, afraid of being discovered.

I did it—but I'd rather not do it again.

Because both Peter and Rebecca were flying on American Airlines—in different directions—they shared a cab to LAX on Monday morning, waited through security, and settled at a cramped table in Burger King to have breakfast. Rebecca was short on sleep because her head had been buzzing with memories of the premiere, amazingly good memories that were somehow in the process of freeing her from the paralyzing fear that had followed her around for years. So quickly gone. Like finally being able to float on her back or balance her two-wheeler. One moment there was anxiety; a moment later it didn't exist. She finally dozed off around four. Her wake up call from the hotel's front desk came at 6:30.

"Did you get any sleep, Bec?"

"A couple hours. Too much happening in my head. You?"

"I did fairly well. Maybe because I'm still on New York time." He ordered orange juice, coffee, a breakfast burrito and hash browns. "It's a long flight. No telling what they're serving in business class. I miss California-style Mexican food."

Rebecca only wanted a plain croissant and coffee. Lots of coffee. "With any luck, I'll be home by lunch."

"May I come visit you?"

"Of course. Anytime." Both stopped short of acknowledging what had happened the last time he'd asked to visit her. "Will you stay for the run of the play?"

"Yes. There's talk of putting together a road company. I've never gone on the road. Might be interesting."

"And hard."

"Probably. It'll be good to do something different. I've discovered it's too painful to keep doing what I was doing before. Changing the game plan helps."

"That's why you've sold almost everything?"

"I need a fresh start."

Oakhurst had been Rebecca's fresh start. Maybe she was due for another one. Too much in Oakhurst reminded her of Alex.

When their order number was called, she went to pick up the trays, grateful for the interruption.

Once Peter had finished his breakfast, he pushed the plastic plate aside, holding her eyes with his. "Becca, darling child, I'm so sorry about your childhood, about putting you in a position where you felt you had to hide from us and the world."

Sorry.

She wasn't prepared for an apology—in Burger King of all places—and had no idea what to do with the olive branch he was offering.

She'd spent years nursing her self-righteous anger, blaming her parents for everything. Martyrdom had become comfortable. If she forgave him—and Hillary—she'd have to look at the world and herself differently.

"Becca?"

"Umm, well—thank you." An inadequate response.

"I know it's rather late for me to become a parent but can we at least be—friends? Please. I've enjoyed your company over the last months though I wasn't very good company much of that time. I'd like to get to know you, really know you, and have you know me—instead of hating me."

"I guess. I'm so used to blaming you and mother that I—"

"Becca," he leaned forward, "you can continue blaming me if you need to, but you don't have to stay tangled in the past, trying to fight your way out. It can't force itself on your present life without your permission." Megan had made the same point. "The present is precious; don't waste it on what can't be changed. You're a smart, beautiful woman. I'm very proud of what you've accomplished. You don't need to hide. It's time to let the past go. Get over it."

A quick flash of anger invaded her. *Easy for him to say.*

They sat in silence while Peter finished his coffee.

Just like that? *Get over it.* A quick fix, as though she were a petulant, sulky child who'd dropped her ice cream cone.

When it was time for Peter to board his flight, she walked him to the gate, hugged him briefly but still couldn't say anything.

In the face of her silence, he was uncertain. "I'll call you tomorrow."

"Be safe."

After handing over his boarding pass, he paused in the doorway and turned to smile at her before disappearing into the tunnel.

Her flight to Fresno would leave from the Commuter Terminal in another hour. As she rode the shuttle to the one story building in the middle of the airport's tarmac, all she could hear was Peter's *Get over it.*

Chapter 29

It had been a year since Rebecca had written anything worthwhile. Every sentence seemed clumsy, the characters uninteresting cardboard. Even though her father was settling in to his new life and the ever-present media, for now, was less of a threat, Rebecca was at sixes and sevens with herself. Every time she sat down with a pad of yellow paper, her mind developed a bad case of ADD. The slightest movement—Tinker brushing against her ankle—or sound—the rain slipping down the window—distracted her. *What ifs* were everywhere. Especially what if Alex appeared on her doorstep or she appeared on his.

After this year of having her life turned upside down, she had lost any clear sense of what she wanted for herself. Though she was back in Oakhurst, sitting in her beloved studio, the cats demanding their dinner—she wasn't happy. Alex was lurking at the edges of everything she did.

Because her house had been fending for itself for the last year, there was plenty for her to do in the yard. Manual labor might restart her brain. She hired Trudy's nephew, who was always looking for extra money, to help her cut back the bushes, then haul away the leaves and needles that had piled up. There was kindling to be ordered as well as a couple of broken gutters to be repaired. The list was long.

Emily's call inviting Rebecca for Thanksgiving dinner in Berkeley was a welcome diversion. "Jake will be flying out for the holiday. I want you to get to know him."

"Because?" Rebecca was pretty sure she knew the answer. Since August, Jake and Emily had been collecting frequent flyer miles. The first weekend of each month, Jake came to Berkeley; the third weekend, Emily flew to New York.

"Because we're getting married on New Year's Day, here in Berkeley. Jake's family is coming out."

"Oh Em, that's wonderful. I'm so happy for you."

"I'm happy for me too." She sounded happy.

"Are the girls okay about having Jake in their lives?"

"Ambivalent but so far not hostile. I have my fingers crossed."

"And how does Jake feel about being a stepfather?"

"He's terrified actually. Would you tell Peter about the wedding? I know he probably can't get away. I miss our talks."

"I'll mention it. He has an understudy who would undoubtedly love to have a chance to play Charley."

They talked for a long time. Emily was making Storytelling contacts in the New York area, and Jake was spending his free time driving around Long Island, checking out schools and looking for houses to show Em when she was in New York. "Instead of the streets of Cairo, he's cruising the suburbs, looking for the perfect picket fence. Sorry, private joke."

For Rebecca, two good things had come from this painful year—having Peter in her life and her friendship with Emily.

And now Emily was getting married. Over the next few days, Rebecca experienced moments of deep envy. Emily was courageously moving on, asking her daughters to make room for Jake in their lives.

Huge changes for everyone except Rebecca, who was in a holding pattern, unsure how to go forward. Even her ability to write had deserted her. Liv's anxious phone calls about her progress on the Acadians didn't help.

On the way to meet Karen for their usual Monday morning coffee, Rebecca walked by Sierra Sports just as Jorge was taping a large banner across the plate glass window. In bright red letters: **Going Out of Business: Everything 50% Off**

"Jorge."

He turned.

"Hi, do you remember me? Becca Sawyer?"

He smiled, "Sure. Haven't seen you in a while."

"I've been in Los Angeles for a few months. Why is the store closing?" Had Alex's father had another heart attack?

"The Zimmermanns are retiring and bought one of those big RVs to travel around the U.S. They've leased this building to an Italian restaurant."

More changes.

"What about you? Do you have another job lined up?"

He stood back to check the banner. "I guess a little crooked won't hurt. I'm going to work for Alex in Squaw Valley."

Alex.

"Doing what?"

"He's managing the ski school and sporting goods store that his friend Jay owns. I'm going to be in charge of the store. You didn't know?"

No she didn't. After her behavior the last time she saw Alex—nearly nine months ago—she didn't deserve to know. He'd moved on too.

It was an epidemic.

"Alex has been taking business courses since he quit teaching last spring. *She hadn't known that either.* Jay's starting up a second ski school in Breckenridge, Colorado, and can't be two places at once. The timing is perfect for me. The Zimmermanns are closing this store the day before Thanksgiving, and I'm supposed to go to work in Squaw Valley on December 1st. Between now and then, I have to drive up to Tahoe City to find a place for my family. Alex sent me the name of a rental agent."

"Congratulations. Is your wife happy about the move?"

"We both are. We've never lived that far from Mariposa before."

"Good luck."

She walked to the coffee shop, slowly re-playing her conversation with Jorge. Obviously, Alex wouldn't be coming back to Oakhurst for a while. At some naïve level, she'd been hoping that, when he visited his family the next time, the two of them would accidentally meet, she'd apologize and—

And nothing.

While Karen was holding forth about how an art dealer in San Francisco had ripped her off, Rebecca was only half listening. Jorge's news about Alex and his parents had taken up all the space in her brain. Working on her house and waiting for fate to get its act together was not fixing her life. She needed to see Alex and apologize. And get over herself.

"Becca, you're not paying attention."

"Sorry, something's come up and I really need to be going. I promise I'll listen better next week." *If I'm here next week.*

She almost ran the two blocks to the parking lot. It was 10:20. She could be in Squaw Valley by late afternoon. Her apology should be made one-on-one, looking into his eyes and telling him that she was sorry she'd pushed him away. That she missed him.

At her house, she put out enough dried cat food, milk and water for a couple of days, once again asked Trudy to pick up the mail, stuffed extra clothes in the duffle suitcase, and tossed her parka and snow boots in the back of the SUV. Whatever else she needed, she could buy or do without. A stop at the Valero station to top off on gas, and she was ready to hit the road.

Alex had just finished a grueling two-hour meeting with Jay's accountant in Tahoe City, trying to absorb the incredible complexities of payroll deductions, unemployment insurance, and W2 forms—foreign concepts his mother always handled for Sierra Sports. His mind was spinning. Jay's school and store had both part time and full time employees—Alex had never been responsible for so many people. Fortunately, Jorge was willing to move to Squaw Valley to oversee the day-to-day operation of the store since the current manager, Ruth, would be going to Breckenridge with Jay. Jorge had learned a lot during his year with the Zimmermanns and was good with customers. He'd be an asset.

When Jay proposed that Alex take over the management of the school and store, Alex had been hesitant—going from ski instructor to boss was a huge change.

"Who else?" Jay argued. "You understand skiing techniques better than I ever will. And your connections with the ski world will be useful because there's a big instructor turnover every year."

Not something to look forward to.

"But you understand the business end. I've only completed four business classes at a community college. I've rarely been careful about balancing my own checkbook."

Jay was not dissuaded. "Put me on your speed dial. Most of the staff, except for Ruth, are staying. They'll help you get your feet under you, and Gwen will keep the office running. The best way to learn how to run a business is to run it. No classroom can give you what you'll learn on the job."

Once Alex agreed, he and Jay spent long days going over all aspects of the business. Alex had never worked so hard or worried so much. Being an adult with a real job was not easy. No more laid back lifestyle. Jay was giving him an opportunity, and Alex prayed he wouldn't screw it up.

It was almost dark when he drove into the Village already blazing with holiday lights. Before he went over to the ski school office to pick up the work schedules Gwen had been filling out, he bought enough groceries for a day or two and dropped them off at the two-bedroom townhouse he'd moved into last month. For once, he had the money to rent a comfortable place for himself. The townhouse had a view of the ski slopes and was an easy walk to the Village, though he never seemed to have time to walk.

Thanks to early November storms, the slopes already had eight to ten inches of base, and three of the lifts would open next week. Even though he was looking forward to opening day, he was scared stiff.

He parked his Explorer around back and unlocked the rear door of the office. The lights were still on. Perhaps Gwen was finishing up.

Instead of Gwen, Becca was sitting at Gwen's desk, flipping through a ski equipment catalog, her back to him. When she heard the door close, she turned around.

Genuine surprise rooted Alex to the floor. Though he hadn't seen Becca in months, standing this close to her felt as natural as if he'd seen her this morning. Natural and very right.

Not sure of her reception, Rebecca smiled hesitantly. "Hi."

"Hi."

"Someone named Gwen said I could wait in here. She said you'd probably come by before you went home because you needed the schedules tonight." She pointed at the stack of paper on the desk. Having no faith in the whims of cyberspace, Gwen believed in making hard copies of whatever was in the computer.

"I stopped at home first."

"I hear you're in charge. Congratulations."

"As hard as that is to believe, yes I am. My mother is sure Jay has lost his mind. She may be right. My track record leaves much to be desired." It wasn't going to be easy to go from the playboy of the western world to being responsible.

Alex moved to the other side of Gwen's desk and sat down so he could look straight into Becca's eyes. She was wearing her hair longer, chin length. He liked the way it curled against her cheeks. She looked more rested than when he'd seen her in February, calmer.

She closed the catalog, "I—uh—came to say I'm sorry about, well, that day—at my father's—I wasn't—it was a bad time. I apologize for just walking away and leaving you alone like that. You didn't even get lunch."

Alex couldn't take his eyes off her. God, she was so beautiful and so close, within reach. But it was too soon to touch her. Maybe she didn't want him to touch her—ever. And yet she was here, on his turf.

"A long drive to apologize."

"Apologies over the phone or in e-mails are cop-outs. Eye contact is a prerequisite. Thus the drive."

"Okay, apology accepted." *And this was going where?*

"I hear your parents are going on the road in an RV."

He smiled. "Yeah, Randy and I have a bet going—will they last one month or two. For decades, they've done nothing but talk about the store and the family. I doubt they'll be able to hold another kind of conversation longer than five minutes."

"Parents can surprise you." *Look at Peter.*

"How's your father?"

"Doing better than I expected. He might join the play's touring company in the spring. Megan and I attended a performance last month."

"And Nate Pullman? He was really generous, letting me stay at his place."

"He's fine. I think he's romantically interested in Mikaela, my mother's publicist, though neither one is letting on they're seeing one another. I sold him the movie rights to *Spring Farm*."

"That was brave. Will you be able to handle the publicity?"

"Maybe. Maybe not. I sold it because I've said No to too many things for too long. It's time for a few Yeses. Liv and Kurt are ecstatic."

"Besides apologizing is there another reason you're here?"

He'd deftly hit the ball into her court. During the drive from Oakhurst, she'd worked and reworked how she'd ask him whether there was anything left between them. She was sure—mostly sure—she was ready to commit to more. Hopefully, she wasn't just afraid of being alone. "I wondered—well—if there's a chance that we could—if there's a way to find a connection or—I realize it's been almost a year and you've probably—well—" She was having trouble finishing the sentence.

He grinned. "Yes."

Quick and simple.

She searched his face and found his eyes were already seducing her, reminding her of all the nights he'd shared her bed in Oakhurst. "Yes?

Really? But being with me will bring complications." Her heartbeat increased. "Do you need time to think about it?"

"Not at all, but there's a catch."

There's always a catch.

"You'll have to move up here. I've signed a two-year contract with Jay."

He was right. That was a catch. But his job was here. She should be able to write anywhere. She heard Peter's *Get over it* loud and clear. It was worth a try.

"Is there enough room—I mean—" Not a particularly romantic question.

"The second bedroom can be your studio. It's not as large as your studio in Oakhurst, but there's a view of the slopes and of course I'll be there."

"You have two bedrooms?"

"I've gone upscale. Two bedrooms, two bathrooms, two stories, and an enclosed patio."

"What about the cats? They've been on their own for most of the year. I can't abandon them again."

"Maybe the manager will let me install a cat door alongside the patio door." He grinned again. "I'm good at installing cat doors. Remember?"

Her voice softened, "I remember."

Hearing that softness, Alex felt safe enough to come around to her side of the desk. "I've been pretty patient. May I kiss you now?"

When she stood, there were barely two inches between them.

"Please do."

She hadn't forgotten the taste of his lips, the pleasure of his tongue searching for hers, his arms crushing her against his jacket.

She'd been afraid of so much for so long, but those fears would be easier to face—with Alex.

Perhaps she was finally ready to move on.

Chapter 30

When she left for Wellesley, Rebecca hadn't taken anything from her childhood except a few clothes. Not even her favorite alarm clock. Other girls in the dorm kept family pictures on their desks, but displaying pictures of Hillary and Peter would have attracted too much attention. She had, however, worn the Gucci watch her parents had given her for her eighteenth birthday. As soon as her roommate commented on how expensive it must have been, Rebecca hid it in the drawer of her nightstand and bought herself a plain Timex with a tan leather band. Though everyone knew she was rich, she didn't want to look rich so, once she saw what the other girls were wearing, she shopped for the same kinds of clothes.

When she left David, she'd taken her laptop, her clothing and books. Her library, begun with college textbooks, was eclectic and growing.

For the move to Squaw Valley, she brought only winter clothes—Alex didn't have much closet space—, the cats with all their paraphernalia, her cookbooks, pots and pans, and as much of her studio that would fit into Alex's second bedroom.